SHUTTER SPEED

SHUTTER SPEED

A NOVEL BY

Larry Krotz

TURNSTONE PRESS

Copyright © 1988 Larry Krotz

Turnstone Press gratefully acknowledges the assistance of the Canada Council and the Manitoba Arts Council.

Turnstone Press
607-100 Arthur Street
Winnipeg, Manitoba
R3B 1H3 Canada

This book was printed by Hignell Printing Limited for Turnstone Press.

Printed and bound in Canada

Cover illustration: *In a Greyhound Bus Depot* by Steve Gouthro, coloured pencil

Cover design: Robert MacDonald, MediaClones

Canadian Cataloguing in Publication Data

Krotz, Larry, 1948-
  Shutter speed
  ISBN 0-88801-134-2
I. Title.
PS8571.R67S4 1988   C813'.54   C88-098097-4
PR9199.3.K76S4 1988

The author wishes to acknowledge
the support of the Manitoba Arts Council
and the generous advice of friends and editors
in the preparation of this book.

SHUTTER SPEED

In February Danny Hinkle had a fantasy about how the world would end. Instead of spring arriving on schedule, it continued to get colder. A tiny switch hidden somewhere deep in the apparatus regulating the rhythms of the universe failed to connect and the earth sank slowly, like a glass, into a frigid silence as deep as time itself. Life disappeared into an irrevocable frozen sleep and the snows accumulated over decades until only the tops of the tall bank buildings in the great cities stuck out above the drifts. And then they too disappeared.

It was a comfortable fantasy; it did not scare him. He knew what it would look like. He had once flown into Toronto in a heavy fog and while the plane, unable to land, had circled for an hour he had contemplated the city buried below in the white billows of vapour. Only the CN Tower and the top of the Bank of Commerce inched up through the fog.

He knew his fantasy was at odds with the great body of scientific speculation. He had read recently the warnings of a University of California physicist that the carbon dioxide barriers accumulated by a century's worth of the burning of coal and oil were creating a 'greenhouse effect' which was, in fact, causing the earth's temperature to rise. We were, the eminent Nobel Prize scientist warned, more in danger of burning or drowning than freezing. Science, moreover, predicted temperature rises that within 50 years would start the melting of the polar ice cap, raising water levels to flood coastal areas while heat and lack of rain simultaneously turned the interiors of the continents into deserts. As well, the ozone layer was said to be disappearing and that would fry us too.

But Danny Hinkle preferred his own fantasy. It was less violent than the holocaust; he knew that death by freezing came through a rather peaceful sleep. There would be, perhaps, a brief, fear-driven madness as the world grew steadily colder; there would be a period, a few months, when people would scrabble and gouge, cheat and steal, hoard, lie and try for advantage, locking their doors and barring their windows to keep their neighbours from grabbing their dwindling piles of kindling wood and stashes of food. But that, sadly, was how the world worked anyway, already. In the end it would quiet down. People would huddle by their furnaces until the fuel ran out and then everyone and everything would give up and drift off into a rest that was quiet and blissful as a smile.

More than that, and the thing that excited him most, was the fact that cold preserved. Everything as he knew it would be preserved, completely intact, like the bodies of the big, hairy ice-age mammoths under those billowed piles of ice and snow. At heart Danny Hinkle was both an anthropologist and an archaeologist; he believed things should be preserved for study even if it had to be in some future moment when there was more time. As a photographer, which was both his passion and his trade, he tried unsuccessfully to make moments stand still. He rushed around like crazy, documenting everything he considered of value, snapping, developing, printing; asking people to stop for a moment to face the camera, asking them if they wouldn't mind repeating what they'd just been doing so he could get a photo. He roamed his city, he roamed his country. He dreamed of buying airplane tickets and roaming the world. There was so much to do, so much to see. The world reverberated like a giant billiard-table on the break, balls bouncing every which way, off every rail. He wanted to get pictures of it all—all the people, all the things, every birth, every death, every tryst, every embrace, every fight, argument, explosion, every breath. He wanted everything to hold still.

He fought a losing battle. In the whirlwind of everything he frequently felt overcome with an enormous burden of futility. His life would never be long enough, he feared, nor would the chaotic world around him ever hold still to allow him the understanding he needed. A human baby was born on the planet every third of a second; 120,000 trees died every hour. Automobiles rolled off the world's assembly lines at a rate of 87,000 a day; a square kilometre of grassland or forest or swamp went down in the path of a new Searstown or K Mart parking lot every five minutes. How could he possibly keep up with that? Life was an act of juggling an impossible multitude of objects; everything up and not knowing what would come down. You just send up the orange and the milk bottle hits you on the head. You win the lottery, you get cancer; you fall in love and World War Three breaks out. Nothing holds still.

But after the freeze, if not himself then an inquiring spirit of some future age, arriving perhaps in a green polymer space ship, could have the leisure to chip away the ice and poke around, to pick up the congealed and rigid pieces, take them back to the lab, study them, pore over them, analyse them and perhaps at last make some sense of it.

In Winnipeg, in February, his fantasy was very much alive. The ice crystals that formed like Christmas ornaments in the bright blue air in front of his breath made him think all the more of frost-created vacuums, nothing moving, everything still as silence and perfectly preserved.

1

Boris Podolski examined his face in the mirror. In the bright, high light of late morning it looked puffy, weary, tender. As if, should he touch it, his finger might leave a mark, a dent. He touched it, pulling his four fingertips firmly from the bottom of his left eye down his cheek to his jaw; the jaw a little rough already with today's stubble. His cheek was red for a moment where it had been pressed. The rest of his face was white.

He had come in at six and slept fitfully for five hours. The girl was a graduate student at the university, psychology or sociology. Something to do with people's behaviour. She had a paper to deliver this morning and said she wanted to wake up alone. He told himself that was okay.

Would it be possible, he wondered, to get laid too many times? Was there a number, pre-ordained, in everyone's life and after you had that many, that was it? No more? If that was the case, could you waste them? Would one night with a graduate psychology student mean one less with Monica, the television weathercaster in Vancouver, of whom he was very fond? And would a night with her be one less for his wife Lucy, the Bank of Nova Scotia credit counsellor in Toronto, should it ever work out that they got back together?

What about masturbation? Did those moments count in the overall tally? He liked better the advice given more frequently now in even the earnest and serious journals, that the more you did the more you could do. Like anything else in the body or mind, sex was muscular activity, enhanced by use and exercise. Use it or lose it was the dictum. Boris worried that he could never use it enough. He worried about getting old. He looked at his face again; what if there was a nuclear war before he could get in enough screwing?

Boris walked from his bathroom mirror back along the hallway to his bedroom and opened the closet to look for some clothes. He had to go out soon. He had agreed to meet a man named Burrows at the steam room at the Club. A steam would probably be good for him, the way he felt this morning. Or it might do him in completely. Boris felt a small anxiety that was other than sexual start to tingle in him and make him jumpy.

He had met Burrows for the first time yesterday at the North End Gym. A short, squat man, surly with a concave face; a face like an empty pie plate. He looked like Edward G. Robinson in *Little Caesar*. Well dressed—impeccably, expensively.

Boris was watching some kids working out. Since Billy, the Indian kid, had broken his hand and gone back up north, the fight business had gone downhill for Boris. No Mike Tysons coming out of this town, that was for sure. But Boris kept looking. Often he just liked to be in the gym, a place whose

old boards smelled of sweat and linament, a place crowded
with half-naked muscular bodies while he was in his pressed
suit smelling of aftershave. He liked that contrast too. He
liked his familiarity with all these little worlds, worlds he
could breeze in and out of even though he didn't have the time
or the talents to be fully a part of them. That's why he liked
being the agent. He couldn't box, but he could help make it
happen. And that role gave him access—to the gymnasium,
to the jockeys' room at the race track, to the dressing room at
the hockey rink, to Danny Hinkle's photo studio, to the apartments of the long-legged models. He cultivated acquaintan-
ces with the people who guarded the doors in such places:
Smitty, the rub-down man at the gym, the doormen at the
clubs and bars downtown, the trainers at the track. He liked
to be recognized when he walked through the doors; he
wanted to be welcomed. Boris Podolski never wanted to feel
left out.

The kids sparring in the two rings were just that, kids.
High school drop-outs with only the vaguest of hopes or possibilities of making it big. He had sat on a wooden stool and
watched for a while before Smitty, the aged trainer, caught
his attention.

"I want you to look at this kid," he said. Boris turned to the
corner where a lithe, sure-footed black boy rhythmically
pounded dents into the big bag. Thunk, thunk, thunk, thunk.
His body shone with sweat, every muscle in his shoulders,
back, upper arms stood out as if polished. His wiry black hair
glistened, drops of perspiration jogged down the sides of his
face.

"Quite a slugger, eh?" said Smitty.

"Impressive," answered Boris. And he was. "What's his
name?" Boris turned to the little trainer standing beside him.

"Afraid he's not available," said Smitty, almost apologeti-
cally, avoiding Boris' eyes.

"What do you mean?" Boris asked.

"Because he's ours," said the Edward G. Robinson

character who stood directly behind them.

Boris turned.

"Sugar Ray," the man said softly, his mouth breaking slightly into a swollen-lipped smile.

Boris didn't know the man; Edward Burrows, he said his name was. He thought he knew all the fight people, a generally unpolished lot in this, a mid-sized city on the circuit. But he didn't recognize this man. They stood for a couple of minutes in silence, watching the fighter. Out of the corner of his eye, Boris was aware of Burrows standing a head shorter beside him.

"This isn't really our business," the man had said, taking Boris by the elbow as they moved from the gym to the street. He spoke in the plural, we, us. "We feel, however, we might make it our business."

His cockiness had caught Boris off guard. But it wasn't unfriendly. Boris was intrigued. The man talked on about the kid they'd watched punching inside.

"We know you, you know," he said at last. Boris started. Burrows, who still held him by the elbow, laughed. "Not like that," he said, almost gently.

"Come on, Podolski," he said after a minute. "Forget the fights. I want to talk to you about other things, bigger things." He slipped two business cards into Boris' hand and gave him a firm smile. Boris looked at the cards; one was Burrows', the other was for a man named Sidney Blumthorp. He looked back at Edward Burrows. His smile had not been that of a man who produced them casually.

After he dressed, Boris took the elevator down to the main floor of his apartment building and walked out to the street. The noon sunlight was warm. It made him feel good, springy, like a colt. The bubble of anxiety of an hour earlier was gone and with it the pallor of his complexion. He felt colour warming his face. What a day! He smiled broadly to himself and saluted the two elderly ladies returning to the building, pulling behind them their little cart laden with groceries.

He thought about Edward Burrows. Whatever the man wanted, he felt confident he would be able to fit in. To Boris, life was a never-ending kaleidoscope of opening possibilities. He felt the change in his pocket, he felt the flat security of his wallet in the inside breast pocket of his jacket, he checked discreetly that the fly of his trousers was done up.

He would take a taxi, but he would get a newspaper first. He crossed the boulevard humming a few bars from "The Sunny Side of the Street." "... if I never had a dime I'd be rich like Rockefeller. ..." "You should be able to tell," he remembered his father once saying to him, "when something good is going to happen. It's like a sixth sense. And when you get the feeling, always go with it. Lucky people always trust their instincts." This, just before his father disappeared. Run off, his mother explained, with a woman he met while travelling. His father, the agent in the western half of the continent for a sewing machine manufacturer, was always travelling. They spent the next six years, Boris and his mother, living with his grandfather, a prosperous importer of coffee, tea and Indonesian wood carvings. An aunt who'd suffered the same misfortune as his mother lived with them too, with her children, twins, a boy and a girl younger than Boris. The grandfather made certain Boris went through law school.

Perhaps he'd got lucky, his father. Boris didn't think about him much anymore, although sometimes he fantasized about what he would look like now, what he might be doing now. He wouldn't have said he felt any lingering bitterness toward him; curiosity, mostly.

Thinking about possibilities always made him a bit antsy. Boris had an acute sense of the passing of time. He had an acute sense also of the line, rigid unbendable line, between medium achievement and the big time. And the other line, the one between the big time and the big, big time. He thought sometimes about the leaps over those lines; he thought about the things that governed such moves—luck, acts of will. He thought now and then of taking his brief-case to New York or

Los Angeles. Setting up operations there. But, save for the odd trip, he never went. And on those few trips he often found himself so uncertain about what to do that once he landed, got out of the plane, drove into the city and checked into a hotel, he sat looking at the phone, not knowing whom to call.

He took this as an indication he wasn't ready to move. He stayed where he was. He travelled but stayed away from the big places; he worked his accounts here. Someday the big break would appear around the corner—the smash literary property, the model too hot to handle, the fighter or the running-back who was a sure ticket all the way to the bank, the deal of a lifetime. He would recognize it when he saw it. He had to be ready and open to each possibility as it offered itself. He thought about Edward Burrows.

He got out of the taxi and hopped up the four stone steps that led into the Downtown Businessmen's Health Club. He checked in at the wicket and got a towel, then went downstairs and followed the long corridor toward the steam room and the lockers. He stripped naked, hung his jacket carefully and tucked the rough white towel around his hips. The stone floors were damp. Moist, humid air suffused the entire building. He met one man coming toward him but the place was almost empty, the crowds of noon-hour businessmen already gone, the after-work customers not yet arrived. He passed a window and looked through it into the steam room. Through the billows of white vapour he could make out one body on the long granite benches. He squinted. Red and rosy and slippery, pudgy and wet, his black hair slicked down from the heat. Looking sleepy, Edward Burrows. Boris reached for the handle of the door. He felt lucky.

2

Every morning at about ten o'clock, Danny Hinkle took himself from his apartment on the south side of the river across the bridge to his workroom, his studio, a bare two-room suite above an Armenian bakery. He'd moved there after the dilapidated, half-empty, turn-of-the-century building downtown which housed his first studio, next door to one occupied by Boris, was torn down. After he checked for mail (usually none) he slipped in past the heavy, bready smells of fresh buns and cakes, and bounded up the rickety stairs.

The front room was large and well lit from two big windows that faced above the street. The floor was uneven and it was difficult to keep the place clean from the grime and dirt that sifted in around the windows from the traffic and the street.

But he liked the room. He liked the way light filled it in the mornings and he'd given the walls a coat of white paint to enhance that, to give the feeling he was enveloped by light. A painter had had the place before him, a madman who believed, literally, he was Jackson Pollock and worked all night on huge canvasses and drank rubbing alcohol. The residue of his life and work was still splattered on the wood floor—spots of red and purple and yellow paint. In one corner, just under the window, a large pool of black paint had dried where a whole can of the stuff had tipped over.

The little room in the back had a sink. Danny fixed it up with shelves, trays and his enlarger, with light-sealing tape around the door frame. It was his dark-room where he developed and sorted and printed. When he had work.

When he didn't have work, he sat in the other room, the large one out front. In the cold white light of winter or the steamy heat of summer, he thought and dreamed and fantasized. Waited for the big break. Listened to the rumpa pumpa rumpa of the Armenians' dough-mixing machines and savoured the sweet-smelling yeasty heat as it pushed up against the floor.

It was an awful and wonderful and frightening thing, being out in the world alone at 29 years old. Sometimes, after he'd only just managed to scrape up the rent, Danny would stand in the bright white entrance to the studio and wonder, what in hell am I doing?

He would get work. Boris got him jobs. Some, he found himself. This morning he had a set of prints to make for a sales flyer. Bicycles. Six of them standing by themselves like cars in a showroom; three others held up by kids along a school-yard wall, ready to take off. He had taken the pictures two days ago. The art director—as advertising flack men now called themselves—wanted the prints by afternoon. On the weekend he had a bar mitzvah to shoot.

He turned down a wedding for Saturday. He used to do weddings; he'd hover in the back of the church behind all the nicely dressed people until the vows had been said. Then he would jump out like a jack-in-the-box to catch the bride and groom and company coming down the aisle, down the steps, enduring the confetti shower, getting into the limousine. Later, he'd leap around like a clown on the bright lawn of Government House or some suburban park with two cameras slugging him on the chest, trying to get all the attendants lined up, trying to get their attention, trying to get them all to smile at the same moment. The job distressed and disconcerted him. Something about it was not quite right. He frequently felt forlorn and lonely, to be in the midst of so many happy people and not know one of them.

Photographing weddings every weekend was, as well, a substantial reminder that he might never do anything else. He knew those people who got stuck forever photographing weddings; they got joked about at the Photographers' Group meetings. They were the guys with the same desperate look in their eyes as shoe salesmen. Most of the photographers, like Danny, liked to picture themselves in other ways. So he quit weddings.

He wished he knew what he wanted so he'd know how to get it. When he looked around, everybody else seemed so sure of themselves; all those business people, professionals, civil servants locked firmly into their career tracks. Not him, though. Maybe if he just waited things would become clear, he thought, like his photos appearing in the developer.

His ambitions were not really fantasies of becoming famous, another Henri Cartier-Bresson or Andre Kertesz, for example. Well, sometimes. But sometimes he just wanted to make a lot of money and have a BMW to drive around in. That would be good too. Usually, he simply wanted to do some really fine work. He wanted to focus all the energy that made him jumpy and locate the big, perfect, final opportunity to make resounding sense out of everything he saw. He knew he would have to look for the job; he couldn't rely on Boris to come up with it for him.

He'd had some good jobs. He surprised himself thinking back on them. Once, for eight months, he'd worked providing pictures for a weekly feature documentary in the newspaper. He collaborated with the writer; they went all over the place. He wrote the stories and Danny provided three or four photos for every piece. They always got a two-page spread and even won a press award. Then the writer was picked up by a paper in Vancouver and Danny was back to square one; only his portfolio to show for it. That's how it goes: one day you're on top of the world, the next day you're waiting for the phone to ring.

It's a funny thing, having a camera, Danny thought. Right away it alters the relationship with everyone and everything. When he left his house in the morning, practically no place was off-limits to him, there was no life he couldn't jump into. The world was his orchard and he could climb any tree he wanted. The camera hanging around his neck and the pretentious title of freelance photographer combined for a wonderful ticket. Virtually any door could be opened, as he first discovered as a 12-year-old kid with the Brownie Instamatic his father had given him. Older cousins who normally wouldn't give him the time of day stopped what they were doing, primped themselves up and shone away when he came along at family gatherings, offering to take their pictures.

It was the vehicle, he discovered immediately and to his delight as soon as he quit the University of Toronto and enrolled in the Polytechnical Institute, that could get him into a room with young women whom he'd never met before. While he was setting up his tripod and lights, they would take off their clothes and pose for him. In the name of Art. Human Figure Study. Now, a guy without a camera, where would he be? Certainly he'd have no legitimacy in that room.

He'd been in jails and cabinet ministers' offices, kindergarten classrooms and Indian reserves. He'd stopped drunks in back alleys and beautiful women on the street. All because he had a camera. The camera gave special privileges, added the extra dimension with the living, he felt, that an undertaker must have with the dead. A one-step-back interpretive role; he'd always felt lucky.

Other people would think of it in funny ways. For most people, the opportunity to pose was beguiling, seductive. They were loath to turn it down. In fact, they'd tell the most personal details about themselves so they could be helpful in the choice of how to photograph them. And they would, nine times out of ten, do any absurd thing the photographer asked once he was ready to snap the picture. Danny had found that no matter how nervous or tentative he'd been in approaching a stranger, he rarely came up dry. They were so eager to accommodate him that he always wondered afterwards why he had been so hesitant in making his approach.

Maybe, he thought, it's the world of pictures we live in, this *People* magazine world. Could it be a tentative crack at immortality? The one chance in a million a person might become one of Walker Evans' sharecroppers or one of August Sanders' Germans, framed in time for all to see? Or maybe a vanity, a chance to leave behind an image no matter how poorly done or poorly circulated? In a world where most people are invisible, an image gave you attention, substance, if only for a moment. It could even be a secret yearning to get on stage and act a small part in life's absurd theatre. How else could you explain powerful businessmen who take nonsense from no one allowing themselves to be photographed out of focus or standing on their heads on their desks for the nation's glossiest monthly magazines?

What was it Susan Sontag said? Photography had screwed up the world. It had objectified everything—people, events, landscapes—so that we believe only in images. Maybe she's right, Danny thought. Once he had gone into a prison shaking in his shoes in anticipation of having to get hard-boiled arsonists, safe-crackers and rapists to stand still while he took their pictures. But he barely started before the word spread and they lined up—cons and thugs with LOVE/HATE tattooed in blue ink across their knuckles—to clutch the bars and press their faces to the tiny opening, or sit on the narrow cot beside the toilet, or stand in the corridor in front of the cells, flexing a Mr. America pose. All for the camera. His problem turned into the opposite of what he had anticipated. He had expected to have trouble getting pictures; instead, he was there all day. He ran out of film and had to leave with 20 men still waiting in line.

Another time, on a Toronto street in the middle of a hot summer afternoon, he spied through a plate glass window a beautiful young woman in a short green dress perched on a stool at a cappucino bar. He stopped to take a long, perspective look. The whole place was chrome and glass and mirrors. In chromium sunlight this lovely woman in the green dress reflected a dozen times in the plate glass, on the rail of the counter, in the mirrors beside and behind the counter. He screwed up his courage and walked in. She demurred for only a short 30 seconds, until it became obvious he would take her reluctance literally and leave. Then she said of course he could photograph her. So he did, for the rest of the afternoon.

When he first started this work, his father kept asking what he was doing, and he'd scramble in his head for his best recent job. "The chairman of the city council's finance committee for the cover of a brochure," he would say. "Hmmm." His father would peer over the tops of his glasses. "And how are you doing, are you making a living?" Always, Danny mumbled an answer that drew on some fiction. It was hard to admit, especially to himself, how precarious things were.

Maybe it's mostly for his father, he thought, that he really wanted the big project, a book or an exhibition that appeared in recognized places, to show something to him. Sometimes when he looked over his shoulder, he thought he could see his father sitting there up high, about where the wall met the ceiling, looking down at him. Whispering over and over again, "Do something."

Once when his father came to Winnipeg, Danny showed

him his studio. And when he came back to the room after getting coffee downstairs, he found him sifting through a pile of current work on his table. Storm windows and awnings for a sales flyer and, underneath, some rejects for one of Boris' bright ideas that he could persuade the Peek A Boo Boutique to shoot their own lingerie ads. A girlfriend of Boris', who was in pharmacy school, was their model. When he came back into the room his father set the photos back on the table, carefully placing Mimi LaBlanca in her lacy brassieres to the bottom of the pile. And he took his coffee.

3

Boris was in a particularly good mood. "Danny O," he hooted as he bounced into the front room of Danny's studio, his big face all lit up. The interruption irked Danny; he was just getting started, searching through the refrigerator where he kept his film stock cool, rummaging behind the boxes of Tri-X for some orange juice so he could feel it was morning instead of almost noon. Then he remembered he had forgotten to pick some up. And now he had the roll of bicycle pictures to print and Boris would delay him. When he looked up, Boris was beaming like a billygoat.

"It's a wonderful day," he said.

"You must've got laid to be so chipper," Danny said. He meant it to be sarcastic, to slow Boris down.

Boris let out a chortle and jumped over to the refrigerator. "What you got in here?" he asked.

Boris reminded Danny of a bull. He had been married three times. His third and current wife lived in Toronto, where she had a high-level job with the Bank of Nova Scotia. Danny had seen pictures of her. She was beautiful; she looked like Lauren Hutton, right down to the little gap in her teeth when she smiled. "How could you leave a woman like that?" he once asked Boris. Boris suddenly looked glum and gave a small, helpless shrug. "I haven't left her, exactly," he said.

And that was true. He still saw her on trips to Toronto, stayed with her sometimes. They would stay together for a few days, have, by his accounts, a good time, then they would be glad to be rid of each other, glad for the break. Or so Boris said.

On Boris' trips to Vancouver, he always moved right in with another woman who did the weather for a television station. When in Winnipeg, he had long, syrupy telephone conversations with both of them. He loved making up pet names and growling into the phone at them. He called them 'my bauble,' 'my little orchid,' 'treasure,' 'sweet stuff,' interchangeably. Sometimes Danny doubted Boris could remember which one he'd called. When they teased him back, he was in heaven. Boris loved those 1500-mile romances.

In Winnipeg he didn't see anybody for more than a night or two. The potential complications were too great. Boris liked to keep a free rein, keep his options open.

To Danny, Boris was a man of wild contradictions. He travelled half the time and always stayed with his women or in the most expensive hotels. Yet he never seemed to have a dollar on him when he was out eating lunch and the cheque arrived, or when he stopped in some place for a couple of drinks. "Can you loan me a few bucks until I see you again?" he would say, even if his companion was impoverished. He had a collection of $600 suits and silk ties in every colour of the rainbow, but he lived in an apartment with barely any furniture. It was an expensive apartment in a high-rise with windows that looked out over the river and the legislative buildings, but it was as empty as a hockey rink in summer. Just acres of pale grey carpet and a couple of folding chairs. It was so empty it echoed. There were magazines all over the floor, a bright red push-button phone, and a huge rented television set so he could catch all the Blue Jays games. The bed in the other room was never made.

Boris could jabber on for hours about Dostoyevsky and Baudelaire, but he didn't have a book in his possession unless it was one that was overdue at the library and had just turned up after being lost for a month among the dirty laundry under his bed.

He treated women with a disregard that was utterly cavalier, yet, almost without exception, they fell in love with him, found him charming, amusing, and were ready to jump in the sack with him. At a party, he could make a young junior analyst from the civil service go all moony by telling her about his time at the Sorbonne, even though he was there for only one afternoon during his life's sole two-week visit to Paris. Even his wife, who must have been sick to death of him, couldn't summon it from within herself to tell him to get lost permanently. Only once did a woman give him what he undoubtedly deserved. She was a lawyer he dated a few times. After he stood her up twice (he protested that work emergencies came up and he forgot), she chased him out of her house, brandishing the poker from her fireplace set. As he took refuge inside his rented car with the doors locked, she swung the fireplace iron like George Bell and broke both his headlights.

Boris was pudgy and slack-muscled and ten pounds overweight, but when he slipped into his bright red sweatsuit and laced on his skates for the pick-up hockey games he and Danny played in winter, he could go like the wind. Long after the others, including those younger than him, were draped over the boards with tongues hanging out, faces grey, zeal long flagged, he'd still be skating, ragging the puck and shouting orders. That was Boris.

Boris was a lawyer by training, but he didn't practise law. He was a salesman, an agent, with interests all over the map. He had a soft spot for artists and writers, and had sold some of Danny's work as well as that of other photographers and a little stable of writers. He bought, he sold, he made deals.

He played both ends. Publishers paid him to find writers, writers paid him to sell their work. He organized stringers and correspondents for newspapers and magazines all over North America. He persuaded manufacturers to advertise their products and found writers to write the ads. He found photographers to shoot the pictures and drummed up models for the photographers. "Just a minute," he would say, "I think I know somebody you might use." He got good rates for everybody and kept a percentage for himself.

Boris was behind Danny's biggest project to date, a calendar of sailboats which they had made together for the Lake of the Woods Sailing Association. Boris went to Minneapolis and told the yachtsmen, "I've got a great idea and I've got the boy to take the pictures. Pay me, we'll put it together and the calendar's yours; you'll make a pile." They bought it and so did every would-be sailor in the midwest.

Boris' fondest hope was that he and Danny would find the perfect Miss July for *Playboy* magazine. "They like Canadian girls down there," he pointed out more than once.

And now, "C'mon," said Boris, straightening up after an unsuccessful rummage through Danny's fridge. "I think I have a job for you, but I don't want to talk about it here. Where's your car?"

"I can't go anywhere," protested Danny. "I've got to work. I've got to get these bicycle prints out by three."

"Such a responsible boy! I like that."

"Then Alice is picking me up."

"Hey," said Boris, feigning an extravagant wink, "the kid's still travelling in fast company." Boris had met Alice.

Danny shrugged, embarrassed.

Boris' energy dazzled and sometimes overwhelmed Danny. From the outset theirs had been a lopsided, one-sided relationship. They met just when Danny had decided to be independent, a full-time freelance photographer. He had no idea what kind of work he'd do. He rented a room in an old office building and moved in, waiting for business to arrive. Boris was next door. They met in the hallway and within a week Boris had given him his first job, a set of publicity shots for a boxer, a young kid he was trying to promote. When he liked those, more assignments followed and within a month he'd set Danny up with little tastes of the kind of work he'd only dreamed about. He'd introduced him to the art director of a big Toronto magazine, an old crony of his, who needed photographs of a famous surgeon who happened to be coming through town to give a lecture. Danny, who thought earlier he might starve to death, now thought he was on his way, all because of Boris.

Sometimes Boris irritated him. Like when Boris bragged about his conquests, or said he'd show up at a certain time and then didn't. Boris irritated him in ways he thought only women could. Sometimes Danny figured he should learn to do without him, not allow himself to be lured into involvement with him. Then Boris would show up, a snowball of energy, and it would be back to the beginning; he would be dazzled by and indebted to him.

"C'mon," said Boris. "I can't hang around, I'm flying to Chicago at supper-time and I have a million things to do first. But one of them is to check out if the photographer would like a chance to travel and get rich. Let's go somewhere where we can talk."

In a few minutes they were heading downtown, across the bridge. Danny realized that the mere mention of jetting off to Chicago had been enough to make his own day and obligations seem trivial. What were a couple of bicycle pictures in the company of international airline tickets, bags always packed, world-beating, deal-making?

Danny knew that in the grand scheme of his hustling, Boris couldn't get rich from him or people like him. Although, where a dollar was concerned, it was likewise true that he was neither so proud nor so careless as to spurn the small jobs. "It all adds up," he would say, putting his big hand on Danny's thin shoulder and delivering his earnest smile of reassurance, his nothing-can-go-wrong smile. "I give as much attention to you as to the big accounts." And he was right, thought Danny. That's what he did; he never ignored the small accounts. In his romantic life as well. If it was ten o'clock and he had nothing going for the night, he would pick up a likely-looking girl at a cocktail lounge in the suburbs or a lonely secretary at the edge of a dance floor downtown. Even though he knew he'd never see her again after nine the next morning, he would romance her as if she were Queen of the Prom—a candlelight dinner at midnight, a drive by the river and out around the golf course. Boris was like that. "They all add up," he would say.

Where Boris really wanted to hustle, though, was not with writers and photographers and models, but in sports and politics. The 'big tickets,' he called them. He tried first with boxers. His first, a big blond kid with the staying power of a steeplechase horse, could have gone a long way but was bounced out of the fight business when he got arrested with a briefcase full of amphetamines. "You can't trust them with tying their own shoes," lamented Boris. "You can't let them out of the house alone."

His second protégé, an Indian from up north whom he named, absurdly, "Billy Boxing Brave," broke his hand, and when complication after complication set in so it looked as if it would never heal right, he gave up and moved back to The Pas. Boris was still looking for the sure-footed slugger with the certain shot at the title, confident that he lurked just around the corner, in the next barroom or the next high-school gym.

He wanted to manage famous football players and negotiate million-dollar contracts for star centres and NHL goalies, but so far they had eluded him. He did find two hockey players in Saskatchewan whom he parlayed all the way to the Minnesota North Stars, but neither became a great light in the firmament. Yet Boris remained hopeful. "You watch," he would say, "they'll find their legs and when contract time comes round again I'll make them rich."

In politics he billed himself as a consultant, which can mean, of course, almost anything. A few years ago, when it was still legal to do so, he persuaded a group of orthodontists and chiropractors to secure a healthy tax loophole by investing in 'scientific research.' Boris relieved them of numerous thousands of their dollars and delivered the money to five guys in lab coats who'd rented a warehouse in a small town near the U.S. border. Using contacts he'd assiduously cultivated in the federal government, he put together a fat proposal and won the little company $3.5 million in federal grants.

For a while, everything clicked, everything was rosy. But then reporters started sniffing around. Turned out that Boris' little group of researching scientists was no more than a band of latter-day alchemists using a second-hand boiler to cook the life out of poplar logs. Given that the province's sugar-beet industry had just laid off workers and lowered prices due to a glut on the market, the group's protestation that they were researching ways to manufacture sugar from wood chips fell on deaf or scornful ears. "It would make more sense," announced one town councillor in the little burg where they were located, "if they were to make wood out of sugar." The government, embarrassed by the publicity, cancelled the grant and rescinded the tax break; the orthodontists and chiropractors scrambled to extract the little of their money that was left; the project fell apart in a shambles. The white coats headed for the hills with the legal actions of angry oral surgeons at their heels, and Boris never made a penny.

But he bounced back. After a period of laying low, he inched back up to his current point, where he billed himself as the confidant of the Hon. Peter Alverstone, federal minister of Labour and Opportunity. When Boris realized the government was about to change, he saw for himself a chance to start afresh. Democracy is a forgiving way of life, after all, he said to himself. He looked around and his eyes settled on Alverstone, an attractive young man with a movie-star head of blond hair, a Ph.D. in economics, mediterranean blue eyes and a perpetual tan. When Alverstone, pushed by the polls, leaped from the faculty club into a federal election campaign with an eye to the cabinet, Boris was right in there pitching— volunteering himself as 'media advisor' and handling the PR and advertising. For the month-long campaign he bounced around town 20 hours a day in the cause of Peter Alverstone.

When it was over, Alverstone was put in the cabinet. But by now Boris didn't know what he was going to get out of it. The aftermath of the campaign was a huge let-down. He kept his brave, chipper smile and passed on the gossip as he heard it third-hand from Ottawa to anyone who would listen, but he never got to go to Ottawa himself. Nobody knew what he expected; maybe he believed that as Alverstone's lynch pin he'd be in the capital every week, hob-nobbing with the high rollers, partying with Mila Mulroney, maybe named to the board of directors of Air Canada. He was invited once, on Alverstone's stationery, to a dinner commemorating the founding of the Canadian Labour Congress. But that was it. At political and party functions in Winnipeg Boris stayed at the edge, twirled his drink, smiled like crazy, tried to play the big shot. But nobody let him all the way in.

They drove, under Boris' direction, through a few downtown streets, parked in a back lane and walked to a white building whose doorway was framed by blinking pink and blue lights. In a minute their eyes were adjusting to the dark interior of a room about the size of a bowling alley. Boris, who'd put on his grey worsted jacket but no tie, bounded to a table right at the front and pulled out two chairs.

Danny looked around. It was a huge room with a low ceiling. An expansive stage jutted out into the middle, taking up almost a third of the area. On a lightbulb-lined runway were displayed a gymnasium's worth of gadgets: a brass pole like the ones in a firehall and a trapeze-style swing that hung from the ceiling, a big iron bathtub and, at the front, a little raised dais.

Even though it was barely 11 o'clock in the morning, the bar was already half full with city streets-department workers and delivery-truck drivers taking an early and prurient lunch. And the first of the girls pranced like a showhorse up and down the runway. Boris ordered two Labatts from a waitress in black leather hotpants. "Isn't this great?" he said. His face beamed in the blinking lights.

Danny took a long draught of beer from his bottle. It tasted furry so early in the day. He felt nervous and when he looked at the girl he felt depressed. He wondered how quickly he could crank out the bicycle prints and deliver them. "What's the job?" he asked, trying to get Boris' attention away from the stage.

"Look at this!" exclaimed Boris. The dancer, a tall redhead with sinfully long slim legs, had pulled her miniskirt up to her waist and was rubbing herself against the shiny brass fireman's pole. The city workers hooted, the truck drivers banged their bottles on the tables. "Hoo, hoo," Boris shouted. Danny looked the other way to where a couple of motorcycle gang members in leather jackets watched the scene flatly from behind unwashed beards and pimple-scarred faces. Both had their hands clasped in front of their stomachs as if to hold something in.

"It's still a bit up in the air," said Boris. Then, seeing the look of skepticism cross Danny's face, he hurried. "But I think it could be very big." He reached into his pocket and pulled out a couple of booklets, big, eight-page, brochure-style sheets. Danny moved his beer aside and laid them on the table in front of him. The light wasn't good but he could see well enough, half- and quarter-page glossy pictures of palm-tree-studded islands, families in bathing suits lolling around pools, sunsets on beach vistas, flocks of colourful tropical birds lifting off salt marshes, smiling attractive women drinking from straws out of hollowed-out pineapple halves.

"What are these?" asked Danny.

"Promotions," said Boris.

Danny looked at him again but Boris had turned his attention back to the stage and grinned with glee. The tall redhead was now bereft of all her clothes except for a pair of white pumps. For a couple of minutes, to the cheers of the audience, she flopped around almost desperately on the little front part of the stage which had, almost magically through the push of some hidden button, raised itself up hydraulically about three feet amid more coloured flashing lights. Then she climbed off and began to move along the front row of tables, accepting tips by pressing her white breasts together and encouraging the audience to stick folded dollar bills down between them.

"Listen," said Boris, "I can't tell you too much yet because it's still an idea. I just wanted to see if you were interested." Danny refolded the brochures. One had been soaked by spilled beer and the picture of a blond man and woman riding motorbikes up a flower-lined drive almost disintegrated between his fingers. "The dough," Boris paused for emphasis, "should be very good. This is a class project." He put a little extra on the word *class* and smiled broadly.

Danny didn't quite understand and wanted to ask more but Boris interrupted. "Hey," he said, "have you got a dollar?" Danny rummaged through his wallet for a bill. Boris took it, folded it precisely, then stood up. Before Danny knew what was happening, he leaned out over the stage with the dollar stuck in his mouth like the beak of a woodpecker. His white teeth gleamed at both sides of his mouth as he motioned the sweating redheaded girl to bring her breasts up so that he could peck the money down between them.

4

When Danny got back after leaving Boris he was in a hurry—two and a half hours to get the bicycle pictures out and then Alice was supposed to pick him up. The red light on his answering machine was on and two pieces of mail were stuck under his door. One was a thin business envelope from Toronto with the address and crest of York University in its upper left-hand corner. The other was a postcard from his father, sent from Plantation Key, Florida. The picture was of a brown pelican sitting on a post in front of a blue sky and a choppy sea.

He felt a catch in his chest when he saw his father's handwriting. His father lived now in Florida, in a condominium on Plantation Key, two hours south of Miami. He returned to

Canada each summer to visit his family and his former parishioners. He stayed in the small town of Treeton where he'd spent 43 years as minister of the United Church and where Danny had grown up; or in Kingston, the gothic Lake Ontario city where Danny's younger sister Leslie now lived. She was a psychiatrist who, with her husband John, worked out of a hospital at Queen's University. His father hadn't been to Winnipeg to see him or his older sister Samantha for the two years since he'd retired, and Danny felt a little guilty because last summer he hadn't been able to rouse himself to make the obligatory trip to Ontario. Maybe he could go to Florida. He looked at the message on the back of the card. A shot of irritation passed over him before he consciously dispelled it. He felt that he longed for something from his father, something interesting or new, something engaging. Something to force them to turn a corner. What he always got, it seemed, was the same old stuff. "Back again for the season and have settled in. Weather is hot but what can you expect. Best wishes, Dad."

He wondered how his father lived, what his apartment looked like. It had been a long time since his mother had died, when he was 11. How frighteningly lonely it had been then, the cancer almost dissolving his mother. He remembered his father, then, and how his mother's death had changed him. His father had seemed to retreat, to disappear into his study and his work, preparing sermons and making endless, constant trips to meetings and conferences. If Danny expected him to bring light and warmth back into their lives, it never happened. Danny was left with women: his two sisters, little Leslie and Samantha, and, for a couple of years, Aunt Bea, his father's younger sister who'd come to stay with them to try to take hold of the fractured household. His father was like a shadow.

The town thought him a hero. When he retired a couple of years ago, they held a week of receptions and farewells. The church, too, regarded him highly. Over the years he had been chairman of some of its most important provincial and national committees. But to his family it was as though he'd missed a step.

One summer Danny's team had won the juvenile 'B' baseball championship. He was 14. In the wake of their victory he and two friends had rushed, still sweating and dusty, into the house with the news, only to be shushed by Aunt Bea. His father was busy writing and couldn't be disturbed. For an awkward moment his friends looked to him to see what he would do, and then they all got on their bikes and went out to the river. A few days later, as if to make up for it, his father, dressed in a tie, white shirt and vest, had suggested they go out into the backyard for a game of catch. Danny had been looking at a book. They commenced a desultory game; the first two throws sailed high above Danny's head. Then, feeling embarrassed and clumsy, they'd given up and returned to the house.

Now his father had disappeared almost completely, to Florida. To his children it was an astonishing move, although Danny could not have said what sort of move he should have made. At his retirement he had announced he was going south, "like a bird." Then he modified it with a rationale about his health. His rheumatism was starting to bother him, he said, so he didn't like the cold. But he didn't move with the rest of North America's arthritics to the dry heat of Arizona; he went to the damp, oceanic humidity of Florida, following the advice of his sister, Danny's Aunt Julia, and of one of his old parishioners, a real-estate broker with his own house near Fort Lauderdale. "Try it, Albert," they told him. "See how you like it." "I can get fresh oranges right off the tree, grapefruit, pomegranates," bragged the real-estate man.

He went first to a hotel on Miami Beach's strip, then to an apartment in Coral Gables. And then, by late winter of his first year, he took his savings and poured them into a bone-white, cement condominium apartment on Plantation Key.

Danny tore open the other letter. The one from York

University. It surprised him. It held out the possibility of a job. Work. It was from a man he had never heard of, a Professor Bellows in the faculty of anthropology. "I am presently involved in an extensive study of the Cree people of northern Manitoba," he wrote, "and would like to accompany my work with a collection of photographs taken in a number of present day communities.

"I am familiar with your work through having seen your pictures from Wasagee River published in *Environmental Accent* magazine last year, and through contacts I have with Dr. Lawrence Charlton at the University of Manitoba who recommends you highly." He went on to propose that everything from their collaboration would be published in a book, that Danny would be paid handsomely—all expenses and a retainer as they went along plus a fee for every picture used. And he asked, should he be interested, for an opportunity to meet in Winnipeg. He signed it Prof. James George Bellows BA, MA, Ph.D., York University Faculty of Anthropology.

Danny looked around at the current state of his studio. Of course he was interested. He had the bar mitzvah on the weekend. And maybe Boris would get him more work for Sears or for the Waterbed Palace. Or maybe the scheme for the promotional brochures on the sun-splashed beaches would turn into something. But there was precious little else on the horizon; he needed the work.

But more than that, he realized with a sudden eagerness, this might have grander possibilities. It had the potential of a body of work with focus. This could be exciting. He imagined trips in buzzing little six- and eight-seater airplanes, skimming across the rocks and trees and lakes and rivers and muskeg of the north, being carried further and further from civilization. He imagined them landing, with their bedrolls and his Minolta and a bag of film, on little sandbar airstrips with motor canoes waiting to haul them, him and the professor, further up rivers to places where they could step ashore and there, photograph Indians!

And the cheque. He did a quick calculation of some of the figures the professor had alluded to in his letter. He came up with a sum and mentally tacked it on to the existing estimate of his present and next year's income carried around, always, in the back of his brain. The new figures inflated the tallies nicely. He was reassured; he was buoyed.

He pressed the rewind button on his answering machine. "Hi, it's me." It was Alice. "I can't make it this afternoon but I'll see you sometime. Bye." Blithe and cheery as a bird. He stood for a second, then wound the tape back and replayed the message. What did she mean, "I'll see you sometime"? He picked up the phone and dialled her number. No answer. His stomach constricted with a disturbing though familiar mixture of jealousy, anger, frustration, longing and lust. He felt irked.

Alice was a difficult girlfriend, if he even dared call her that. Elusive and whimsical as a chickadee, she had the power to throw weak men (and something in her chemistry made all men weak) into realms of prolonged torment. Currently she was throwing him.

Probably he shouldn't even be involved. Being with Alice was like going downhill skiing when it was basketball you were good at. But here he was: a chirpy non-explanation on a magnetic tape, a broken date, and him holding his groin in perplexity.

He found it all paralysing. He didn't know what to do. He felt ensnared not just by Alice, but by women. Women were at the very centre of the great hole of his wanting. The female —body, face, clothes, smell, voice, touch, sex (or more accurately the prospect or possibility of it)—was the fulcrum upon which all reality turned. He felt it must be so for every man. How could it be otherwise, since for him the need, the awareness, was so ever-present, so close at hand, so powerful?

Yet of the men he knew the approaching, and so perhaps also the need, definitely differed. His friend Roger, for example. Roger lived alone in a room in an elderly downtown hotel where he worked every day writing a great long book on 'relationships in the 20th century'. Roger was a romantic with the will, stated repeatedly, to support, nourish, love and champion a woman. But he was so shy and awkward he couldn't meet any. His life was defined narrowly; it revolved around the neat pile of his developing manuscript, his old Underwood typewriter, his little second-floor room in the decaying Prince George Hotel, his friendships with Danny and perhaps three other people, bicycle rides to his mother's house on Manitoba Avenue, afternoons, evenings and weekends at the movies (he saw every movie that came to town at least twice), and falling impossibly in love.

"Impossibly" because his love grew in impossible situations, with women he couldn't have or didn't even know, in situations where there was no hope. Because he was so shy when it came to meeting real ones, Roger fell in love with pictures of women in magazines or newspapers; he fell in love with sales clerks or with women waiting at red lights. They, of course, never fell for him in return; they didn't even know he existed. Danny tried to tell him that this was one reason why he wrote; maybe if he were famous he could get all the girls he wanted. Like Leonard Cohen. They would read his words and see what a sensitive, perceptive fellow he was, and then they would fall for him the way he fell for them.

He was currently in love, or thought he was, with a bureaucrat at the National Arts Endowment Fund. Gillian spent much of her time travelling across the country, talking to people who wanted money. Roger met her when he was applying for a grant. "Should I ask her out?" he demanded of Danny. "What should I do?"

Or Boris. Boris, to Danny, was a rollicking bus on its way to the carnival. A dozen girls a week loaded on for the ride and then dropped off. No discrimination; the slightest willingness to engage was the only price on the ticket. When the ride was over, a friendly wave. No hard feelings, see you soon.

What Danny needed and wanted most and sought to find

wrapped in the soft flesh between the arms, between the breasts, between the thighs, in the warmth of the voice, was a friendship that would melt him wholly, yet would not consume or frighten him. At age 29 he still had not found it.

Sometimes he wondered if there was something in the fact of his mother's dying early, abandoning him before she could shepherd him into that world where the sexes knew how to behave, how to treat one another, how to get along. It was a self-pitying thought, he knew, but when you're approaching 30 and have had nothing but false starts, you have to look somewhere to place the blame.

When he was 27 he had met Rosalind. Rosalind was 15 years older and worked for an art gallery. She was a tall, willowy woman with large nervous eyes and dark chestnut hair that she kept piled and pinned in a bun. She had exquisite taste in clothes and furniture, and an adolescent son. Her husband, a research physicist for an aerospace corporation who travelled all over the world, had ignored her for years.

Her husband had led her to believe, she confided, that she was frigid. Rosalind wasn't frigid at all. Hurt and humiliated for years in her exquisite suburban house, she took an instant liking to Danny when he walked into the art gallery looking for a deal on second-hand picture frames. And he found himself pleasantly though warily attracted to an elegant woman with a nice house and wardrobe, more than a decade his senior and already a mother. On nights when her son was at his father's, they lay curled on the huge waterbed she'd bought the week after her separation, underneath a whorehouse-size chandelier, and she stroked his hair and fed him cakes and liqueurs. At noon on days when she worked, she came to the narrow bed in his apartment or to the roll-out piece of foam rubber he kept in his studio. Taking off her wool skirts and her silk blouses, and shaking her hair loose from its bun, she climbed on top of him and worked like a journeyman trying to achieve those possible but all too elusive orgasms.

The intensity was exhausting. Danny was fascinated by
the beauty of the thin older body, the child-bearing creases on
the lower belly, the breasts small and slightly dropped like
lightbulbs, the flat behind, the feet long and bony. Her face
was elegant as a Modigliani painting. Yet Rosalind frightened
him. He felt he was making love to his mother. She panicked
too. She started phoning him at all hours; she wanted to line
up future dates three at a time. Danny felt overbooked. He
made excuses to give himself more time. He told her he had
to go out of town and then hid out at Boris' apartment for two
days, sleeping on the couch. Finally he went to her lovely
house, sat among the muted colours of her living-room and
told her he didn't think he could do it anymore. He felt stifled;
it was too much for him. An enormous river-sized hurt welled
up in her eyes. She turned her head and asked, facing away,
if they couldn't make love one last time. He felt his heart sink
in his chest like a balloon leaking air. But he began to un-
button his shirt.

When they were finished she turned to rigid fury. While
he was still getting into his clothes she was at the door, holding it open for him to leave her house. For weeks after he
would find notes, short, one and two sentences, under his
apartment door or in his studio mailbox.

Then he met Alice, who didn't want him at all. Or she
wanted him as part of a team of opthomologists and olympic
volleyball stars she somehow needed to keep her going. Alice
was a 25-year-old medical intern with the kind of thighs in
bathing-suit ads. Firm, brown, pliable, long. A romance with
Alice was not a romance like any other. It was a ride to outer
space in a shuttle that might blow up at any moment. There
was no compatibility, only frenzy. But as long as it lasted the
ride was so terrific that Danny couldn't blame himself for not
wanting to get off.

Alice would have liked to have been a tennis pro or a scuba
diver working off the California coast. That she liked him both
intrigued him and served as a marvellous aphrodisiac. But

she also liked big houses, holidays in hot places, and men who owned Mercedes. She always kept a couple of dentists on the line. She liked to offer Danny unsolicited advice about his career and his life. "You should advertise," she would say. "You could make a lot of money doing what you do but you have to do it differently. Go see my father, see what he can do for you." Her father was a businessman with connections in the Conservative Party.

Or she would tell him how he should get his hair cut or what kind of clothes he should have, or she would criticize his studio, calling it an office too shabby to be an office. "It's not an office," he would protest, angry. Alice didn't understand anything, he told himself.

Then she'd say, "You should move to the country." This on an afternoon when they were driving down back roads like gangbusters because she liked to drive fast with Bruce Springsteen screaming on the tape deck. "You look good out here. A little cabin would suit you." She would give his shirt collar a tug, but then they'd have to go back to the city because she'd arranged to have dinner with her father.

She talked about sex all the time but somehow something always happened before they actually got to it. She realized she had to get up early. Or she had to call her father or one of her girlfriends. Or the hospital called her. Or she would have a strained back from that afternoon's tennis lesson. Or she would have a date with one of her dentists.

But she had that wonderful, pliable beauty. And when they did screw—Alice always called it "screwing," never "making love"—it was another world. Being with her was like living in a movie. They were driving in from the country one hot afternoon in late summer and she said, "Let's go by the hospital."

"What for?" Danny asked. He was afraid she had to work.

"I want to do it in a hospital bed." She leaned over and bit the sleeve of his shirt.

He looked at her. "You're kidding."

"No," she said. She sat up. "They'll think we're visitors and we'll find an empty room." She tucked her brown legs up underneath her on the seat.

"Alice. . . ." Danny said. He didn't know what to say; he feared they might have to go through with this. "Why don't we just go to my place?"

Danny would have loved to be the kind of guy who could play along with Alice's schemes. But he was not. He tried, sometimes, but she was so wacky and thought so fast that he couldn't keep up. It was a tennis game and he couldn't return the serves. Embarrassed, he would start to close up while watching himself with growing disgust, wishing he were different. But there seemed to be nothing he could do about it. If there was a course he could take to learn how to be wacky, he would have taken it.

"Come on, I've always wanted to make it in a hospital bed," she said. "That's why I studied medicine."

"Are you sure we can get in?" Danny asked. This was seeming more and more crazy, yet plausible.

"Sure," she said. "I once made it with a doctor in the O.R." His mouth dropped.

She giggled. "It was late at night, there were no more operations for that day."

"Jesus," he said. He started to feel depressed.

She didn't notice. She continued, "He had an appendectomy at nine the next morning and there we were at midnight, right on the table he'd be using."

As they drove Danny thought about this; he started to get a feeling low in his stomach and through the sides of his neck, reckless and excited.

But something strange always happened with Alice. By the time they got to the place where they could turn off for the hospital, they had talked themselves out. So they kept driving and he took her home instead.

5

Late in the afternoon Danny dialled Alice's number once more. No answer. He was still at his studio. The emptiness of his white front room made him anxious, a feeling almost like the panic he got when he was late for an appointment. He sat down and listened to the silence for a minute. He could hear himself breathing. Impulsively he picked up the phone again and dialled his older sister Samantha, though half-way through the action he didn't know why he was doing it. When he was depressed a conversation with Samantha certainly never helped.

His niece Prissy answered the phone. "Hello?" Her six-year-old voice turned the greeting into an exaggerated question. He smiled. Prissy always made him feel better. She was the one thing that made Samantha's living so close to him, in the same city, Samantha with all her problems, tolerable.

"Hi kiddo, is your mom there?"

"We're moving." She announced it as if it were news of winning the lottery.

"I know."

Samantha and Prissy moved regularly, at least once a year, sometimes more frequently, from one square, box-like, single-mother's apartment for which she could barely scrape together the monthly rent, to another, another so similar Danny always wondered why she went to the effort. Maybe it was some sort of forlorn quest for a better life (or for life, period) to be found through slight variations in kitchen/dining-room/living-room layouts. Or it was trying to find a life that fit, like trying on dresses until she found her size. Or maybe looking for new apartments and moving was simply something to keep her busy. Since Ray, her swaggering high-school-beau-cum-husband, had moved her and Prissy to Winnipeg in search of elusive adventure and riches and then had moved on (alone) in search of still further elusive adventure and riches, Samantha had been in an ongoing, confused quest to occupy herself. She was now in her third year of it.

"Mom, it's Uncle Danny," Prissy's perpetually optimistic voice chirped at the other end of the phone.

"Hello." Samantha's voice. Flat and unexpressive as it had been when she was a teenager. Then, after their mother died, she, the eldest, had somehow internalized (as Leslie would explain it) all her terror and had put her head down, skipping school to do housework in a valiant effort to fill their mother's vacant shoes. An effort that drove their father to distraction and embarrassed everyone else.

"I got a card from dad today." He tried to sound cheerful.

"Oh."

"He didn't say much, it was just a card. He's back there."

"I'm moving," she said. "Do you think you can help?"

"Yeah, sure." She'd sidestepped his entire message about their father and he didn't know how to remake the point. If he did, she'd avoid it again. Some day, he knew, they'd have to get into it; he would have to summon the energy to referee a 20-year-overdue confrontation between his sister and his father. And she might have to do the same.

"We're moving Saturday morning at eight. I really like the new place."

"Eight o'clock in the morning? That's awfully early, isn't it?"

"That's when Al can get a truck." She sounded suddenly irritated.

"Okay, I'll be there."

He hung up the phone, turned out the lights, locked up the studio and went downstairs. The Armenian bakers had quit for the day and everything was silent. He went around the building to his car, an oversized and out-of-date Pontiac, a decision forming in his mind to drive out by Alice's place. Making such a drive would use up some of his anxious energy, but he didn't know what else it would achieve. In the back of his mind he knew it was a stupid thing that would only irritate him further. But people, he mused wryly, not knowing what they really wanted, did such stupid things all the time.

Alice lived in a low, three-storey apartment building on a clean street in River Heights, a building not dissimilar to the one Samantha would end up in but in a better neighbourhood. Danny parked the Pontiac half a block past her building and walked back, entered the door and pressed her number. There was no answer.

He waited a minute, then walked back and got into his car. He was about to pull out when he looked in the rear-view mirror and saw a red Buick stop in front of Alice's building. In a moment Alice stepped out of the passenger's side. She wore a little white dress and when she bent over to say something to the person in the driver's side, the breeze blew it against her.

Danny turned around. A serious-looking man in his early 30s, wearing a light suit and a nice haircut, got out, carefully locked the door on the shiny new car and walked around to join Alice. The two of them went into Alice's building. They had not seen Danny.

He sat for a long minute. He wasn't sure what to do or how he felt. Finally he started the car. It was starting to become dusk. He drove to the end of the street, then turned and drove slowly around the block. When he passed Alice's building he slowed down even more. The light in her living room was on. He re-parked his car and sat there. Then he got out; the early evening air was chilly. He crossed the street and walked back past Alice's building. He knew he wasn't being as nonchalant as he liked to think he could be; if Alice and Haircut happened to look out the window and see him he would feel very foolish. He glanced up. The living-room window was now dark and her bedroom window was lighted through its blinds. The shiny red Buick, not a mark or a speck of dust on it, sat like a mocking sentry on the street. A good kick at one of its hubcaps might make him feel better.

There was a young spruce tree on the lawn by Alice's building. Its limbs looked sturdy up to about the place where her bedroom window started. He glanced back and forth, up and down the street. There was no one on the sidewalk. It took him an eighth of a second to recall a full litany of the frustrations he'd had over the months with Alice. This guy's a goddamn dentist or a goddamn accountant with his goddamn account number tattooed on his pecker, he thought. I wonder if he can get it up or if she just wants to look at it. He took a step toward the tree and then was startled by the loud squawk of a tailpipe scraping on the pavement. A car halfway down the block backed out of a driveway. He stepped back on the sidewalk, breathing quickly in short, hyperventilating puffs. His head felt light. He walked to the end of the street and then back to his car.

He stood for a half minute leaning against his car door. It

was getting darker and the light in Alice's bedroom stood out like a beacon. He got in, started his car and drove to the end of the street. A phone booth in front of a 7-Eleven store was lit like a glow-worm. He left his car running and put money in the phone. He dialled. It rang. It rang again, seven times. He waited. He heard it lift on the other end and Alice's voice said "Hello?" Far away and small. "Hello," she said once more. He hung up. He got back in his car, still running, and hit the steering wheel as hard as he could with his fist.

Danny drove home and climbed on his bed. His hand throbbed. Maybe he had broken something. He felt foolish. He hated himself for his reaction to Alice, but it was her fault. He sat in the silence of his apartment. He wanted the phone to ring so he could refuse to answer it.

It was almost dark in his bedroom. He heard noises from outside and went to the window. Down below, a drunk was getting sick against the wall of his building. People drank in the park up the street and from time to time the odd one would end up in his courtyard. The drunk, a middle-aged man, heaved and coughed and banged his head against the brick wall of the building. A woman in a white smock that almost glowed in the low light stood behind him, her hand on his shoulder, steadying him, or herself. God, Danny felt suddenly lonely; his lip quivered. His irritation at the drunks passed. Someone across the courtyard opened a window and shouted at them to leave. The woman looked up and raised her hand in a defiant gesture, almost losing her balance in the process. "Fuck you," she shouted in a high, nasal slur. But they left, the man still coughing and staggering.

Danny turned from the window, needing to do something. He washed his hand in icy water. He wanted to talk to someone. Boris, he remembered, was out of town. He wished there was another woman he could see but he couldn't think of any who would be happy to see him. He couldn't call Samantha, he didn't need a sister. Maybe Roger could go somewhere with him and get something to eat, have a drink.

But Roger couldn't meet him. "I've agreed to go to this party; some teachers, at a friend's house," he explained on the phone. "I sort of like the guy, I used to work with him." He paused. "Why don't you come along?"

Teachers were doing okay these days. Roger's pal lived in a suburban split-level on a street heavily treed with Chinese elms and blue spruce. The neighbourhood was like a forest: houses in subdued, discreet colours tucked back in the trees behind lawns studded with juniper and various other tamed bushes, all strategically placed to give just the slightest hint of wilderness.

When Danny and Roger arrived, the driveway and the street in front were full, parked with sensible, understated cars, Volvos and Subarus. Nothing flashy, very sensible engineering. *Consumer Reports*. A couple of Soviet-built Ladas for the social scientists. They parked the Pontiac.

Roger's pal's wife, a sprightly woman in a lively yellow jumpsuit, met them at the door. In the background they could hear the din of the party, the hubbub of talk. Roger was immediately ill at ease.

A large man with wavy brown hair broke away from conversation with an earnest East Indian man in one of the doorways and came over, steering a drink in front of him.

"Roger," he exuded in an accent that was more than slightly English. "So glad you could come."

Roger smiled. "Hi," he said. Then, almost as an afterthought, "This is my friend, Danny. I brought him along."

The Englishman fixed Danny with a level blue gaze. "Fine, fine," he said. "The more the merrier. Alan," he introduced himself and reached for Danny's hand. "How do you do, Danny?"

The handshake was the hearty, aggressive kind Danny associated with assertively friendly people who get drunk before a party's over and tell you too much about themselves.

But they always resent you later for having the knowledge. Roger's pal took a deep draught of his drink. "Help your-selves," he said, motioning expansively with a sweep that took in the whole of the room, if not the house, although what he meant mainly was the table filled with liquor bottles, mixes, potato chips, and sliced vegetables and dips.

Although the night air was chilly, a number of people had spilled out through glass patio doors into a backyard. They stood in little groups between the house and a small, kidney-shaped swimming pool that was still filled, although it was late in the season. Roger got waylaid early by people who knew him and Danny drifted, as if island hopping, from one small cluster of people he didn't know to the next. Just about everyone was a teacher, or spouse of a teacher, or friend of a teacher, or an educational administrator. Shop-talk and gos-sip; only photographers, he thought, are worse. One short, blocky man, who punched the air incessantly with his cigarette glowing like a signet ring in his curled fist, ex-pounded about contracts.

"If the government wants us to keep working for a pissing three percent, I say balls to them. Let them put something on the table too."

"But Harold," said a woman with a sharp face and sandy-coloured hair starting to grey, "it's a buyer's market. There's not much we can do. I talked to friends in Toronto"—she pronounced it deliberately, To-ron-to—"and it's the same there."

"Bullshit. If we all walk out we'd see what kind of buyer's market it was."

Danny reached the side of the swimming pool and turned around to survey the crowd. Someone had turned on a spot-light at the corner of the house and it bathed about a quarter of the yard in a pale, yellow glow.

He looked over the women, one by one. Despite Alice, or because of her, he felt pointedly on the make. What else was new? He realized he was almost always on the look-out. Even when doing something as innocent as buying groceries or doing his laundry, there was always the possibility that a real good one would walk by. Some days that possibility was all that kept him going.

There were lots of women in Alan's house and on his patio; any gathering of academics or teachers is bound to have its share. Danny spotted two standing just under the eaves of the carport. One, a tall girl with pale skin and black hair bobbed short in tight curls all over her head, struggled to open a bottle of beer. He stepped closer. She grimaced.

"I hate these screw caps," she said, turning uselessly at the neck of the bottle. "I think I cut my finger." She stuck her finger in her mouth.

Her friend, a short, pudgy blonde, a little drunk already, started to giggle, snorting away like a tractor.

"Here, let me try," Danny offered. But before he could take her bottle, two well-tanned Lothario types stepped up. Bandit moustaches and shirt-fronts open. More and more teachers are like this these days, thought Danny.

"I can open it with my eye socket," said one. This announcement sent Blondie into such gales of tittering she had to turn away and hold her stomach.

"I can open it with my teeth," said the other.

The curly-haired girl handed the bottle of beer to the fellow with the teeth. He stuck it in the side of his mouth and, sure enough, popped the top. He held the open bottle out, triumphant. Foam ran down his chin and dripped onto his chest. Danny walked away.

A woman with short brown hair sat alone on the deck by the pool, her chin resting on her knees and her arms hugging her legs. She stared into the water, seeming oblivious to the party that dinned in the background. Danny watched her for a minute, then fumbled for an opening line. No matter what he said, that's what it was going to sound like.

"Nice water," he said.

"Hmm?" she said. She turned her head only a fraction, but

her eyes looked into his. Her eyes were green. Danny squatted down so he was at her level.

"I'm not a teacher," he said.

She laughed.

"I don't even know the addresses of any schools." He was trying hard and felt a little embarrassed but she laughed again and he felt better, confident. She had perfect teeth.

"I guess it can be a bit tedious," she said. "I'm not a teacher, either."

They managed only a few more sentences before Big Alan, the host, cruised up. He landed a large hand on Danny's shoulder. "You seem to be faring well," he boomed. Then, before anybody could phrase an answer, he said to the girl, "Well, Rita, your man Harold never stops, he's going to have us all on strike before the night's out." He laughed. Rita sniffed but didn't answer. He turned to Danny. "I say, I've got a little dark-room in the basement you might like to see. Nothing much, but my little corner."

Danny didn't want to see it in the least. Looking at Big Alan's dark-room was the last thing he wanted to do. Rita was already getting up to move back toward the party. "See ya," she said in a low voice.

"I mainly do pictures of nature, birds. And the kids," said Alan. "But I have the whole Nikromat system. Cost me thousands. It's a beauty." He led Danny away.

When they emerged from Alan's basement, Danny passed Roger in the kitchen. Roger was pushed back against the counter, looking helpless and stricken as the Pakistani geophysics professor regaled him, close up, his nose three inches away from Roger's, hands flapping in animation, about some problem he had solved after months of experimentation. When Roger moved his head back an inch, the professor compensated, zooming in closer.

Alan pushed past Danny to pour himself almost a full glass of gin. In the doorway to the living room Rita was cornered in a triangle of men. One tall, thin fellow with a sad, hound-like face and a tweed jacket expounded about Yeats. "They wanted me to expand the paper and make it a book," he said. "But I told them, where would I find the time?" Rita stood on one foot, the other hooked behind her ankle, leaning on the door jamb. A half inch of ash fell from her cigarette onto the front of her silk shirt; she brushed it off with two quick flicks of her hand and exhaled a stream of smoke into the conversation. Danny wondered if he should break in, then decided not to. The circle was too tight; he didn't want to be just the fourth man. He turned in the other direction. He thought Rita caught his eye for an instant as he slipped by.

In the hallway leading to the bathroom two figures squirmed frantically in the shadows. It was Blondie, the giggler, and the guy who could pop bottle caps with his teeth. He had one arm moored against the wall behind her head and his free hand up under her sweater. "Don't," she said. "Oh, mmmm."

Danny made his way toward the patio where he encountered Harold. Harold was propped in the doorway, swaying slightly. One hand held a half-filled glass, and the other gripped the doorway to keep him steady. He looked at Danny. His eyeballs looked sunburnt. "Last year I got some of 'em over the 40 thousand threshold," he slurred. He fixed Danny in his gaze. "I negotiated it. But do they appreciate it?" He raised his eyebrows and swayed dangerously.

Danny shrugged; he had no idea how to respond.

"Naw," Harold continued. "They don't 'preciate it. Some of 'em even want me out. Well, I say," he took a drink from his glass, "if they don't 'preciate me, screw 'em. What do you say?"

"Yeah," Danny said, "screw 'em."

Harold chortled, letting him past. "Hey, wait," he shouted, but Danny kept on going.

In a few minutes Danny returned to the house. Harold was no longer in the patio doorway but had moved into the den, a sunken room just off to the side and filled with plants. He lay on the floor with his head in the lap of the woman with the greying hair. She stroked his head absently. He appeared to be asleep. Danny looked for Roger.

Down the hall he caught a glimpse of Rita talking to Alan. Alan had his right hand on her arm. Then he moved it and rested it on her hip. She took hold of his wrist and lifted his hand off. He returned it, with a pat, to her buttock. "Stop it," she said sharply.

In the kitchen Alan's wife, in the yellow jumpsuit, was cornered by the geophysicist. "It was all I could do to contain myself," he was saying. "The director was ecstatic, the president was ecstatic. We are on the verge of a giant breakthrough, he told us."

Danny looked for Roger but couldn't find him. He returned to the hallway and encountered Rita coming the other way. His heart skipped. During all his aimless wandering, he'd been half looking for her, half avoiding her. Now, in the commotion of leaving, here she was again. "This is getting ridiculous," she said. Danny was not sure what she meant. Maybe it was time for a joke. He reached desperately. "Want to run away with me?" he offered, working hard to concoct a broad, show-business smile.

"No," she said. His smile disintegrated, embarrassing him. "Wait," he said, "I was just kidding."

She gave a weak smile. "Have you seen Harold?" she said.

All the way home Roger was depressed. He had drunk enough to take off his nervous edge, but the liquor had submerged him into a pool of melancholy. "I shouldn't have gone," he said repeatedly. "I'll lose two days trying to get back on keel." He always worried about the book he was writing and that anything that required energy distracted him too much. He stared out the window at the passing streets. Danny wanted to talk but couldn't get the word in to start. Roger obviously had no interest in Danny's preoccupation, and Danny didn't care about Roger's. Whatever it was that was bothering

Roger, Danny was a million miles away. He was thinking about Rita.

He dropped Roger off and headed home. All night he thought about Rita. He slept fitfully, clutched at his pillow and thought of her sitting beside Alan's pool. The green eyes, the white teeth. He slid through a couple of vivid fantasies, miserable and ecstatic at the same time. At five a.m. he was still wide awake. He got up and went to the bathroom.

6

In the morning Danny went to his studio. He was in a restless mood, discontent and weary. He stared out the window. The day was grey. Boris would be back from his trip later and they were supposed to meet. He looked at his cameras and tripod, ready for the bar mitzvah shoot, then picked up the letter from Professor Bellows, still lying on his table.

In his fitful sleep, somewhere near morning, he'd had a dream. And in his dream the book the professor wanted to do had appeared, clear as day: *Anthropology of the Northern Cree*. Photographs by Danny Hinkle. In the dream it was all completed and awards were being handed out. He was in a big room, a hotel ballroom, for the awards dinner, Associated

Photojournalists of America. He took his place at the banquet table, bashful, beaming, waving off the applause. Around the room his blown-up prints of Cree fur trappers were on display. The mood of the photographs was perfect; they brought tears to the eyes of those who viewed them. Soft blacks, toned whites; old women stringing designs of beads on threads, young men pushing boats into mirrored waters, children gathered outside cabins. Everyone had seen them, everyone had been enthralled.

Life magazine had bought two of them, the Museum of Modern Art another. The room was full of people from the photography business. The editors from the big magazines and the big companies were there; black ties abounded, beautiful women and tinkling glasses. A rich expectancy filled the room. Then for a moment during the speeches the attention shifted to him, the new boy from the north country and his trail-blazing book. Rookie of the Year. He was at the front and the crowd was rising. Applause filled the room like an ocean. He looked around, overwhelmed, his eyes misty. He scanned the room until his eyes came to rest on a table near the front and there, clapping harder than anyone, face glowing with adoration, was not Alice but Rita.

Rita! He realized he didn't even know her last name. The thought plunged him abruptly back into the present.

At that moment his doorbell buzzed. The mailman stood there with a plump package wrapped in brown paper. It was from his father, the second offering in two days. He read the letter that was the first thing out of the parcel.

"I'm back. The drive was pleasant though by the time I got to the southernmost states it was hot going."

His father never flew, always drove these trips alone in his little yellow car. He set out early each morning and followed the highways like an explorer.

"We had a good stay with Leslie and John in Kingston," he wrote. "Their life seems settled and they are both progressing in their work." Danny prickled slightly; a veiled reference, no doubt, to the unsettled lives of his other two children (who never seemed to progress in their work). "Missed both you and Samantha. And Prissy, of course. Wish you could have been there."

Enclosed in the letter—indeed, causing the main bulk of the envelope—but without explanation was a folded, 38-page tract entitled *The Voice*, produced by the Full Gospel Business Men's Fellowship International, "a worldwide evangelistic fellowship of Christian Businessmen; Cosa Mesa California U.S.A." Danny thumbed through it. Now why in the world would his father send this? Was it a gift or a message?

In the back of the magazine, in a section entitled "Fellowship news from here and there and around the world," was a list of the organization's international directors—U.S., Canada and Global. He skimmed through them. Maybe his father was the surprise new member of the directorate of this outfit, although he'd never mentioned it. But no, he was not on the list. Danny glanced through the articles at the front of the magazine to see if there was a clue; an article about something he might be interested in or had been involved in or, worse, some pointed message directed at a perceived vacuum in his life. But he could find nothing that made sense. One piece dealt with how "God used yodelling to change my life." Another, entitled "Run Larry Run," described the life of a middle-aged chap from Burlington, West Virginia, who went from one near disaster to another, including car accidents, business bankruptcies, a severe industrial accident and an undiagnosable disease, until the Lord started working in his life, healing him and performing a series of miracles that allowed him to open a showroom of antique cars where not only could visitors see some beautiful automobiles, "but he could share the gospel with them as well."

An article described a Full Gospel Businessmen's convention and banquet on the *HMS Queen Mary*, docked permanently in Long Beach Harbor, California, with colour pictures of portly salesmen and store owners in applause and at prayer.

And another story explained how "modern technology can provide an exciting new way to express our love for Jesus," and recounted the work of someone in Huttonsville, Virginia who beamed gospel television programs into a jail.

But no clue as to why he was the recipient of this missive from his father. He set it aside, a bit baffled, and folded the letter.

Danny had to meet Boris later. But first he thought about Rita. What do I know about her? he asked himself. Nothing. Roger didn't know her; he was so preoccupied with his own melancholy on the drive home that he didn't even catch on when Danny tried to pump him. He told him only that the guy she was with, Harold, was an asshole. Roger's words, but sort of Danny's impression too. But brilliant in his own way, said Roger. A fanatic organizer in his teachers' union. A tough negotiator. Not married.

Danny didn't see any ring on Rita, either. He always looked. During their brief conversation he thought she said something about working for the CBC, the television network. It was hard to remember—he hadn't been listening very well. He had trouble concentrating on his approach to a woman and listening at the same time, especially when he was being assaulted simultaneously by a party and a man who wanted to show him his dark-room.

Christ, I'm stupid, he thought. I didn't even get her last name. Now he couldn't look her up in the phone book. He could go to the CBC offices and ask for 'Rita,' but they'd think he was nuts. What would he do? Say he was researching television employees for a photo-documentary? What if he met her and she thought he was nuts? Maybe she wouldn't remember who he was.

Yet they had been conspiratorial a couple of times, he believed. For a moment. He was depressed and excited at the same time.

What would Boris do? Boris would say, "Bide your time, this is a small town. Everybody turns up again sooner or later." He didn't think he could do that; he was impatient like crazy.

Boris wanted to meet him at the Wellington Hotel. The Wellington was a dive: bookmakers, hookers and drug dealers even in the middle of the afternoon. But then Boris sort of liked that about himself, a little sense of unpredictability, a notion that he could turn up anywhere, he could move in all circles.

Danny arrived at the Wellington. The place had slid so far it had almost ironically turned a corner. Although sleazy, it was certainly less depressing than many other drinking establishments in the city. Most bars were characterless. The liquor laws prescribed a deadly uniformity, a hold-over of the country's founding puritanism: you don't deserve to enjoy drinking so you shouldn't be allowed to do it in places that are either pleasant or interesting. The government had closed all the old all-male beer parlours and only recently could rooms where drinks were served have windows onto the street. The newer drinking places on the main city routes were like factories—huge, dark, chilly, echoing rooms filled with cheap Formica and vinyl furniture and garish purple lighting. Danny hated them and wouldn't have gone into most of them even if it was his job.

This place was old, with its own circus of low life. A stripper on the small stage slapped her full breasts together and taunted two elderly Chinese men sitting at a nearby table. The old men were unperturbed; they both grinned like banshees and leaned forward for a good look. The stripper squatted down, opening her legs wide. The old men applauded.

Two hookers sat at a table by the door, dressed as if they had to catch a cocktail party in River Heights at five. Danny couldn't see Boris right away, so he asked a couple of young Indian fellows in Caterpillar baseball caps what time it was. They both sported brand new Bulova digital wrist-watches. "Two thirty seven twenty five," they said in unison.

Then he saw Boris along the wall, bent over the screen of a video game. The green light flickered off his face and his hands shoved the levers feverishly. Zap, zap. Shooting down space invaders.

"Hi ya, Danny," he said, looking up. He wore his blue silk suit.

Danny intended to tell Boris about his letter from Bellows but didn't get a chance. "Come on," Boris said, almost as soon as Danny was seated. "I want to show you something."

Boris led him back outside into the sunshine and around a corner into a lane. Between two buildings was parked a shiny new, startling white Cadillac Biarritz with a leather sun-roof. Danny looked at Boris.

"Like it?" he said, beaming.

"Well, sure," Danny said. He didn't know what to say.

"Got it this morning," Boris said. "Just walked in and picked it up. Hop in."

Danny was incredulous. Boris never had a car of his own before. He never even seemed to have any money. A lot moved past him but he didn't seem able to hang on to much of it. He pulled smoothly into the downtown traffic, then accelerated across three lanes. Danny felt as if they were floating on air. Boris chuckled like a happy bear.

"I have to stop in here for a minute," he said, pulling into a parking spot in front of the Bank of Montreal building. "Come on up if you like."

Before Danny knew it they were whisking skyward in an elevator. Boris straightened his tie, looking to the ceiling as if he could see where they were going.

"What's up?" Danny finally ventured to ask. For the last 20 minutes it was as if he had been in a whirlwind, unsure what was happening.

"Big things," said Boris with his confident, confidential smile. "Big things, my boy. Deals. I had a very good trip."

The elevator stopped and the door opened directly into a plush suite of offices. Wood panelling, lush green big-leafed plants, paintings on the wall all over the place. A stunning auburn-haired woman looked up from the reception desk and adjusted large-framed glasses on her nose.

"Hi," said Boris. "I'd like to see Sidney."

"He's in," she said. She got up from her chair in a rustle of silk and moved two steps to the left to stand beside her desk.

Boris stepped past her and entered an office behind the desk. "I'll just be a minute," he said. Before the door closed Danny caught a glimpse of a plump, tanned man with a head of wavy white hair. His two fists, knuckles bejewelled with gigantically stoned rings, were at rest atop a sleek, bare desk.

The woman gave him a brief smile and sat down again, returning to letters or reports or whatever they were on one corner of her desk. It was also nearly bare. Danny sat on a white loveseat under a lamp and noticed that the offices were actually smaller than he had thought at first. But very well appointed. That was the clincher in the first impression.

He picked up a copy of *Time* magazine but before he could get it open Boris was back out.

"We're off," he said expansively, winging Danny toward the door and the elevator. Just before they passed out of sight he half-turned back to the woman at the reception desk. "We'll have to have lunch sometime," he winked. She looked up with a startled toss of her magnificent head. She didn't smile.

In Chicago, Boris had made a deal for some real estate. Not Chicago real estate, but ranch land in Idaho, ocean-front lots in Florida and some more land in Alaska.

"You know why the land in Idaho is so valuable?" he asked. "Water," he said before Danny had a chance to think of an answer.

They were at Joanna's Bar on River Avenue. Boris was explaining, spreading his hands before him on the low table. Boris was buying the drinks.

"The water is the clincher," he said. "Underground rivers.

They'll be needing them in Phoenix and Los Angeles before too long," he said, "and we'll have 'em."

Who'll have 'em? Danny started to ask. Sidney? Boris? Who? He didn't know what to say. Boris seemed so satisfied with his enterprise that he sat there preening himself like a fat cat.

"Did you see them?" Danny asked him.

"What?" he said.

"The rivers. The underground rivers that they're going to want in L.A."

"Of course not," he said. "I was in Chicago. But I dealt with the agent."

Boris loved the word 'agent'. Especially since he was one himself. An agent, now, with a new white Cadillac.

"Did you know," he leaned over the table, "that eventually a third of the North American continent will exist just to provide water for Los Angeles and the southwest of the United States? Controlling some of that water will be like being a sheik in Kuwait. Bigger than that. In comparison, oil will seem . . . like nothing." He snapped his fingers. "Already," he spread his arms, "they have a computer in California that regulates the flow of the Colorado River. You might think that the Colorado River is for drainage and watering cattle and deer and for putting some water in the bottom of the Grand Canyon to float rafts down. But it's not. It's for jacuzzis and swimming pools in California and Arizona. When they need the water down there the computer opens up the dams and lets it flow. When they don't need it, the computer slows it down."

Boris nodded okay when the waitress asked if he wanted another drink. "I might go to Florida soon," he announced. "Sidney wants me to slip down and take a look at the other lots I optioned."

He didn't say anything about any work he might want Danny to do. He didn't mention the promotion brochures or the pictures of women sipping drinks from pineapple halves. Danny decided not to push it; it would come in its own time. Besides, he had other things on his mind.

"My old man's in Florida," Danny said. "I just got a letter."

Danny was buzzing nicely after the drinks, even when he got home. It was late afternoon but not too late. What the hell, he thought, he'd give Rita a call. He looked up the number for the CBC in the phone book. The main switchboard.

"I don't know her last name," he told the operator. "But she works there." He was just nicely beyond caring but still coherent. Nobody could tell from his voice. He stretched out his legs luxuriously on the coffee table in front of him and leaned back in his chair. The telephone receiver, smooth and cool, felt comfortable, reliable, like a charm. He tucked it between his chin and shoulder and thumbed through *American Photographer*. He still felt cocky but was losing it fast. If they didn't hurry up and find her the nerve would be gone. Maybe he should hang up. He put the magazine down and took hold of the receiver again.

The girl at the other end had decided to work for him. She came on the line again. "It could be Rita Eller," she said. "She's an assistant producer over at news specials."

"Yeah," Danny said. "That sounds good."

"I'll put you through."

Rita Eller wasn't there, but a secretary took his number and promised to have her call back. Maybe not until tomorrow, though.

Danny hung up the phone. He felt okay. Now it would be her calling him and somehow he liked that better. He sat for a moment before he remembered to call Samantha.

7

There was no return phone call for Danny from Rita. The next morning was Saturday, and he got up early and headed over to Samantha's place. Getting her moved early would leave him lots of time to get ready to photograph the bar mitzvah later.

It was a bright day, the kind of clear, bright, sunny day possible in the middle of the continent with those lingering high-pressure weather systems; the kind of day that made him feel expansive, as if everything, both himself and the world, would go on forever.

The television was on in Samantha's apartment and already soap-opera characters in some far-away city were engaged in the dramas of their lives; broken hearts, broken promises, little treacheries. Al and his truck were nowhere to be seen.

"I got up early and had my palm read this morning," Samantha told him when he walked through her door. "And then I had her read my tea leaves and cards," she added, "just to be sure."

Fer Crissakes, Danny wanted to say. A fortune-teller. There was always some reason to make him want to say "fer crissakes" to his sister. But he held his tongue.

Samantha's move this time was to a smaller place across the river. "It will be better for Prissy; she can walk to school," she said. "It will only be a block and a half. Also it's less money." Samantha had quit her job with a telephone-answering service more than a month ago.

"I couldn't do it, Danny. They wanted me to come in at seven in the morning for a while. Then it was the afternoon shift. Then they wanted me to work evenings; four o'clock until midnight. I told them 'I have a kid, I can't come in just any time you want me to. Why can't you just give me a regular shift, same time every day?' Then they said they have to treat everybody the same, that lots of the girls were in the same boat as me. But I don't see why they couldn't have set us all up in some way regular. All the other girls felt the same way. I couldn't get a sitter anymore for all the strange hours, a different time every day." Her voice trailed off. She shrugged.

Danny helped her get organized, moving some of her big things and shifting things around. Samantha had moved so many times all her belongings had a kind of mobile look and feel to them; highly adaptable. Danny had helped her move so many times that he instinctively knew the weight and bulk, the feel of every piece of her furniture, her belongings. He knew that everything would be easy except her maroon hide-a-bed. It would be heavy as blazes and it would want to unfold just when they had it half-way through the door.

At 9:30 they were still working alone. Still no Al and no truck. They had packed all the small things, dishes, knick-knacks, into boxes and had lined them up in front of the door and out in the hall. They had taken the curtains down from the windows, removed the pictures from the walls, the garish bullfighter from Seville, the chubby, impish baby pictures of Prissy. Danny had packed the Willy Nelson and Kenny Rogers records into a wooden crate; Prissy had been helpful in the kitchen, dumping pots and saucepans into cardboard boxes. Periodically, Samantha went to the window to search up and down the street.

"Where the hell's Al?" Danny said finally. "I thought the reason we're here so early is because he got a truck." He knew he was starting to sound impatient.

"He'll be here," said Samantha. "He's just sometimes late."

Danny looked at her.

"You don't like him much, do you?" she said.

He shrugged. "I don't even know him."

Danny had only met Al, Samantha's part-time boyfriend, once. He didn't like him much. He was short and scrawny, and had the manner of a small man continually trying to compensate for his size. He was puffed out like a rooster. But Danny knew a comment from him would only drive Samantha to feel she had to defend Al. And she blessedly never asked about much in his life. It was as though they had an unspoken agreement.

"We'll give him a few minutes," said Samantha. "Can I make you some coffee? Do you want a beer?"

"Sure," Danny said. "Whatever."

Danny watched his sister move toward the refrigerator. He remembered what it had been like when they were kids. Samantha had had a really hard time when their mother died. She was 14 then, the oldest of the three of them. It knocked something out of her that she'd never been able to replace or get back. She became angry and, although she wouldn't admit it, she'd been angry, he felt, ever since. He had been only 11 but he remembered when their mother died how Samantha started to work. Never cried, never laughed, just worked. She was in her second year of high school, a really bright girl, but every morning she'd be up at six and for the next hour and a half she'd be running around cooking breakfast, making lunches for Leslie and him, doing laundry, vacuuming the house. At four-thirty when she got home from school it would be the same. She took it all on like some enormous load she had to carry over the mountain by herself.

Their father begged her to stop; he hired a housekeeper, a local woman who would come in for a couple of hours every afternoon to clean and shop and get dinner cooking. But Samantha wanted to beat her to it, to have it all done ahead of time so that every day when Mrs. Foster got there she'd have to hunt around for something to do. It went on like that for months. Samantha's schoolwork slipped and her teachers started to call their father in for talks. But their house, the parsonage, was spotless. Their clothes were always ironed and their lunches always made. Samantha walked around with bags under her eyes and looked like she would collapse in a heap if you got to her the wrong way. But she never cracked. She had something either to prove or to exorcise and she was determined to get on with it.

Their father didn't know what to do. Maybe he had other worries, other preoccupations. Grief, for instance; their mother had been sick for months before she finally died. And he needed to get back to work; he had two churches to serve as well as work on larger provincial and national committees. And if he needed help with his children, theirs was neither the community nor the family to seek it from outside. There would be no visits to family counsellors or psychiatrists specializing in adolescent anxieties (even though a psychiatrist is what their younger sister Leslie became years later). Albert Hinkle was a strict Methodist in personality and belief, and Danny now believed that in many ways he admired and was pleased by the seriousness and responsibility with which Samantha applied herself. But his father also became alarmed when her ferocity took its physical toll, when she started to lose weight and the teachers called to see him because the schoolwork of this obviously bright girl was slipping badly.

Their father's solution was to bring another woman into the house, full time. To restore the equilibrium, fill the gap, provide once again the adult female figure they all needed and that Samantha, to her destruction, seemed so bent on supplying. The woman was Aunt Beatrice, their father's younger unmarried sister; a round, friendly, uncomplicated woman of unwavering generosity and self-sacrifice. Samantha resented her mightily.

Aunt Beatrice, who insisted they all call her 'Bea,' moved with three suitcases into the spare room at the end of the upstairs hall, and immediately took on the roles not only of cook and housekeeper, but of everyone's supporter and encourager. They were roles she'd been waiting all her life to be called upon to play, but no one had ever asked. The younger children thought she was great. She spent most of her time preparing food, always smelled like a combination of a bakery store and a garden of violets, and asked no more complicated questions than "What did you children do in school today?" They accepted her as they'd always known her; she wasn't their mother, but she was Bea. But for Samantha, now well into her adolescence, and a smart and complicated girl, Bea was never enough.

Of course it wasn't Bea's fault. Even less so, Danny would have said, than the confused and listless woman Samantha had turned into was her own fault. Bea was a product of her times and particularly of the small towns where she'd grown up, places that expected very distinct roles of women. And if a woman wasn't married by the time she was 25 her life— contrary to much experience nowadays—became not wider, but much narrower. Bea's common reaction to almost any event in life or the world, whether it was an earthquake in Central America or a death in the family, was philosophical. "Well, it must be for the best because the Lord knows what he's doing." And she'd return to more practical matters like getting the scalloped potatoes in on time. She was a sentimental woman who would never do anyone harm, idolized her brother and his work, and heaped huge dollops of her own brand of affection on the children. But she and Samantha could never connect. For Samantha, the rationale that "the Lord knows what he's doing," a philosophy that was certainly shared by more people than Aunt Beatrice, was far from good enough to explain the months of her mother's agonized, cancerous suffering and final death.

For their father, the breach that hurt the most and that became unbridgeable was the defiance during her later teenage years with which Samantha treated the ten-minute time of prayers he insisted on every morning before break-fast. Danny, at age 29, could still shiver at memories of the strange mortification he felt when compelled to pray aloud while other people, even if they were his own family, listened. He could pray privately; usually when he was in a jam, making little deals with the Creator. Aloud and in public was something else. But partly for the sake of his father, and partly because he didn't know there was any other way, he did it.

And he could still see his father, his eyes clenched tight as if in pain, hands clasped so rigidly the knuckles shone white, imploring his deity to come to the aid of the little amputated family with gifts of strength and wisdom.

But in the midst of it, in the streaming morning sunlight while little Leslie, always the angelic good girl, and Aunt Bea sat, closed-eyed portraits of bliss, on the other side of the table Samantha stared at the floor. It made Danny angry, her attitude. She looked out the window while their father summed up. "What is family, ahem," he would say, looking up and clearing his throat, "if not a unit that can worship God together?" And Samantha would rise abruptly and brush past everyone, hurrying out the door.

Their father didn't know what to say. Especially when Samantha started to miss the rituals altogether with a flimsy excuse like an unexpected volleyball practice at 8:30 and she had to skip. The rebellion cut to the quick of his authority and his beliefs. He muttered and sputtered. For a while he let it go; but finally he exploded.

He grabbed her arm one morning as she rose to leave before even the amen was formed on his lips. He dropped his prayer and dropped the teenage girl to a chair and shook her by the shoulders. "What's the matter with you?" he shouted. He grabbed her hair and shook her head. The rest of the family sat paralysed. Danny's mouth was dry with fear. Finally he jumped up, flinging himself at the back of his father's legs. "Leave her alone," he screamed. "Let her go."

"Go," their father ordered. "And until you wish to be a part of the rituals of this household, don't come back."

Samantha left immediately. Their father's eyes, in the wake of his words, were round with anger and terror. She left and stayed away for a week. And when Danny knew there was real trouble was upon his entering the high school and learning in short order, in the unimpeachable manner knowledge spreads through the boys' locker room, that the common wisdom of the older guys in the school was that the United Church preacher's daughter was the easiest girl in town.

By ten o'clock Al still wasn't there with the truck.

"When are we gonna move?" said Prissy.

"Maybe I ought to call him," said Samantha.

"Maybe you ought to call him," said Danny.

Samantha went to the kitchen to phone. When she returned she looked resigned. "He slept in," she said. "He'll be right over. Can you help us a bit longer, or do you have to go?"

8

On Monday morning there were two phone calls for Danny. He was in the dark-room developing the film from the bar mitzvah shoot—three rolls of Tri X. The colour he had sent to the lab.

He was just setting up when the phone rang the first time. The water was running and he was trying to get the right temperature before unloading the film. He shut off the water and ran to grab the phone. I should have taken it off the hook, he thought.

"Hello."

It was Professor Bellows calling from Toronto.

"Yes sir, I got your letter. I replied Friday. You won't have it yet."

"Yes, I'm sorry," said the voice. He sounded precise; clipped, serious, businesslike. No humour, no jokes; not even much of an attempt at introduction between two strangers on the long-distance wire. "I find out this morning that I'm to be in Winnipeg earlier than I had anticipated," he said. "Thursday, in fact, to attend a conference. I wondered if I might see you then?"

"Certainly," said Danny. This is sprinting right along, he thought. "Whenever you like."

They agreed to meet on Thursday and hung up. Danny bounced back to the darkroom, elated, thrilled by his luck. He started to feel important. He could work straight for 20 hours.

He got the first roll of bar mitzvah film into the developer when the phone rang again. Again he had forgotten to take it off the hook. He thought about letting it ring, then decided to take ten seconds to answer it, ask the caller to call back, and jump back in time to keep the film agitating. On the fourth ring he grabbed the receiver. It was Rita.

"Danny?" she said. His heart careened northwards into the back of his mouth.

Rita apologized for not calling back sooner. She said "don't be silly" when he said he didn't know if she'd remember who he was. She is wonderful, Danny thought. He suggested they get together. She said that yes, she thought she could manage it. He was ecstatic.

Rita said lunch. They tried for Tuesday but it was out for her. They tried for Wednesday, then agreed to Thursday. Danny remembered that Bellows was coming to town that day. So they jumped to Friday.

"Bye," said Rita, bright as a little bird. Danny was in heaven.

When he hung up the phone he nearly popped through the ceiling in his exuberance. He felt as if he could give all his belongings to the poor without a second thought, so great was his good will, his enthusiastic contentment with the world. Then he remembered the film.

He rushed into the dark-room and looked at the timer. It was a six-and-a-half-minute job to be done precisely to the second. The film had now been in for over nine minutes. Danny tore the lid off to rescue it from the chemicals. The little bar mitzvah boy and his proud mother and dad and grandfather and cousins would be black with contrast; the over-development would make the grain on the rabbi's face suggestive of a fatal skin disease. He plunged the film into the stop bath.

Shit, he thought. Which roll was this? He tried to think what else he had on the other films. He might, after all, have to work for 20 hours.

Danny met Dr. James Bellows first on a chilly Thursday morning. The weather had turned the night before. It was now October and the switch had been pulled. In the morning a raw wind under a slate grey sky gusted dead leaves and the previous day's newspapers down the streets and across the sidewalks. People wore coats with the collars pulled up tight to their chins. In six hours everyone had forgotten that summer had ever existed. Even though there would be more bright orange, sunny days, within a month snow flurries would be swirling. As Danny left his apartment to walk downtown, a straggling flock of geese flagged by overhead, just over the tops of apartment buildings, looking for the river that would highway them south.

The professor wanted to meet for breakfast in the coffee shop of the Marlborough Hotel, where he was staying. When Danny got there, only one person in the room was alone at a table; a table set with white linen under a high window.

"Doctor Bellows?" he asked.

"Yes." The professor got up and reached to shake hands, bumping the table. "Have some breakfast," he said. "I haven't ordered yet."

Bellows was a small man, mid-40s, Danny judged, with thinning, sandy hair above a face that was red and finely defined. His hands were small, like a girl's. When they shook, Danny caught himself pulling back, afraid to be too vigorous, afraid to hurt him.

"Welcome to Winnipeg," he said.

"Yes," said Professor Bellows. Nothing more. He seemed shy.

Danny was nervous too, and he didn't feel much sympathy for the professor. After all, he was the one being interviewed. He wished the professor would do something to put him at ease.

"You have experience, I believe, in some of the communities I want to visit." The professor was getting right to the point.

"I was in some of those places five years ago when they had the fight about power dams," Danny told him. "I did some pictures for magazines then." He paused. "And I've been back since then. I think you've seen some of my recent stuff."

He and the professor were checking each other out like a couple of kids on a blind date. The whole thing made Danny uncomfortable. He had felt green when approached by the professor, inexperienced. His few trips north had whetted his curiosity but had certainly not made him an old hand. Compared to the professor, though, he didn't feel green at all. Looking over the tops of his plastic half-glasses, looking over his plate of soft-boiled egg on brown toast, looking through the sedate morning light of the Marlborough Hotel breakfast restaurant, the professor admitted he had never been to northern Manitoba, although he had spent two weeks once at a cottage on Lake of the Woods near Kenora.

"It was hard to forget the Indians in Kenora," he said in his stilted way. "Very pathetic samples. From an anthropological standpoint, almost totally at a loss for identification, culturally off their moorings."

This observation startled Danny. He wasn't sure what the professor meant. Then he wasn't sure what sort of discussion he had expected the professor to offer. A slight cloud of apprehension passed in front of his brain. He would have to get used to thinking of Indians as 'samples.'

He tried to remember. He'd always been fascinated by Indians. For the first part of his life it was because he'd never seen one; only pictures in books or on television. When his family went on trips through Algonquin Park, his father sometimes pulled over at those busy roadside souvenir stands where they could watch a bear cub in a chicken-wire cage, get some cream soda to drink and buy 'Indian goods,' things like a beaded belt or a small tom-tom, a drum whose birch-bark frame was stretched over with soft inner-tube rubber. Once, for 89 cents, he had bought a head-dress, cardboard with eight brightly dyed feathers.

But Treeton had no Indians, even though it was in country once inhabited by the Hurons. He and his friends used to search the clay banks of creeks and rivers for buried arrow-heads, but they never found any. No Indians in the school, or in the stores, or walking down Main Street on a Saturday afternoon, either.

But he had never thought of them as 'samples.' When he was up at Wasagee River taking pictures of pathetic, weathered plywood houses that were about to be torn down to make way for the flooding of the power dam, he had thought of the Indians as good fellows despite their tribulations. The ones who had been assigned to shepherd him around never stopped joking with him, even amid their growing horror and anger about the imminent rising waters. "I guess we'll have an indoor swimming pool, right in the living-room, eh?" they had said.

He had trouble thinking of 'samples.' But what about his own urge to do good? To get away from bar mitzvahs and bicycles, lingerie and politicians' faces. To take his cameras and do a wonderful photo-documentary that would change the world, save a whole people. Turn the world around, rescue somebody whether they needed it or not. The Indians, for example.

He snapped his attention back to Professor Bellows. The project, the professor was saying, would be to measure the responses of people in hitherto isolated communities to the strengthening influences of extra-cultural stimuli. That is, he wanted to see how they liked television and radios and airplanes and newspapers and telephones, electricity, record players, running water and trips to Winnipeg. And Danny was to take their pictures enjoying those various amenities. The bridging of the worlds.

A lot was riding on this for Bellows. "I consider it my most important research to date," he said. "The university is solidly behind it and the anthropological community," his mouth twitched in a grin, rather smug, his first demonstration of anything remotely emotional, "is, I believe, a bit envious. Can you handle it?" asked the professor, leaning forward across the table. Danny felt more nervous. What a responsibility! What if something happened and his pictures didn't turn out?

"I would very much like to do it," he said.

Late in the afternoon Danny dropped in to see Roger. He wanted to tell him about Bellows; he needed to tell him about Rita.

The day had turned to drizzle; a fine, chilling drizzle that misted the whole of the afternoon into an endless grey. The city was a damp cocoon. Danny zagged through the streets and alleyways to the Prince George Hotel. A black Lincoln idled by the front door, lights on, windshield wipers flapping. It belonged to the bookie who worked out of the back room on Roger's floor. But no one was inside. A drunk wearing only a pair of trousers reeled out of the Angelus Bar across the street and then stopped and looked up, astonished at being rained on. Danny dashed through the darkening lobby of the Prince George, past the tired, bleached blonde at the desk, and bounded up the staircase to Roger's room.

Roger had the television on. Danny could hear it before he

came to the door. He stood in the doorway with his jacket on and refused to sit down. The news hour on the television rattled away about a strike at a paper mill and the layoff of 60 or 70 employees at Boeing Aircraft. Then the Minister of Finance came on the screen. He was in town selling an audience at the Holiday Inn on a new plan for fighting inflation.

"Will you look at that!" Roger waved one long flapping arm at the Minister of Finance while he groped through the pile of clothes on his bed, looking for a shirt.

"Listen to this," he said again. "I'm sick to death of it all; I'm sick to death of the economy; I'm sick to death of the news."

The Minister of Finance was joined by a local labour leader. They had just dined together on Cornish game hen and fresh oysters at the Holiday Inn luncheon but here they were squared off across from one another. Each used his hands to emphasize his points like a pair of shadow boxers or Hagler and Hearns at their weigh-ins. A diminutive reporter with curly blonde hair swung her microphone back and forth between them like a referee, then turned to the camera and, with the measured earnestness of a war correspondent, summed up the dismal state of things as of the moment.

Danny thought of Rita.

Roger flicked off the switch. "You know," he said, turning to Danny, "all of this"—he motioned toward the now silent TV set—"is built on our 'right to know', our right to be kept instantly up to date. What if we don't want to be up to date? What if we don't want to know? What if we're better off not knowing? Are we really better off knowing what's supposed to be going on in the mind of the Minister of Finance? Why is it such a treat," he demanded, "to be constantly reminded that the world is in fact even more banal than you would have imagined it to be?"

Danny shrugged, as if to say 'don't blame me,' but Roger pressed on, dissecting the brief bits of news they'd just watched item by item, declaring his profound belief that not a bit of it would make a whit of difference in his world.

Danny looked at the blank, grey-green screen. He and Roger were members of the last generation able to recall life, however dimly, before television. His parents bought their first TV when he was three years old. It was a big clumsy Motorola in a heavy cabinet (they really made them pieces of furniture in those days) and was always breaking down in the middle of "Rin Tin Tin" or "Dragnet" or the "I Love Lucy" show. His father got so exasperated at calling repeatedly for the repairman that he threatened numerous times to junk the thing.

For a long time, he remembered, his father questioned the morality or even the utility of such an invention as television. He thought it an invasion. He was one of those people whose difficulty with current technology is an automatic tip-off to their age and generation. He couldn't relax with a telephone, either, thought Danny; his voice still got a little louder when he spoke into the mouthpiece. Word processors, computers and VCR machines stymied him completely. It was instructive to observe him and his granddaughter Prissy watching television together. Prissy had extra chromosomes, modified genes that allowed her to absorb the myriad messages that emanated from the screen during "Magnum P.I.," "The Price Is Right," "Miami Vice," or re-runs of "The Beverly Hillbillies." She accepted it all; it was a world, a lifeline, a diet.

She didn't believe it all, but that was not the point anyway. It was all things: mystery, instruction, fantasy and the fantastical, laughs, jokes, all in a stream. It was the mainline she couldn't imagine being without because she'd never lived in a world where it didn't exist. When Danny's father reminded her that in his life there was such a time, and a long time, when television hadn't even yet been invented, he might as well have been talking about a time when dinosaurs roamed the earth, so far off and unimaginable and unreal would such a time seem from Prissy's perspective. She curled up on the rug instead, a cherubic smile dotting her face, her eyes wide as saucers. She accepted it all with equanimity, whether a royal wedding, war in Lebanon, Bugs Bunny, "Dallas" or "All Star Wrestling."

His father, Danny realized, did not have such a mind. He prided himself on his ability to discern, to separate the useful from the useless, the important from the unimportant. He put everything into well-defined compartments and watched television for two reasons: to glean information from news, public affairs and weather programs as he would from a newspaper. Or—and being a Methodist, a Calvinist, he only permitted small doses of this—to be entertained. The television for him, with his logical, left-sphere brain, was a re-invention of two old comforts: the newspaper and the movies. It could never come close to providing either the satisfaction or the meaty support of a good book.

Not so for Prissy, a child of the right hemisphere, the 21st century. Newspapers and the movies were anachronisms. Television was the connector to everything and to the source. Prissy and her grandfather sitting together in one room in front of the same little light-emitting tube were worlds, ages, solar systems apart; Prissy swimming head first into the mainstream, her grandfather, like some aged brontosaurus, seeing his world around him evaporate into dust.

Danny attempted to explain this dichotomy between the generations of his father and Prissy, but Roger interrupted him. "You know what television is?" he asked. "It's a carnival." He got up off his scrambled bed where he'd been sitting and walked over to the TV set, framing it with his hands. "In the old world," he said, "they had great market-places, Baghdad, Istanbul, where all the commerce of the world came together. Some of it was important, wonderful stuff. But a lot of it, likewise, was pretty shoddy. The important thing was that there was no differentiation in the ways those old bazaars treated the stuff. Everything was all mixed in together, the good, the bad, the significant, the scandalous. And this today," he patted the wood-grained metal top of the TV, "is just the same. Turn the knob and look what you get. Immediate access to every wacko society produces, every gizmo and hard sell, lottery tickets, breakfast food, automobiles, storm windows. Every tidbit of juicy sex or maudlin sentimentality, half-baked politics or suspect theology, every little titillation for the mind, the appetite, the soul, the libido. . . . Over here is a guy on a soapbox talking to you about corruption in the society; over there, a war in the Middle East; around the corner a politician offering a cure for crime in the streets; next to him, some headache pills. Another channel and you get an out-of-work football player, an ex-convict and a pretty woman who used to be a model for Richard Avedon holding hands and praying in a living-room setting with a jungle of huge ferns looming behind them. A little switch and people with funny hats are being insulted by the appallingly rude host of a game show while they endure it all hoping to win a new Ford Fiesta or a trip for two to Disneyland. . . ."

Danny thought of Boris. The difference between Roger and Boris was that Boris loved all that. He thought it wonderful; infinite possibilities. Already he was trying to line up cocktail waitresses and students at the theatre school of the university to make blue-movie videotapes. Roger, on the other hand, was more likely to be plunged into despair. Both of them knew what television was about. Boris knew what it was all about and that's why he was so happy; Roger knew what it was all about and that's why he was depressed.

Danny looked up at him brightly. "Remember, though," he said, "one time you were on TV." Roger grinned sheepishly. Roger was a writer. All day in his little room he hammered out short stories on the shaky old Underwood machine and mailed them off to *Playboy* and the *Atlantic Monthly*, to *Saturday Night* and *Canadian Fiction Magazine*. When they were rejected, he banished them to his filing cabinet, or popped them into another envelope and fired them off again. Sometimes they didn't come back. Sometimes one would get accepted and Roger would get a cheque. That's what kept him going day after day, week after week, up in his room.

Roger's mother lived in a little house on Manitoba Avenue. His younger brother, who was going to architecture school at the university, stayed with her at least part of the time. Roger's mother worked in a cardboard box factory until her fingers gave out. Now she stayed home, collected a pension, had a big garden and worried about her sons.

She wanted her sons to be professionals. Mostly so they wouldn't end up in a cardboard box factory or working for the railroad as Roger's father had to do. Doctors would have been nice. The younger boy becoming an architect was okay but not quite as socially useful. But a long shot ahead of what Roger had become.

For a long time his mother was not sure what he was. He'd been a teacher briefly after university, but then he had a fight with the principal over how he was handling noon-hour playground supervision. For three years he had been writing and doing bits of substitute teaching, maybe a day or two a week. But how do you tell someone you're a writer when they've worked in a cardboard box factory and want you to be a doctor? All you are is a failed teacher.

Roger typed his stories at four o'clock in the morning— words spilled from his typewriter like flickering beacons into the terrible darkness of the world. Or on a Sunday afternoon. In the middle of the week, in the middle of the day, if he was out of ideas, he went to the movies. A good time; there was nobody else there and he could have any seat he wanted. Or he would go for long walks by the river or long rides on his bicycle.

One Wednesday afternoon at two o'clock Roger's mother was leaning over the back fence at the bottom end of the garden, talking with a neighbour who hadn't seen Roger for a long time. Her boy Hubie, the neighbour said, now had a good job at the University of Manitoba, an assistant professor in the chemistry department at only 29. They wanted him to give a lecture at Princeton, she said. And how's Roger? "Oh, Roger's doing well," said Mrs. Smerno. "We don't see him much; he has a good job with the government."

Just then Roger rode up the driveway on his bicycle, wearing his green army pants with the tear in the knee. The neighbour looked up. "The government must have got out early today," she said.

"You humiliated me," Roger's mother said to him after. "Why can't you get a job?"

But then, not long after that, Roger had a story in an important anthology put out by an eastern publisher. Somebody at a local television station heard about it and summoned him to be a guest on the mid-morning talk show. Roger got his suit pressed and bought a new tie.

He got seven minutes. Right after a cat- and dog-veterinarian and right before a group of well-scrubbed young people who were promoting the annual visit of the "Up with People" show.

The talk-show host remained confused throughout the interview about which story in the anthology was Roger's, but enthused energetically and at great length about what a wonderful thing it must be to be able to create such fictions. He concluded the interview with a wink at the camera and a warning to James Michener, if he was listening, that a writer from Winnipeg was not far behind him. Roger looked embarrassed.

After the show he was depressed. He stayed in his room for a day and a half reorganizing his emotions. He contemplated suicide or leaving the country. He vowed never to go on television again.

But on Manitoba Avenue he was a hero. Mrs. Smerno had watched it all with tears of joy welling in her eyes. The people up and down the street had all seen it. So had the woman across the back fence whose boy was supposed to lecture at Princeton. So had the manager of the meat market at the corner of Salter Street. For days afterward, when Roger's mother walked up and down the street, when she did her shopping, when she rode the bus downtown to Eaton's, she held her head high, beaming like a saint. She was proud. Doctors were a dime a dozen. Her Roger was something else. Hadn't they seen him on television?

Roger hadn't been on television lately. His current book was stalled somewhere near its final stages. Danny got the feeling that he didn't want to talk about it. After the diatribe about television, he sat exhausted for a long moment. Then, unexpectedly, he broke the silence.

"I think I'm going to have an affair," said Roger.

Danny sat down.

"Gillian?" he said, after a pause. "You talked to Gillian?" Gillian the bureaucrat, he meant. Roger had been pining over her for a month.

"No, not Gillian," he said. He was lying flat out on his bed and staring at the ceiling. Danny could tell he was nervous. "Claudia," he said. He rolled on his side and looked at Danny.

Danny's mind raced. Who the hell is Claudia? Roger caught on to his confusion.

"The other night," he said. "You met her the other night . . . at the party. It was her house."

Jesus, Danny thought. Roger rolled away and resumed staring at the ceiling. "Alan's wife?" Danny said. He knew he must sound incredulous.

Roger rolled to the far side of his bed and sat up on the edge, his back to Danny. He stared out the window at the pigeons huddled under the eaves of the Angelus Bar across the street.

Well, Danny thought, what the hell. "Are you sure?" he blurted out. Then he realized how stupid that must sound. It was as if Roger had just announced he was pregnant.

Roger sighed, then got up and walked over to the window. "I'm in love with her, Danny," he said. "I just realized it the other night. All this time I've known Alan I've been secretly falling in love with his wife. I couldn't help it. The other night when we were there, when I saw her, zappo, it all came clear. It's irrevocable." He collapsed on the chair by his work table and his hands fell helplessly on his thighs. He looked miserable.

Danny didn't know quite what to do. In the silence of the damp, dusk-filled room he offered Roger a little grin. "Have you done anything yet?" he asked tentatively.

Eighteen hours later Danny was sitting across a restaurant table from Rita, whom he first laid eyes on a week ago, whose last name he didn't know until four days ago, whom he now, in the brief space of a 50-minute lunch, was hopelessly smitten by, dangerously infatuated with.

The eyes seemed to do it. The smile did it; the rows of perfect teeth. The way she lit her cigarette, even though Danny didn't fully approve of smoking. A little awkwardly as though she hadn't quite perfected it, hadn't yet got perfect grace in the movement of match to cigarette, the coordination of bringing the hand up, the head forward, so that the tip of the cigarette meets the match; as though she still needed to practise.

Maybe, he thought, it's because she never quits talking, even when she's lighting her cigarette. She keeps jabbering away and the cigarette keeps bouncing around, not holding still for the light. He found that utterly charming.

Then she got it going. A deep drag; she took it out of her mouth between lovely tapered fingers and exhaled a thin vapour of smoke. A pause for breath, and the dazzling smile, green eyes dancing like footlights. Danny wanted to grab his breastbone and fall to the floor.

For the first part of the lunch Danny felt that Rita was flirting outrageously with him. She did it with her eyes and the way she shifted her shoulders. A little twitch, nervous perhaps, but sexy as hell. As if, under her sweater, she was going to shrug her bra strap off her shoulder.

Rita had been early. She was there before Danny, waiting

by the cashier at the front of the restaurant, leaning against
the desk with her elbows on the partition. She was wearing
a wool skirt and leather boots that made her look like a
Cossack. Big, round, gypsy hoop earrings.

My God, Danny thought. "Hi," he said.

"So how's life at the CBC?" he said, suddenly, stupidly
aware that this conversation was now loaded, dangerous;
they weren't in the safety of a casual, accidental meeting at
a party.

"Have you ever been married?" she asked in return. They
were seated now.

"No," Danny laughed. "You're a producer, what do you
produce?" He lurched the conversation back onto the job and
biography track.

"Public affairs shows. Have you ever lived with a woman?"

"No. Well, briefly once, I guess, if you can count that."
Danny flushed. Her directness confused him. This was quite
an opening.

"I was married briefly when I was 19. Now that was too
young." She emphasized the word 'that'.

"What are you going to eat?"

"Salad. I think a salad. What's the soup? Let me get a
cigarette."

"So, how's life at the CBC?" Danny said, again.

"What kind of pictures do you take?" she countered.

"Almost anything they'll pay me for," he laughed. "Actually, I just got a big job. Well, not that big. I'm going to be going
up north. For a book."

"I think this whole thing between men and women is
doomed."

"What?"

By half-way through lunch things had settled down. By
the time the coffee arrived, Rita had told him the story of her
life, the skeleton of it anyway, and he had done the same. It's
remarkable, thought Danny, that I can summon up the zest
to do it. It takes a lot of energy, meeting someone new. It's

hard work, dredging out the information you need to give them about yourself. How does Boris do it, meeting a new woman once a week, sometimes more? He told her about growing up in Treeton and managed to make the couple of anecdotes seem funny. At least she laughed. So far, so good, he thought.

He tried to pace himself. Too many people tell too much too soon. Then they're left high and dry at a later moment when the story would have been more appropriate. When that happened to him he sometimes found himself telling the story again anyway, but timing is important in the moving of information, in the letting out of your stories. He avoided mentioning Alice. Only obliquely did he refer to her when they got to the point in the conversation where it was necessary for both of them to drop hints that not all was going well, currently, on the romance front. That too is important, to keep the other interested, let them know there's a chance here, some room to move. The whole business is a delicate enterprise, Danny realized. You don't want to put yourself in a bad light through it; you don't want to give the impression that the reason things aren't going well, the reason you're on the lookout for new romance, is because in your past you were an incompetent schmuck, insensitive, unresponsive, difficult, moody, jealous. Danny watched Rita and tried to figure out what it was she liked. At this stage in the relationship he would do anything; he was a chameleon. If an airline pilot was what turned her on, he would learn to fly. He leaned forward across the table and fixed her in mid-forkful of Greek salad. "Despite what anybody says," he said, "intelligent, interesting people are a rare commodity."

That did it, he figured. He had let her know he considered her a find. And she beamed in response. He had let her know he had high standards, though reasonable ones. He had said 'people,' not women, just in case she was one of those feminists for whom gender words are a problem. And he'd made the point that being 30 years old and unattached had nothing to do with his being weird or impossible or unlikeable. It's the luck of the draw.

She countered. "When I met you at the party last week, I'd just about given up. I despaired of ever meeting a man who truly interested me."

Danny's heart soared. Did she really say that? Does she mean it for me? he thought. He wanted to dance around the room and kiss people on the tops of their heads.

"Can I borrow a cigarette?" he asked.

9

On the plane Boris had read a book by Robert Ludlum. It made him feel chipper about his own enterprise. The bizarre things that happened to the Ludlum characters in their various intrigues—walls caving in on their apartments during the three minutes they stepped out for cigarettes, drugs showing up in their drinks—would never happen to him. But in his mind of the moment, the world was or could be such a place. A place of trips to strange hotels in strange cities, money in brief-cases, bank-account numbers memorized.

Boris was going to Chicago again, to meet a man he knew this time only as Mr. Thomas at the Marriott Hotel, the one near the airport. Through Mr. Thomas he was, after perusing some alternate packages and using his discretion—"we know you have it, Boris, that's why we're sending you"—to spend more of Sidney Blumthorp's considerable money on more land options in Florida and Idaho.

"Trust your instincts," Edward Burrows had said. "We don't even want you to call us. In fact it's best if they don't know exactly who is behind these investments, if you know what I mean." He smiled. Boris thought that a bit enigmatic, but shrugged. He felt immensely flattered. He trusted his instincts too, but when someone else reminded him that his opinion of himself was shared, it made him feel eight feet tall, chest round as a barrel.

Thomas would be, like himself, an agent. An agent for some other unknown principal. A middleman. They were the middlemen, he and Thomas, in a world that was filled with middlemen. Agents. And agents for the agents. But they carried the money and they carried the papers in their soft leather briefcases. And they did the flying to exotic places. Boris was exhilarated.

The land in Florida, he had been told, was to be divided into lots for waterfront condominiums for sale to Canadians. Blumthorp would not build the condominiums, he would hold the land for a while and mark off the lots, pump it up a bit with some well-placed ads and get rid of it. The Idaho land, as he had explained to Danny Hinkle, was different. It had to do with water. To get hold of it was like buying oil land in Texas in 1870. What Blumthorp and Burrows told him sounded so lucrative he wished he had money of his own to put in, and for a day and a half he had scrambled about trying to borrow some. Edward Burrows held him off. "Don't worry. There'll be other ventures in the future and if you handle these for us well, we'll make sure you can get in on some of them."

He'd explained the water business to Danny Hinkle, but poor Danny Hinkle. A funny little guy, Danny Hinkle; earnest as hell but he didn't understand the world, how it really ran.

He'd just sat there in the bar wide-eyed; the idea of gathering up options on water land wouldn't even have occurred to him. The thought made Boris laugh out loud for a brief second, right there in the airplane. You had to be able to second-guess the future. Once you got into the right way of thinking about things, it wasn't that hard to do. Now Danny Hinkle, if he could second-guess the future in a photographic sort of way, anticipate what books they would be looking at, anticipate what kind of shows would be turning them on big in Chicago or Toronto or New York or San Francisco in a year's time, then he might really make his reputation, really put himself and that eye and that camera of his to work. But he wasn't sure if Danny had the instinct. Boris pondered that for a moment above the clouds, 35,000 feet up in the air, while the stewardess brought him another drink.

Boris had the idea that he might take Danny down to Florida and come back with the makings of a sales brochure to flog Blumthorp's ocean-front condominiums and lots. An irresistible sales brochure; state of the art. Wonderful moody photography to plug through realtors and investment-house offices, through Saturday supplements in the *Globe & Mail*. It would be a surprise for Sidney; Sidney hadn't asked him to do it. It would demonstrate to them his initiative. But he didn't know for sure about Danny.

Danny now was all hepped up about going off with some college professor to take pictures of Indian reserves. Boris had no part of it, Danny had landed that job himself. That was all right; that didn't upset him in the least. If he was upset, exasperated was a better word, it was because of the waste, the misguided notion. At 30 years old Danny Hinkle should not be spending his time and energy doing jobs for university professors; he'd never become famous in an academic book.

What Danny was short on was good ideas, and good ideas were what made the world go round, what made the difference between the winners and the losers, the champions and the also-rans. Boris took a sip of his Bloody Mary.

Boris felt that he had a good idea for himself. He'd been plotting it for some time and before leaving on this trip he'd made his move. Senator Stern, the old boy from the party, had helped him—but only that; essentially, Boris was going to do it on his own. In a few weeks there would be an election of officers for the executive of Peter Alverstone's constituency association. Because Alverstone was in the cabinet, it was the most powerful constituency association in the city, in the province. No point in running a political organization where your man wasn't a winner, didn't have clout. And who had helped make him a winner? Boris. Boris believed so with all his heart and mind. And everybody who had their eyes open, who had been watching things, should know that.

Not that it would be easy for him. He had no illusions about the party brass, those men with soft white faces and thinning hair on top who all knew each other from way back. They had run the many campaigns, losers and winners, together and had spread the largess around—to one another's law firms, accounting firms, ad agencies. And they suggested names for judgeships and memberships on federal commissions. Many didn't like him, he knew it. He felt it every time he entered their rooms, their forced smiles with the cheek muscles too tense. Many more were indifferent to him, taking him for a joe boy, a hypster who had been useful to them once. But he had his own ideas. And any opposition on their part would only make him grittier. He caught himself gripping the armrest on the seat of the DC10, he caught himself holding his Bloody Mary too tightly; he caught himself with his teeth grinding in a mix of anger and anticipation.

There were five running on the ballot for four spots and his name was number five. When the party in all its finery— lean, careful, stringent men; tall, intelligent, proficient women—met in the ballroom of the downtown hotel, he, Boris Podolski, would somehow execute the squeeze play, right up the middle, startle them all. It would make Stern beam and laugh. He hated them too, and would be happy to find a way to knock them on their heels. It was a calculated move for Boris, not in the least whimsical. It would cement his business: government and party contacts. It would cement him socially, those junkets to the National Arts Centre receptions the Prime Minister gave. Most important of all, it would make him, Boris, a somebody; somebody to be taken account of, somebody to reckon with. None of this "good job on that, Boris, now see what you can do for us over here." He intended to go first class from now on. He had his Cadillac, he was making his deals. The money was sure to follow. And through the force of his will and his determination, his position would follow too.

He felt the slide as the plane started to go down. At the same moment the captain's voice advised that they were descending to O'Hare. He pushed his toe against the edge of his briefcase planted on the floor under the seat in front of him. He had yet to locate and meet Mr. Thomas but he marvelled at how easy this all seemed, nonetheless. He was cut out for this kind of work, he thought to himself. When the plane was down he would pull the briefcase out and march into the airport, into the city, like a soldier on a mission. A little wink for the stewardess. How long it would take him he didn't know, had no idea. Probably not long.

"Don't haggle," Edward Burrows had instructed him. "Just take a good look at the properties and get rid of the money." A joker, Edward Burrows, Boris thought. And he liked him despite the flicker of unease he'd had at first impression. But Boris was good at overcoming unease. One of his talents, he thought. And with Burrows it had paid off. He was much more relaxed with Burrows than with the other man, Blumthorp. The latter was busy, preoccupied, curt. Sitting in his polished office in his big chair with his short legs not reaching the floor. Worrying. He made Boris feel nervous and Boris didn't like that. But he didn't have to spend much time with Sidney. Thank God for that. Although, given time, he believed he could warm him too. "Never met a man I couldn't like," he had boasted on occasion to Danny Hinkle. "Or who I couldn't make like me." Actually the comment wasn't original; those were phrases his father had used and he now incorporated them. There was very little in his legacy from his father but he made use of every bit he could.

10

In a week Danny got two letters, again on the same day. Again from Bellows and his father.

Bellows: "Dear Danny. I appreciated the opportunity to meet with you and discuss the possibilities of our working together on the Northern Cree project. . . ." Yes, that's fine, thought Danny. But he went on, ". . . I regret that it looks now as though our travelling should be undertaken later rather than earlier."

Maybe not until spring, Bellows said in the letter. It was still on, he seemed assured of that. But the idea of putting it off deflated Danny. What in hell was he to do for four months or six months or however long it took before they got going, before he started getting paid? He got a panicky, fear-filled, starvation-just-around-the-corner feeling. It was a familiar feeling, working for himself.

He would have to find something. Maybe he'd have to go back to shooting weddings. The thought depressed him. The whole thing depressed him. A wave of irritation coursed through him. This should be his grand project; this should be the one where all his work and his career came together with a resounding clang.

The job still excited him but his first meeting with Bellows had taken away some of the edge of anticipation. He had felt awkward. Was it because of the professor, he wondered, a feeling that their personalities might not be in sync? Was it because of the project? Maybe despite all their good intentions they would only do harm. A couple of strangers with over-developed pretensions, full of self-importance, probing intrusively into other people's lives. There was an uneasiness, to be sure, about the professor's inability to be specific about exactly when they could get underway. Danny wanted to do it right away, he wanted to do it yesterday. Now Bellows said perhaps not until spring.

And yet, Danny realized, this is how it goes. Nothing ever remains perfect. Everything is at its best during those first few moments of conception. An idea, a thought, a concept then is as roundly perfect as it will ever be. An idea in his head for a picture, the idea, no doubt, in the head of a writer for a book or of an architect for a building. The first flashing moment was the moment of pure excitement and pure joy, unencumbered by thoughts of the work and the compromises and the frustrations that must follow. For follow they would, as they were following on this project with Bellows, now. The best you could hope for, he sometimes thought, was to get the job done quickly before your compromises had the chance to destroy it completely.

Still, he was angry. An artesian well of frustration and anger bubbled up inside him. He didn't know what to do; he wished things wouldn't go like this. He looked around his room, then grabbed an empty Molson's bottle from the chaos on top of his desk, stood up, poised himself like Trevor Kennard and drop-kicked the brown glass vessel across the room. It hit the ceiling, bounced to the wall and scuttled in a thousand shards across the floor. He picked up the letter from his father, found the knife on his desk and sliced it open.

He had written to his father when the work with Professor Bellows had opened up. He had been careful to sound nonchalant, but he had been excited too. This project was exactly the kind of news he had been waiting for years to deliver to his father. He was anxious to see what the response would be. Eagerly he looked over the letter but there was no mention of his news.

"We had a storm last week," his father opened, "that blew waves in from the Atlantic side that were higher than the breakwater. I've never seen anything like it. The palms were blown back until their fronds almost touched the ground. I thought for a while that the whole building was going; you could feel it shuddering and pressing, holding onto its foundations for dear life. A Winnebago was blown right off the highway and ended up on its side in a mangrove swamp. How is Samantha? How is Prissy? I think of you often."

The letter was lumpy from, Danny discovered, an added insert. Folded in the back of the letter was a single page torn from a magazine, a page of shiny, high-quality paper with an editorial-style message. In the top corner of the page a photograph showed a snowy-haired man billed as the founder of something called the Worldwide Church of God. He sat relaxed on the edge of his desk, hands placed casually on the well-creased knees of his trousers, a benign smile printed on his plump, smooth-cheeked face. The editorial was entitled "As Knowledge Doubles, So Do Troubles. Why?" Danny's first reaction was one of vague irritation, but he began to read.

"Poverty, illiteracy, crime are growing, not diminishing," it began, all in capital letters. "World troubles and evils have escalated. Weapons of mass destruction exist by which man can blast mankind from off this earth! The whole world today stands on the brink of human extinction. But *Why*?"

Why, indeed, Danny wondered.

"The whole world went along on a fairly even keel with little agricultural, mechanical or industrial progress for almost 5500 years," he read. "Transportation was by foot, mule, camel-back, rowboat and sailboat. Communication was by written letter carried the same way.

"Then, just over 500 years ago, the printing press with moveable type was invented. About 300 years ago came the first beginnings of modern science. This advancement of modern science and technology is so recent that 90 percent of all the world's scientists *who ever lived* are alive today! In a brief span of time this world has passed with lightning speed past the age of invention, the machine age, the major developments in science and technology, the nuclear age and the space age!

"The world thinks it is wonderful.

"*Progress—Advancement*! The world's fund of knowledge doubled in the decade of the 1960s and again in the 1970s. But in each decade the world's troubles and evils doubled also."

Father, Father, Father, Father, Danny thought. What is going on? Why are you sending this nonsense? Do I want to know all this? He already knew all this. The stupendous statistics carelessly whipped out. Knowledge has doubled, what do they mean? Did he know twice as much as he knew in 1970? Did everyone know twice as much? If everyone knew only half as much, what would they know? Would it suffice? Or would they feel empty, half full, needy for more knowledge?

If they got twice as much again in a decade, what would that do? Circuitry overload. It was like he wanted to say to Boris every time he rhapsodized on about the 'communications explosion.' "There may be a communications explosion," Danny wanted to say, "but no one has anything more important to say than they ever did."

But Boris would only look at him blankly, as though that were irrelevant. Communications explosions, sexual explosions, population explosions, knowledge explosions; 90 percent of the scientists of all time alive and working today. Working feverishly. The image of all this furious activity exhausted him.

He also felt fury building up inside him. Fury at Boris, fury at his father, fury at the Worldwide Church of God. He read another sentence and laughed. A doubling of the world's troubles and evils. A doubling. Not an increase of 40 percent or 80 percent, but an actual doubling. Right on the quantifiable nose. Thank God it wasn't more, like an increase of 120 percent. Or 140 percent. Thank goodness, he thought, that it was only a doubling; there may be hope yet.

For hope he read on.

And, yes, there it was. Hope in the form of the "Unseen Strong Hand From Someplace." The hand that was going to intervene in human world affairs and save mankind from itself.

"I," the writer continued, "am merely a voice crying out in the spiritual wilderness of this 20th century." Crying out from the plush, glass-encased offices of the Worldwide Church of God, Pasadena, California, with offices in Auckland, New Zealand; Bonn, West Germany; Burleigh Heads, Australia; Geneva, Switzerland; Johannesburg, South Africa; Manila, Philippines; Mexico City; San Juan, Puerto Rico; Boreham Wood, England; Utrecht, The Netherlands; and Vancouver, B.C., Canada. Crying out via shiny magazines, second-class mail, submitted for international airlift at Hamilton, Bermuda. "Calling out on people to repent of their false ways and turn to the God who gives us the breath we breathe."

He could feel his anger growing once more. Why in the world was his father sending him this? Were they messages sent for mere intellectual titillation? Or was there something else? Am I missing something, or is my father off his rocker?

he wondered. When I go to visit him, will we have to talk about these things? Will I have to go to see him soon? The pit of his stomach felt uneasy and heavy. As if it was weighted, at its very bottom, by a great, flat, unmoveable plate of lead.

11

Danny thought the city wonderful. Over a few weeks Rita had become his girl. In a manner of speaking—they saw only each other. "I only have eyes for you." All those 1940s songs—he wanted to hum them as he floated through the city. He was buoyant as a hot-air balloon. He walked the sidewalks whistling even when the cold rains of autumn were falling; nothing could faze him, everything was lovely. Winnipeg might well be Paris for all the difference it would have made to him.

He had little bits of work, enough to keep him going until Bellows came through. He puttered around in his dark-room happy as a lark. Then he would come down the rickety wooden stairs, over the methodical chug chug vibration of the

Armenian bakery, and step out onto the street.

The street opened up like a world of wonders. A land he'd never noticed before. A walk down its length took him through a midway of special things: stores with ballooning yellow, green, turquoise, burgundy, blue silk Chinese wind socks hanging in the windows; his favourite bookstore and a store where you could buy Hawaiian shirts; a store where they sold coffee beans and chocolate; a florist with fresh-cut bird of paradise in the window. On the corner was a shop with brass elephants and hanging circles of stained glass and paper flowers. And another, a store with cards and posters, posters of ballet slippers and Marilyn Monroe's behind.

By reputation, Winnipeg was the unadventurous centre of a careful, unenthusiastic country. Demographic reports defined the city as 'stale', a land of missed opportunities and exaggerated pretensions. If fortunes were slow, the city burghers frequently resorted to jingles to try to turn things around, to bring the world galloping to their door (Winnerpeg, some brilliant light had decided to call it). But for Danny, in his current mood, it acquired a magic of infinite dimensions. It was a house of mirrors, an orchestra, a symphony. "Strike up the band!" he wanted to shout. "Isn't this wonderful? So many human beings with so many histories, so many genealogical, chromosomatic lines, so many languages, so many hopes, so many fears, so many misunderstandings, so many possibilities, so many energies, so many fantasies, so many dreams . . . doesn't it make you want to shout?"

He started off on a walk with no particular destination. The city went on forever, following its rivers, its avenues, its bridges, its railroad tracks. At its outer reaches, in every direction, were split-level houses on manicured boulevards, houses with wet bars in the basement and video games for the kids. He turned in the other direction, toward the older city, and after 20 minutes was walking under the overhang of old buildings, elderly warehouses with theatre schools and gung-fu studios on their upper floors. Here and there bright new owners were attempting to make even more dramatic transformations, and sandblasters wearing goggles and masks like spacemen hung from ladders while they tortured the grime off warehouses, trying to convert them into new chic shops and apartments. He stood still on a street corner and watched and listened to the hum of the city. The city was a chaotic mill but it could be, he thought, not a chaos but a ballet. He pictured two directions simultaneously on his downtown street corner and let his mind gallop into a private fantasy of a ballet. A ballet of churches and beer halls and slaughterhouses, union halls and labourers pas de deuxing with hard hats and lunch buckets; a ballet of girls in insurance offices and young men in banks, salesmen in brilliantly blinking suits and car dealers lining the avenues. His mind choreographed elderly women arriving at first bell to Eaton's and real dancers, their bodies taut, emerging from the studios of the real ballet. He imagined the dance of dentists' offices, juvenile delinquents toughing it out in front of arcades, and crazy old men selling the *Free Press* along Portage Avenue by yelling out World War Two headlines; BMWs emerging from the underground parking garages of tall apartment buildings and Indians poking along the banks of the river, pretending that they were back up north in Shamattawa. The music of the street was that of cops in squeaky shoes and, in office buildings, the hum of photocopying machines and civil servants waiting for coffee time. He loved the city, he loved the streets; his heart welled up with affection for all the people he didn't even know. He thought of the places where he found them.

The length of street beyond the door to his studio was called, a little self-consciously, 'The Village.' It was not a village, it was simply a street. But nonetheless he liked to go up into its heart. Sometimes he sat in one of the cafés for an hour by himself just watching good-looking, well-dressed women having lunch. He noticed how unselfconscious they were. And how beautiful they were when caught unaware. He could have watched all day. He was caught between wanting to love them, each one in turn, and wanting to photograph them. Perhaps it was the same thing, a longing to possess, but for only a moment. And he watched them, aware that they were slightly, perhaps subconsciously, aware of him. Women like this, he thought, were subconsciously aware of everything. It was the sort of tension he would have liked to get in pictures but to bring in his camera would have been too much of an intrusion.

"When someone is trying to be natural, or better, when he doesn't know he's being photographed," Golo Mann once wrote, "he reveals character. But if he approaches the camera with a certain solemnity, with the intent of showing himself off, he has become something more than himself. He is revealing a secret self-image."

That's what would happen if he brought the camera in. It would be interesting, but it would not be the same. Just as a woman by herself was not the same; she was wary then, self-conscious. Only rarely would a woman eating lunch alone or walking down the street relax and smile or give a little toss of her head. Women in groups were different; they flirted in safety and with abandon; enjoyed and quite liked themselves. Or so it seemed to him. And the pleasure of watching was immense.

Having a girlfriend like Rita was startling and wonderful for Danny. The first couple of weeks of knowing her put him in intuitive sympathy with all those people who say "All I want in life is to be happy." He was happy. He woke in the morning cheerful as a bird; all the chemicals necessary for seeing the world in a pristine light were flowing in the right direction. He was filled with euphoria, totally unlike the joy experienced upon hitting a home run, hearing he had passed grade nine, or deciding in some sudden moment of high school that he was proud of his sisters. It was a better feeling than being able to sleep late or getting paid more than expected for a job. He was in love, and the feeling was almost uncontrollable.

Everything about this girl was fresh and she made everything in the world seem fresh. When she called him on the phone, it made him want to slide down banisters.

"Hi," her voice would ring like little bells when he picked up the phone, and he would feel he was 15 years old. A kiss, when they had been to the movies, second date, snuggled into the side doorway of an office building in the dark, chilly, autumn downtown night, was as soft and thrilling as anything he remembered from adolescence. Rita's hand sneaked over his jacket collar up the back of his neck, fingers entangling tight in his hair, and she pushed herself up hot against him, her mouth open like a flower. Then she broke away and ran up the street, turned to face him and danced backwards in the shadows of the street light until he could catch her and they embraced once more.

And so it went through the first weeks; life was a picnic. He could have ill will toward no one. He woke in the morning and looked at the ceiling above him and thought himself the luckiest man in the world.

One Sunday morning, early, Rita called him. "What are you doing?" she asked.

He was barely awake. "I was just thinking about calling you," he lied. "Can I see you later?"

"How about right now?" she said.

Rita arrived at his door in a pair of lycra blue tights and a leotard under her coat. She had on running shoes and bulky pink legwarmers. Around her head she had a thin, rolled, pink sweatband. "No breakfast yet," she said. "I signed us up for a class."

Danny stayed calm. "What do you mean, a class?"

"A workout, an aerobics class. C'mon, get some things. You'll like it."

Danny looked at her suspiciously. "You smoke," he said. It was the first thing he could think of. "How can you work out?"

"I'm thinking of quitting," she said. She smiled broadly as if nothing could faze her. She looked terrific.

Danny took a step back into his apartment and Rita came forward into the hallway. He felt challenged. He was in good shape; he did push-ups and played hockey. But he'd never exercised in public.

"C'mon," she said. "We haven't got much time."

They ended up in a wide room where, even though the air conditioners chugged mightily, the odour of perspiration hung redolent from the cadre of tight bodies that had just left when their group came in. They filled the room, about 40 of them, lining up like Chinese soldiers to face a wall of mirrors and a taut, muscular woman in a well-fitted yellow leotard. Rita moved to the front row and rolled her shoulders and neck to loosen the muscles. Rock-and-roll music blasted from the sound system.

The young woman in yellow set a ferocious pace—arms up, legs up, jumping jacks, stretching. When they were down on their hands and one knee with the other leg stretched out in front of them, flexing the foot, Danny's calf muscles felt as if they were being ripped from their connections. When they ran on the spot, raising arms over heads, to the front, to the side, up, down, out, the poor man beside him, a middle-aged fellow with a grey flecked beard, kept hitting him on the shoulder with his hand. He was hopelessly out of step with everyone else and went right when everybody else went left, up when everybody else was down. When they picked up the barbell weights and started a routine that required them to pull the weights back and forth to their chests from a 45-degree angle somewhere in front of them, the young man to the other side of him, one of those arrogant-looking, early-30s homosexuals with an austere head of shortly cropped hair, arched his body intently on the pull with the grace of a cat, the poise of a dancer.

When they were down on hands and knees, pumping the barbells from floor to chest, Danny's face was a serene nine inches from the exquisite behind of a woman, a young blonde about 20. She wore a tight black body stocking accentuated by a lime green bikini bottom whose briefness, cut high on her hips and between her buttocks, would have been outlawed on most public beaches. She tightened the muscles in her rump and he lost count of his lifts.

The aerobics instructor shouted at them above the din of a Madonna song; in the front row, Rita moved like a panther. Danny felt the sweat course down his face, half blinding his eyes and soaking the front of his T-shirt. From the corner of his eye he could see the grim intensity on the faces along his row. His arms and shoulders ached. He thought about eternal life.

When he was younger he would have been in his father's church at this hour. Likewise would the music have consumed the gathered faithful; likewise would the ritual, the congregation kneeling and rising as one, have displaced rational thought. And there would have been people present who never missed a Sunday, turned out in the best of their fashions. Passion and intensity would have filled the faces around him and, not unlike what was happening here, his own mind would have wandered—to random thoughts, to day-dreams about the girl in front of him.

The hour ended as the music slowed, and the people stretched their bodies to cool them. When the last beat faded abruptly, there was a brief, spontaneous applause. Then everybody filed out, wiping faces on towels. Danny looked around; the average age of the people there was probably about 30.

Later, as he and Rita drove home, exhausted, they passed a grey stone church. The only people coming down its steps were elderly ladies.

After a couple of weeks he and Rita decided to celebrate the good fortune of their romance by going to the splashiest place in town for dinner. Restaurant Sarajevo. The gesture, for Danny, was a signal of something serious, a watershed. He couldn't part with $120 for just any old casual affair. He wasn't Boris; he wasn't some hot-shot young lawyer with the Attorney General's Department, who could take these things for granted.

He had a new red tie; 100 percent silk. Little yellow diamonds on it edged with blue. In over his head for that, too; it cost as much as a shirt. He put it on, tied it and pulled the knot up snug against his adam's apple. Looking in the mirror, he couldn't prevent the fat grin that slid across his face. His whole life, he felt, loomed before him like an open football field and he'd just emerged from the tunnel.

He hopped over to Rita's place, a one-bedroom walk-up in a sedate building on the other side of the river. Her apartment was filled with wicker and oriental rugs. Just the place for a girl like her, Danny thought. He looked her up and down: she looked dynamite. An electric blue dress wrapped her up like a present; patent leather pumps and she had her hair done up. Dazzling. He felt as though he'd just been presented with a triple-decker ice-cream cone.

Sarajevo was a restaurant that had taken over an entire old house. It was one of those Old World places that had to restrain itself from showing just the slightest impatience with the fact that its clientele was less European than it was. You should know how to order. And the waiters were ruthlessly efficient, like officers in the Hapsburg army; they were pushed to their limit by conventioneers from Grand Forks and Moose Jaw who wanted to make jokes while they were supposed to be tasting the wine. But what did Danny care? He had a new red tie on, 120 bucks in his pocket, and he was with the smartest and best-looking girl in the place. Clark Gable out with Vivienne Leigh. They were whisked off to a dark corner near the stairs.

Danny settled back in his chair and smiled. Other people, all of whom seemed to have arrived in a Mercedes, were settling in too. Next to them, an old grey-haired man with an

Acapulco tan sat in the company of a dazzling young woman who seemed to be seven feet tall. The old fellow kept smiling and patting the top of the girl's bejewelled hand. At another table, a middle-aged couple were discussing what sounded like the man's desire to quit his vice-presidency of something or other and become a sailor. "I only live once, Eunice," he kept saying earnestly. Eunice seemed to be in a state of mild panic. At another table, an older woman and two young men. "What do you think?" Danny whispered to Rita. "A homosexual couple with A meeting B's mother for the first time," she said. A family at the large round table in the centre of the room was already working at their duck à l'orange. Mother, father, two grown daughters and teenage son. Teenage son had the headphones of a Walkman portable tape player set firmly over his ears, so he could only see his parents' mouths moving in conversation. His head bobbed to his private music.

Amid this, Danny and Rita only wanted to be alone, in their own world. They were in their own world for five minutes.

They'd just started to pull escargots out of their slippery shells with silver toothpicks when a wide shadow swooped down.

"Hi i i i i i i i, I thought it was you!"

Danny looked up; the voice was not talking to him. It was talking to Rita. He looked over at her; she was grinning foolishly. "Hi," she said in a voice smaller than the other, but it seemed to have excited bells ringing somewhere in it. "What are you doing here?"

Danny didn't know if he should put his fork down and stop eating, or if he should continue to work on the snails. The guy standing looking over their table seemed to him as slippery as any one of them. He had a $100 haircut. Danny wondered if Rita would introduce him.

"Oh, Danny," she said, as if she'd just thought of it. "This is Lyle."

Lyle shook Danny's hand. He wore a pinky ring the size of a golf ball. He smiled down at Danny; his face was soft and pink, no leanness. Lots of dinners here.

"I'll catch you again," Lyle said. Not to Danny.

"Who was that?" Danny asked as Lyle's grey-suited back disappeared carefully into the room.

"I used to know him," Rita said. "He sells real estate."

"You used to know him?" A little unplanned emphasis on *used*.

"Well, yes." She shrugged and gave Danny a little smile. What do I say now? he thought. Do I want to know more? Should I change the subject? A quick flash of Alice went through his mind. The waiter brought their salad and the steward brought their wine.

As the dinner progressed, Danny watched Rita taking the pieces of lamb off her shish-kebab skewer. She took a swallow of wine. She talked about having just read a huge two-part biography of playwright Eugene O'Neill. "His mother was on morphine, an addict, from practically the time he was born. He hardly knew her in any other state than that of reclusive, helpless addict. He felt guilty all his life; he thought it was his fault for being born."

But Danny kept thinking about Lyle. He tried not to, but somehow that two-minute interlude had taken the magic out of the evening for him. Something unsaid, something implied in the ease of their greeting. Waves of unfounded jealousy rolled over him. Something about the way he had stood at their table cocked back on his heels, smirking with duplicity, spittle making his lips and his tiny teeth shine when he grinned. Danny could hardly eat.

"What's wrong, Danny?" Rita's eyes were dark with concern.

"Nothing. Nothing, sorry." He tried a weak smile.

"Are you sure?"

"Yeah." He tried to sound bright. He felt stupid.

But when they were having coffee and a liqueur, just when

Danny had calmed down, they had another visitor. A small, delicate man with an older, creased, sensitive face. Like Lyle, he appeared suddenly beside their table, although awkwardly, surprising them. He was a rather rumpled man. The legs of his trousers were too long and they bunched at his ankles just above his shoes.

"Danny, this is Robert," said Rita again after a few moments of exclamation-filled greeting.

Robert was not nearly as sure of himself as Lyle had been. He was shy and perhaps a bit embarrassed to be caught in this place. It was hard to tell. He shook Danny's hand and offered a slightly pained smile.

"I told you about him," Rita reminded Danny. "He's been after me to work on his committee, nuclear committee."

Rita had indeed been telling him about the committee. Her desire to save the world was one factor of her personality he had been trying to adjust to. And here was the personification of her possibilities.

"I'd very much like you to help us," Robert jumped in with sincerity. "We need you if we're to get anything started in this city, in this province."

Rita seemed affected. "I know," she said. "You're right."

Robert smiled. "Does that mean yes?" he asked.

"Call me Monday," she said.

"Robert," said Rita after he left, "is one of the most committed men I've ever met. Really. He's at the university but he spends 20 hours, maybe more, each week organizing the anti-war, anti-nuclear lobby. He's tireless." Her eyes brimmed with an admiration that brought her almost to tears.

12

Rita did call up Robert, the nuclear activist. And before Danny could count to three, she was off every night to a committee meeting.

Rita was ripe for this. She was the kind of person who believed the world could be saved. Over a year she had joined a group advocating free abortions, a committee to build a poor people's health clinic, and the New Democratic Party. The NDP, in turn, put her on a committee to study culture and help the party define its 'Culture Policy.'

Now she had joined Robert's committee to prevent nuclear war, stop poisoning the environment and make the 'Green Party' a force in Canadian politics. Rita loved it all. Nearly every day after work she rushed home, discarded her CBC assistant-producer clothes—boots, tailored suits—for her activist clothes—shapeless corduroy trousers, bulky sweaters, no make-up—and was off again. A second career. She became knowledgeable on all the issues and spouted them to Danny every chance she got. She could cite the most up-to-date death counts from the Chernobyl nuclear accident and the Bhopal chemical spill; she would tell you that although Lake Erie had been 'saved,' through an expenditure of $8.8 billion, the Great Lakes as a whole still contained a thousand chemicals. She had the numbers for the nuclear warhead arsenals on both sides and could explain in detail the going line on how to rid the world of acid rain. All this information didn't destroy her, it didn't cauterize her, make her impotent; it energized her, it sent her off to meeting after meeting to organize the crusade.

Danny hardly saw her. Often she showed up at midnight, or she went straight home to her place and he wouldn't see her at all. He would hear from her the next morning on the phone. Sometimes he felt hurt, neglected. Sometimes he had to resist interpreting her actions as a gesture of moral superiority; the last thing the world-savers had time for was the company of the mere mortals they were trying to save.

When he confessed those thoughts to Rita, she considered him insecure and overly sensitive. "Don't be silly, Danny," she told him. "Sometimes it's a matter of time; sometimes I just want to be alone. It's as simple as that. It has nothing to do with you."

Then he felt foolish. Small and foolish.

While Rita was saving the world, Danny had some preoccupations of his own. Leslie wrote a long letter from Kingston, putting forward her theories about their father. She'd been getting letters from him that were similar to the ones Danny had been receiving, stuffed with clippings. She didn't think it was harmless; she thought he was about to go off the deep end. "There's little rational pattern to the communications he is trying to make," she said. She thought someone should go to Florida and rescue him.

He was also preoccupied with Boris. Boris wasn't himself. He seemed edgy and nervous, overly pumped up. One afternoon he arrived at Danny's studio just before Rita was supposed to show up. He wore his dark suit and a black overcoat; his tie was undone. He looked haggard.

"You've been working too hard," Danny told him.

"I was at the bald doctor today," Boris said.

"You're not bald," said Danny.

"There's a 75 percent chance. That's what the doctor told me." Boris leaned his head forward so Danny could view the top of it. "See," he said, pulling at the hair on the back of his crown. "Look how thin it's getting. I'm worried."

Danny couldn't tell it was thinning. "Who knows, maybe you'll look good bald," he offered. "Lots of guys do. I saw an article once that women think bald guys are sexy."

"Please," said Boris in a voice heavy with burden. "The doctor gave me some stuff to rub on. I'm going to try it. Where there's action there's hope."

Danny was straightening out his negative files. He lifted another tray of them onto his desk. Boris came around to face him. "I need to do something," he said. "Everything's so up in the air, nothing's down to earth."

Danny stopped what he was doing and looked at him. He'd never seen him quite like this before.

"Everything's nuts," said Boris. "I went out last night with Leigh, you know, that model who works for the Bay, the blonde one."

Danny knew her; she had legs 17 miles long.

"We're having a perfectly nice time, getting along great. But do you know what she starts talking about late in the evening, just when it's time to, you know, start thinking about going home? Astral travel."

Danny looked at him.

"No kidding. She has books on it and she does it. She says

she astral travels to California to see her boyfriend. Can you believe that? I say, how do I know you're here right now? and she says, I'm not. What kind of wacko woman is that? What's wrong with them?"

Danny put his hand on Boris' shoulder, Boris' slumped shoulder.

"We gotta do something," said Boris. Then he brightened. "Remember those promotions I talked to you about months ago?"

Danny nodded. The people sitting under the palm trees sipping drinks out of coconut halves.

"I want you to think about doing it with me. We'll go down there, Tampa, Miami, Key West, some place like that, look around, take a few pictures. I've got an idea in my mind. Things with Sidney have been stalling and I need to take an initiative. Will you think about it?"

"Sure I'll think about it," said Danny; thoughts were forming in his mind already about his father and about Florida. "Will you pay?"

"I'll get money, don't worry."

Just then they heard noise on the stairs and Rita arrived, lugging her briefcases, her cheeks rosy from the cold. When she saw Boris she stopped, a little taken aback, wary. Boris looked at her, full of innocence. "Tell me," he said, lowering his head and parting his hair with his fingers, "do you think I'm going to go bald?"

"We've gotta go," said Danny, hoping to move Boris out. "We've gotta go over to my sister's."

After two more phone calls from Leslie, Danny had decided to raise the subject of their father with Samantha. It would be hard to talk to her but he would try. He called her and asked if he could come over to visit.

Rita went with him. Rita had never met Samantha and Danny was worried about what they would think of one another. All the way over in the car he talked too much. "Will you stop it?" Rita finally said. "The way you're preparing me

I feel as though I'm going to meet someone who is incapacitated in an institution. Will you stop apologizing for your sister? This is embarrassing me. She's probably going to turn out to be a very nice woman with whom I'll get along fine."

"I'm not apologizing for her," said Danny. But Rita's observation stopped him. He didn't realize that the picture he painted of Samantha was so bad. Yet he needed to explain. "But she is different, Rita. I mean, she is my sister, but she is . . . a bit helpless. She can't do things. Sometimes she can't function. . . ."

"Stop it," she said.

They drove in silence for a few minutes. "I hope her boyfriend Al won't be there," Danny said.

They reached the apartment block and went up the stairs. Samantha was hesitant when Danny introduced Rita. Shy and a bit nervous. He had told her when he called that Rita was coming along but he hadn't told her, he realized, anything about her. As far as Samantha was concerned she might be a friend of a year's standing, or she might have arrived only last week.

"Come in and sit down," she said. She led them into her living-room and they sat on the maroon hide-a-bed. Danny sprawled down and flung his arm a bit too deliberately across the back of the couch.

Rita sat stiffly. "I like your lamp," she said, pointing to the big stainless steel bowl with a shade on the end table. "I've been looking all over for one myself."

"Yeah, it's new," said Samantha.

"Is it new?" said Danny.

Samantha crossed the room and put a Linda Ronstadt record on the stereo. Then Prissy bounced in from her bedroom and charged up to Rita. "Hi," she said. Danny suppressed an urge to hug them both.

"I got a job," Samantha said.

"Yeah?" Danny said, a little too excited.

"Al set it up for me. Three different hotels and restaurants want me to do their books. I can do it right here at home. I set up a little table in the bedroom and I just drop in to see each of them once or twice a week. Al says maybe I can get some more."

"That's great," Danny said. "That's wonderful. Did you hear that?" he said to Rita. "Samantha got a job."

Both Rita and Samantha looked at him. He shut up.

"My mom's an accountant," announced Prissy.

Samantha poured them each a glass of wine and told Prissy to get some crackers from the kitchen. "I'll help you," Rita offered, getting up from the couch and following Prissy. Samantha sat on the floor across from Danny, next to the stereo. She held her wine in one hand and with the other pulled her knees up in front of her.

"I got a letter from Leslie," Danny said. "She's worried about Dad."

Samantha didn't look up. Maybe she hadn't heard him. Danny could hear Prissy and Rita rummaging around in the kitchen. "I think we should have some cheezies," chirped Prissy's voice.

Then Samantha looked up. "What do you mean, she's worried?"

"I don't know. Maybe she thinks he's too lonely down there in Florida. Nobody to be with, nobody who knows him."

"He's always been alone," said Samantha.

Rita and Prissy returned with a huge plate of soda crackers, olives and cheezies. Rita sat down and Prissy passed it around.

"If she thinks he's lonely," Samantha said, "why doesn't she go to see him?"

"Who?"

"Leslie. Why doesn't she go to see him?"

"I dunno," said Danny. "I guess any of us could go to see him."

Samantha got up to change the record on the stereo.

One time when they were kids, Danny remembered, their
father got sick. Pneumonia, after a bout of working too hard.
They didn't put him in the hospital but the doctor confined
him to bed at home for almost a month. Aunt Bea wasn't there;
she'd gone on a trip as she did every year—Greece, England,
the Holy Land. If she'd known her brother was sick she'd have
been there in a flash, but this was a time when she was gone.
It was exam time and Samantha was in grade 12. She wasn't
having a good year in school, mostly, Danny thought, because
she wasn't paying attention. But she was smart enough that
if she'd applied herself she could have sped through the ex-
aminations. But she didn't. When their father got sick she insisted on staying home to care for him. She kept the
humidifier filled and his pillows fluffed, his juice glass filled
and his blinds drawn. She laundered, she cleaned, she inter-
cepted his telephone calls and his mail. She packed Leslie and
Danny off to school each day, and administered their father's
medicine. He urged her not to; he told her to get off to school.
She refused and insisted on staying right in the house, right
outside his room. She shopped and she cooked. In a month he
was up and well again and Samantha had missed her exams.

"That's what you think I should do, isn't it?" she said.

"What?"

"Go to see him." She turned from where she had been
looking out the dark window at the night outside. "Prissy, get
ready for bed," she said.

"Well, it mightn't be a bad idea," Danny admitted.

"Listen, Danny." Samantha stepped toward him. "It would
be a very bad idea. I can't go and I don't want to go."

Rita tensed beside him on the couch. "Come on, Prissy,"
she said, "show me how you get ready for bed." Prissy led her
out of the living-room and Samantha watched them leave.

"Hold it," Danny said. He wanted to defuse whatever it was
that was building.

"No, you hold it," she said, "and stop trying to manipulate
me into situations. It's not for you to decide if and when I

should go to see Dad and then come over here and set it up so I go. . . ."

"Listen, Sam . . . this is not what I had in mind in the least."

"No. You listen. You and Leslie. I'll make my own peace." She was angry, Danny could tell. Her eyes flashed and her jaw was set, her mouth a thin, pale line.

"Sam, I'm not. I mean, I don't know what I thought. Leslie just thinks somebody has to do something and I guess I agree. Maybe I feel a little guilty."

"Well, if you feel guilty, Mr. Big Shot Brother, do something about it yourself; don't put it on me. And if you didn't meddle maybe you'd have less to feel guilty about."

"What do you mean by that?" Danny was shocked, taken aback by his sister's vehemence. She was breathing hard.

"You should know." She sat down in the chair across from him and hunched forward. She lit a cigarette. "Every time there was a problem with me and Dad," she said, exhaling a breeze of white smoke, "and I admit we had our share, who was right there making it worse? You and Leslie."

"What?" Danny said. "That's not true."

Samantha eyed him silently for a moment. Danny thought she might lose her nerve and change the subject. Maybe they could talk about movies they'd seen recently. That they should get deeper into this terrified him. Still: "Tell me what you mean," he said. "When did we make things worse?"

He could tell she didn't know whether or not to plough on. She looked at the floor for a moment.

"Well," she said, sitting up straighter. "To take one example out of the air, when I had to marry Roy—and don't you dare plead innocence on this, that you didn't know anything about it—who was it who told him? Who went and blabbed the reason I was marrying Roy and why I needed to do it so fast?"

Danny was dumbfounded. He searched back through his memory. Now he wished they hadn't got into this. He looked for a defence. "It made sense," he said weakly. "He was bound to find out. You couldn't have kept it from him forever."

"That's not the point," she said. "I should have been the one to talk to him, not you going like some spy. I was going to talk to him and it would have been better if I had, but there was no point after you got there first. He had his mind made up against us."

"Is that what you did?" It was Rita, standing in the doorway.

Danny felt trapped. He glanced at Rita, resenting her. I don't need her in on this, he thought. He ignored her. "I did it for you," he said to Samantha. "I thought it was best."

"Did you?" Samantha pursed her mouth and refilled her wine glass.

"Yes. I mean, he asked me. What's with Sam? he said. We were all trying to figure you out, he having more trouble than any of us. It wasn't meant to . . . sabotage you."

"Thanks a lot," she said.

They sat there, neither looking at the other. Danny held his glass balanced delicately between the thumb and forefinger of both hands. He looked at the nubs in the brown carpet on Samantha's floor. Then he looked obliquely at his sister. The exchange had deflated them. Danny felt depressed. He could tell Samantha wasn't very happy, either. Rita tried for a moment to keep it going but it was obvious her efforts weren't welcome.

"Will I make some coffee?" Samantha offered.

"Thanks," Danny said. "But we gotta go."

After a few more minutes they left.

"See what I mean?" Danny said to Rita in the car on their way home. "About her?"

"What do you mean?"

"How tough it can be with her."

"I like her," Rita said. "I like her a lot."

13

Danny talked once more to Boris, and then made up his mind. He would go to Florida. He would do the brochure with Boris and he would go to see his father. Two birds with one stone. Boris brightened visibly at the prospect. "You won't regret it," he said. "We'll have a great time."

The timing was excellent; winter was entering its long haul. For a while Danny found it invigorating. Even though it was bitterly cold, the days were bright with blue skies and a far-away yellow dot of a sun. Every afternoon he took his skis for long sprints down the white, frozen stretch of the river. But the days went slowly; Florida would be perfect.

Almost every night Rita was off to a meeting. The NDP culture committee; the women's abortion committee. But mostly, Robert's save-the-world committee. They were organizing a big spring rally that would combine all the anti-war and the environmental groups. Rita was heavily into it. They were drafting anti-nuclear 'statements' and Rita was doing the writing. They were trying to write letters to people in the Soviet Union but they were having trouble getting names. For a week Rita was all excited about starting a new committee, TV Producers for a Clean Earth.

"We have to localize it," she said. "If everybody campaigned in their own area, think what a movement could ensue. Robert says it would be a coalition to end coalitions. You could organize the photographers."

It never went any further. She was too busy with other things and Danny didn't manage to get any of the photographers he knew motivated.

All this time Bellows stayed sporadically in touch. The date for their northern Indian enterprise was now, he said, April or as late as May. Or it could be earlier if he got a break. Danny was becoming philosophical about it: when it happened, it happened. Every time Bellows wrote he sent another hundred dollars to keep Danny interested, he had to say that for him.

All winter Roger had been in such a funk that Danny could scarcely bear to be with him. His potential affair with Claudia never amounted to anything. At least, if it did, Danny didn't know about it. He believed they had tea in Roger's room at the Prince George once. Roger started to imagine things; he started to believe that Alan, Claudia's husband, was after him, that he wanted to break his nose.

"He's capable of it too," he told Danny. "Oh yes, those big Englishmen, despite all their civility and good sport and all of that, are bloody messy when it comes to fighting. They stop at nothing. He's twice as big as me."

Roger took to sleeping all day and only going out at night, when he would put on a big overcoat and slink in the dark from the shadowy entrance of the Prince George to one of the restaurants down the street for a meal. He gave up substitute teaching because of his fear of Alan. He gave up going to movies because he had no money. He slept all day and wrote all night; the hotel manager threatened to raise his rent because of all the electricity he was using.

One day Danny ran into Alan eating dessert with a bunch of teachers at Café d'Ambroise. Far from skulking around like a mafioso, plotting to get Roger, he was open, innocent, perplexed.

"Where is the bloody guy?" he asked. "I haven't seen him all winter. Is he hiding?" Alan didn't know a thing; Alan had no idea.

In December Roger sent his book away to a publisher in Toronto. In January he got it back. It was no wonder. The manuscript was such a shambles of deletions and arrows and writing in the margins they would have had a hard time even reading it. It needed another typing.

He showed Danny the letter. They said some good things about it, even left the door open for him to bring it back. But Roger was not to be consoled. For a week he couldn't work at all.

Sometimes Danny thought of Rita and himself as an old married couple who didn't expect much of each other. The thought depressed him. He worried that she was getting bored. He tried to make himself more interesting but it seemed to be of no use. A lot of it, he thought, was mainly in his head, for sometimes she could be as tender as he could ask. Sometimes she would bring food: sandwiches, pizza, cakes, doughnuts, Chinese lemon chicken from her meetings. Leftovers in tin foil. And in the middle of the night they would unwrap them and spread them out on the floor in front of the TV and have a picnic.

Once, though, she went out for lunch with a network junior executive, in town from Toronto. When she came home and told Danny he'd invited her to have dinner with him too, they had a fight.

"Surely," she said, "it's possible for me to have dinner with another human being."

"Of course it is."

"Then why are you upset?"

"I'm not upset."

"Yes you are. Your fists are clenched. I can see the muscles standing out in your neck. You're jealous."

"I'm not jealous. Jealous is not what I am, Rita. I've never been jealous in my life. I don't care who you have lunch with. You can have lunch with Burt Reynolds. It's just that you're gone all the time."

"And you want me to be here all the time."

"No. . . ."

"See, you can't really care, can you, because if I were here all the time it would drive you crazy. Where's my space, you would say." Her eyes took on a hurt look.

So she went for dinner with this fellow just so each of them could prove their point. And she continued to go to all her meetings, where her idolization of Robert grew to what Danny considered embarrassing proportions. It was like she was spending time with the Mahatma Gandhi. "He's just an incredible man, Danny," she would say. "So dedicated, so patient, so sure of what he believes."

Periodically, more letters arrived from his father in Florida. The diet of clippings and editorials tapered off but never abated completely. Again, Leslie called from Kingston. "I'm getting worried about Dad," she said.

"What kind of letters have you been getting from him?" Danny asked.

"I know what you mean," she said.

Leslie insisted someone go to see him soon, but put in right away that it couldn't be her. She was taking on extra patients at the hospital while one of the senior psychiatrists was on extended leave. And she was starting to do work at the prison; psychotic women. And John was in the middle of another thesis. Post-post doctoral something or other.

"Don't worry," said Danny, "I'm going." He told her he was going on business, which seemed to impress her, but he would make lots of time to be with their father. "Okay?" he asked.

"Okay," she said.

He hadn't talked to Samantha since the disastrous evening at her place. It seemed useless; he didn't know what to say to her. He decided to leave her out of this.

Our poor father, he thought. Elderly parents and middle-aged children. Soon it's going to be us. Already we're buzzing around on long-distance telephone conversations like doctors in consultation while the terminal patient lies in the next room. He didn't know what good the trip would do, but he'd go.

14

Rita wasn't sure how she was going to do it. She was just barely managing to juggle the twin demands of her CBC job in the daytime with the increasing obligations to Robert's committee. It met almost every evening to plan the groundwork for the protest rally they wanted to set up for the spring. "It will be the biggest rally this city has seen," Martin, Robert's big, good-natured assistant, had enthused. "We'll get everybody out; we'll have the premier on the platform and the streets will be full of marchers."

Then her boss, the CBC chief producer, called her into his office. "We're going to revamp news specials," he announced. Rita sat down. "We're caught in the squeeze," he said. He was a short, blocky, untidy man with thinning hair on top. He'd worked in television since its invention. His tiny office was a clutter of framed citations, some hung, some not, piles of unread newspapers and magazines, shelves of dusty film canisters and a desk piled high with videotape cassettes. "They've cut our budget but they're expecting us to come up with more programs."

Rita waited to hear the inevitable, what all this would mean for her.

"What we need to do," he said, turning a long yellow pencil between his fingers as if sharpening it, "is more street work. We're going to use the mobile and we're going to do a new series that we'll call "Neighbourhoods." It'll run with the suppertime news show, maybe three, four times a week. We're going to get out there and show this city to itself. We're gonna scoop the newspapers in the soft-focus lifestyle game. We're gonna find kids and housewives and schoolteachers, hockey-team coaches, corner-store owners, and we're gonna make them heroes. Whattaya think?"

Rita nodded.

"And you," he said, pointing the pencil straight across the desk at her, "are gonna do it."

Rita gulped. "What do you mean, me?" she said. "I'm going to do all of it?"

"It's yours," he said. "The whole shabingo. I had to send Tony to sports; they're moving Mel to Toronto. I told you, they're squeezing us."

Rita went for a long walk at lunchtime to try to absorb it all. She walked along the busy street and then turned into the Hudson's Bay department store and stood aimlessly amid the maze of the cosmetics counters. Attractive salesgirls looking efficient in white lab coats, as though they were scientists or doctors, scurried to deliver tiny sample bottles of fragrances and jars of creams and ointments and cleansers and toners to matrons bundled in fur coats. At any other time Rita would have been ecstatic, enthusiastic about her new job opportunity. Today was different. How in God's name am I going to be able to handle it all? she wondered. The night before, Robert had announced a new strategy; the committee members would take every opportunity to confront public officials. They would go to public meetings, press conferences, wherever and whenever they were held, and they would stand up and demand that the politicians come clean on matters of environmental protection, defence policy and nuclear weapons policy. They would hound them until they were all on the record one way or 'another. They would start, said Robert, at an upcoming community meeting involving the Hon. Peter Alverstone, federal Minister of Labour and Opportunity, and the most up-and-coming politician the city offered.

Rita thought of Danny, now gone off to Florida. A little warm spot, half-way down her sternum, made her smile. She thought of the last night before he had left. He had wanted to take pictures of her.

His going away had, for several days, put an unspoken strain between them. They hadn't talked about it but they both knew it was there. They had circled like boxers in a ring, aware of but avoiding one another's emotions. They were frightened. These were the standard opportunities, in the early stages of relationships, to get out. A trip, a separation, a return and things were never quite the same. A goodbye at the airport, a time to think, an excuse if either needed it to make the goodbye permanent. This was the first stage of the show where lovers could conveniently leave. If they made it through this, they'd be good for a while longer. Both of them realized it but neither knew how to say it.

On the night before he left Rita had walked across the bridge that spanned the sleeping, frozen river, turned up the dark street and knocked on Danny's door. She had prepared nervously, yet carefully. After work she'd spent half her cheque on a tiny bottle of Opium perfume and she'd poured it all over herself. Into her purse she'd put, carefully wrapped in foil, two marijuana cigarettes that had been hiding in the rosewood box on her dresser for a couple of months. She had a chilled bottle of Piat d'Or white in her fridge, left over from a dinner a couple of weeks ago. She put that in a paper bag and tucked it under her arm.

Inside his apartment, neither of them could say anything. They were like bruised battlers who had no strength left; only a huge tired tenderness that they both recognized at once. They embraced wordlessly at the door. Danny led her to the floor in front of his fireplace, which didn't work. He put his television on to the weather channel and turned the sound off. When they turned their backs to it, the flickering red and green and blue light behind them made them think they had a fire. They smoked the joints and began to laugh.

Danny laughed first, choking on the smoke. He hit his chest and coughed. Then Rita laughed, starting with a slow giggle and then, leaning back against the support of the couch, guffawing loudly. Then they both laughed. And laughed and laughed, rolling on the floor, holding their sides, lying on their sides, clutching each other. Then Danny got the idea about the photographs.

"You can be Georgia O'Keefe and I'll be Alfred Steiglitz," he said.

"Or Miss May and you're Bob Guccione," she countered.

"No, no, not that," he said. "Rita Hayworth and I'll be Hurrell."

Rita giggled. She was self-conscious but she was stoned. She opened the bottle of wine and took off her sweater. Danny got the tripod from his bedroom and stumbled, dropping one of his expensive lights on the floor. They both doubled over once again with laughter. Rita took lipstick from her purse and touched up her lips, then put some on the tip of her index finger and applied it to her nipples.

"That's great," said Danny, "I love it." He stood behind his camera, not wearing a stitch. "I want these to remember you when I'm away," he said.

"You want them to show your father," she said.

"That'd be good," he laughed.

Then they both realized again that he was going away.

In the department store, in the midst of the cosmetics counters on her lunch break with too much to do, she thought of all this, remembered it. And an enormous tiredness and sadness and emptiness came down on her.

She looked out across the ocean of heads, heads and upper bodies of shoppers bobbing and darting like little animals among the counters. The rows of counters and attendants made the store look like a parking lot, a bazaar. The midwinter sales banners, *Bay Day 30% Off*, flapped above all of it like heraldic symbols. She was in the middle of it, in the middle of all the darting and bobbing. The sales floor stretched away in all directions until the distance shimmered and blended everything like a mirage. She felt calm in the midst of all the motion, calm and somehow unreal. Her mouth felt dry; she clenched her hands to test her fingertips. She was alone. Very alone.

She turned to leave, then turned around to head in the other direction, to try to find the door at the other end of the store. She had gone only a half-dozen steps when she ran into him. Bang. Surprise. Like an automobile collision when you've day-dreamed your way through a red light. He was examining two pairs of socks. His glasses, a bit steamed, sat professorially half-way down his nose. "Oh, what are you doing here?" Robert.

15

Two women sat at the table next to the one where Boris and Danny enjoyed their first Florida drinks. Danny had a tall glass of mineral water with a lime twist, Boris, a spritzer. "We've suddenly become effeminate," Boris joked.

Danny watched the women. The one with her back to him raised her right arm and snaked a hand over her shoulder, lifting her ash-blonde pony-tail off her neck. Her long, lacquered fingernails caught for a moment in the tangle of her hair. She lifted the hair until Danny could see, and the small breeze that moved across the patio, across the linen tablecloth, could touch, her slim brown neck and the thin gold chain that clung against it. Then she shook her head and the hair fell back onto her shoulders.

Her friend, the one doing all the talking, wore a bright yellow T-shirt, a red skirt and tan high-heeled sandals with a thin strap that buckled across her instep. The heels were so tall they gave her foot an absurd arch. Her face looked fleshy, healthy, like a peach. A peach painted with bright red, round, Betty Boop lips and exaggerated lashy eyes the colour of the pale sky. She complained with determination about someone named Peggy who wouldn't come to a brunch she was going to give on Sunday. Boris looked around impatiently and drummed his fingers on the table.

Their tables butted against a stone railing that ran along the sidewalk. A tall, thin young man with a deep tan coasted by on roller skates. He nodded his head to music that entered his ears through the sponge phones of his Walkman portable radio. Parked across the street was a metallic blue Alfa Romeo sports car. Beyond the car, the Atlantic Ocean lay still in the afternoon. The horizon was in the middle distance and just at the point where the sky started, a brilliant white cruise ship lay at anchor.

Boris and Danny entered America on the same day that President Ronald Reagan assured a convention of evangelical Christians in Orlando that he was not about to change his mind on the Soviet Union; he still viewed it as an 'evil empire' and he was ready with every wile at his disposal to "cut off Communism's toe-hold in Central America." It was the same day that an arbitration panel in Washington awarded a major league baseball relief pitcher five million dollars for three years' work, and the same day a policeman in Stanton, California entered an apartment and shot dead a five-year-old black boy because the child was holding a toy pistol that "looked," said the policeman, "remarkably real."

They flew at 36,000 feet in a DC10. The captain made no announcement when they entered another country, nor could Danny tell by looking out the window. Down below a bank of clouds obscured the 49th Parallel and the whole of the land lay beyond them, still and distant as sleep.

Somewhere below, Canadians were carrying on heated discussions about the levels of interaction they felt appropriate to have with the Americans—in things like trade of manufactured goods and natural resources and defence of the western world—while they sought simultaneously to 'preserve the Canadian identity.' Down below, he also knew, were hockey rinks in American cities filled with Canadian boys playing on NHL teams, just as there were American boys playing baseball in Canadian stadiums in Canadian cities—one of them in the American League. On football teams in Canada the American boys from Mississippi and Ohio were known as 'imports' and the Canadian boys from Nova Scotia and British Columbia were identified by the double negative, 'non-imports.'

On the bus from the Miami International Airport, Boris had to move to the back to get a seat and Danny, seeing no alternative, had squeezed in beside an enormous fat man from Chicago, dressed to go fishing. He was a salesman, he informed Danny right away, a representative for his company in seven midwestern states. And before they were into the downtown of the city, Danny had heard everything he would ever want to know about sliding doors, skylights and greenhouses.

The fat man was on his way to a place called Islamorada to go fishing. He kept a truck, a trailer and a boat there. Back in Chicago he had an answering service. Every two days he would phone back, get his messages and return all his calls. He didn't tell the people he phoned that he was in the Florida Keys fishing. "That would only make them jealous." He laughed a great belly laugh. Then he got serious and told Danny about selling.

He tilted over until the peak of his baseball cap with the rod-and-reel insignia was millimetres from Danny's forehead. "If you want to sell something to people, you don't wanna make 'em jealous of you or have anything but the most undisturbing emotions toward you." It was warm in the bus and the man was sweating profusely. His great body slithered around in his perspiration. He huffed and puffed with the energy of all his talking. He told Danny of great sales he had closed for skylights on shopping centres or in manufacturing plants, quarter- and half-million dollar sales.

"For me it's fun," he said. "I make 'em want it, need it real bad. They're wantin' it for less money; I want to sell it for as high a price as I can. But they already want it. It's like huntin' an animal then, I start closing off all the routes of escape one by one. Then I move in and bam! I've got 'em. I close the deal." He pounded a chubby fist against his knee and sat back, puffing.

The bus trundled through the city. It dropped people at the Hilton and various hotels near the airport, then headed across town toward the Fontainbleu and other hotels on Miami Beach. On the journey it passed through a wasteland of glass-strewn streets and abandoned buildings, a white paved wasteland; buildings four storeys high with every window, every bit of glass blown out like Dresden, dandelions and creepers springing up through broken sidewalks, black children, skinny dogs and winos picking their way through the shards of glass and broken concrete.

Danny's father lived in a condominium on Plantation Key, two hours south of Miami. Danny called him once they got a hotel, a place on Ocean Drive. Unlike many of the other places, it hadn't yet been revamped and had pale green paint peeling off its stucco. He called from the lobby and had to raise his voice and cover one ear to be heard above the commotion of two elderly Jewish men from New York who were rehashing an argument about who was the best fighter: Louis, Dempsey, Marciano or Jersey Joe Walcott.

"Hello, Dad?" Danny shouted into the telephone, sticking his finger in his left ear.

"Dan? Yes, Dan, where are you?" His father now too had a bit of the shake and the shout in his voice that Danny characterized with the elderly of Florida he saw all around him in the hotel lobby. He had been always firm of voice and soft-spoken, Danny remembered, except when preaching in his pulpit. Then his voice rang out like a bell, with a clarity and a resonance that left his hearers almost in awe. Now his voice wavered: aging vocal cords, diminished control of mouth and facial muscles, the slightest touch of Parkinson's and the ever-so-tiny wagging of the head.

"When will you be down? Can I get you? Good to hear you, son."

"I have to do a little work first," Danny explained. "I told you that in the letter. I'm here with Boris; I'll come down in a couple of days."

"Who's Boris?" his father asked.

"My friend, you know, the guy I work for sometimes."

"Well, bring him down then too," his father said.

On the second day Boris rented a car and they drove north toward Boca Raton and West Palm Beach. Boris became all business—a plan was forming in his head. He drove while Danny fiddled with his equipment, fitting lenses to the body of his Minolta, testing his light meter against the bright of the passing day.

"I think I know what we've got to do," said Boris.

Danny looked over at him.

"We won't use models," he said. "We're going to break new ground in naturalist presentations. People know when they're being sold a bill of goods, so we will create something that is definitely not a bill of goods."

"What does that mean?" asked Danny.

"It means," said Boris, patting the steering wheel of the rental car with his hand, pleased with himself, "that we will present life, land, people as they are, as we find them. Our promotion will have no contrivances. Life here will be shown as it really is. It's bound to appeal; people have always respected honesty."

They veered off the highway and headed down a narrow road toward the beach in search of some honesty.

Danny was trying to figure out Boris' angle on all this. As

far as he was concerned, it seemed like a wild goose chase, not very thoroughly thought out. He knew that Boris was doing this on his own, it was not an assignment from Sidney Blumthorp. But it was something he wanted in order to please Sidney, surprise him. He was preoccupied with his work for Sidney and for Edward Burrows; later, when they were going to part ways, when Danny went to visit his father, Boris was going to travel around Florida, go up to Tampa and Fort Myers to inspect the properties he had been buying for Blumthorp. Blumthorp and Burrows probably didn't even know Boris was down here; Boris was doing this on his own in order to go one step further than his assignments required. Not only would he buy the properties for his employers, he would come up with conceptions on how to develop and market them. He would deliver, without their asking, all the brochures to promote them. They would be astounded. What an operator, Boris; he's a genius, thought Danny.

They spent the day driving down little highways and tramping across stretches of beach, looking for the unadulterated reality that Boris felt would sell his conception of Florida living to Sidney Blumthorp's eventual buyers. They took pictures of boys on surf-boards, a young mother with two children building a sand castle, and some old people feeding popcorn to seagulls. They were Livingstone and Stanley traipsing around, their shoes filling with sand. The day turned hot; Danny lugged his cameras and tried to keep them clean. Boris was wearing his dark suit to maintain a professional demeanour and he refused to take it off. But as the day and the heat and their tramping wore on, the suit became dirty and rumpled and blotched with Boris' sweat.

The inside of their rental car took on the characteristics of someone's apartment. Danny's cast-off sweater and shirt and his empty film boxes filled the back seat. At noon Boris bought cartons of Colonel Sanders chicken and cans of Pepsi, and these remains added to the litter.

At five o'clock they were driving down an elegant side

street in Boca Raton when Boris spied through a fence some people sitting around a swimming pool. "There, there," he exclaimed, stopping the car, "that's something we want. We can use that. That's Florida life!"

"We can't intrude on a private party," said Danny.

"We won't," said Boris. "We'll do like we did earlier on the beach. We'll walk up along the street like we're tourists, we'll take a couple of pictures of the trees and the flowers, and when we get close we'll say, 'say, you look like you're having fun, this is just the kind of picture we've been looking for.' They'll be caught off guard and it'll take them less energy to say yes than to say no."

They started along the street. Danny carried his Minolta low on his chest and felt like a fool looking around at the birds and the trees. Boris had put on plastic sun-glasses and, in his rumpled black suit, looked like a mafioso. When they got close to the pool party they stopped at the fence. A half-dozen women and men lounged around the pool, chatting and toying with their cocktails. The women were slim and wore bathing suits; the men, well built in flowered shirts. The house behind them glowed pink; the water in the pool shimmered. Danny pointed his camera toward the street and then turned his body so that slowly, without being too obvious, he could bring the pool party into focus. Suddenly, they were startled by a tremendous volley of barking as a huge German shepherd threw himself at the fence. The people around the pool bolted up. One of the flowered shirts started sprinting toward them. "What the fuck? . . ." he said. Boris put his hands up and unleashed his professional grin as if to say, 'Everything's okay folks.' But he stepped back and before he could say anything, lost his footing in a hole in the boulevard and had to lurch to keep his balance. Danny snapped a couple of quick pictures of the barking dog. The man in the print shirt was nearing the fence, still shouting. Another man came around the corner of the house carrying a black pistol in his right hand. "Holy Jesus," said Boris, "run for your life."

Later, when they were having a drink, Boris seemed unperturbed by the day's adventures. "This is going well," he said. "This is exactly what I wanted." He paused for a drink. "But you know what I've been thinking would be really good?"

"What?" asked Danny.

"Your father," said Boris. "Let's go see your father."

At first, the idea of mixing his father and Boris didn't appeal to Danny. But when he thought about it more, he realized that having someone along to diffuse the intensity of his meeting his father alone might not be a bad idea. He called his father again on the phone and found himself surprised once more with the eagerness his father showed to have company. "Of course, bring him along," he said. "I told you that the other day." His father agreed to wait for them at the end of the road that led to his condominium so they wouldn't get lost.

Danny's father was a small man. Smaller now, Danny realized, when he saw him waiting on the white crushed coral of the roadside, than he remembered. He saw his father first through the blue tinted window of the rent-a-car as they swooped down on the lone figure who stood back from the highway on the shoulder, under the blazing white heat of the early afternoon sun, in the blazing, pale, desert-like wastes of what passed there for land. He was dressed in blue—pale blue slacks held up with a wide white belt, dark blue short-sleeved shirt, white patent leather shoes. The sun glinted off the gold frames of his glasses and burned off the rosy top of his balding head. The land around him was white. The coral and the houses and the haphazardly placed buildings were white as bone, and the tangles of mangrove had a milky whiteness infusing their green, partly from a coating of dust and partly as if their hard leaves were saturated with the calcium they had sucked up from the hard, treacherous spine upon which they lived. Even the sea was pale, and the white cranes that swooped over the mangrove swamp and lifted across the apartment buildings and the pelicans that squatted on posts at the corners of parking lots and by the dock had eyes the colour of slate.

In the car Danny had debated how much to tell Boris about the problems he and his sisters were having with their father; how concerned they were about him and his apprehension about what he would find when he saw him. He broached the subject gingerly.

"What do you mean?" asked Boris.

"We're afraid he might be going a little nuts," said Danny. "He's off on a track, obsessed with things it never occurred to him to think about before."

"And that worries you?" said Boris.

"Wouldn't it concern you?" said Danny.

Boris shrugged. He paused. "Maybe I'd think it was a good sign," he said.

"Hello, Danny." His father grabbed his hand and wrist and gave them both a good squeeze. His grip was still firm despite his apparent frailty. "How do you do, Boris?" He climbed into his car and they followed him up the narrow road.

To get into his father's house they had to deal with three locks. The first was on a huge, elaborate, black wrought-iron gate that barred the parking lot and grounds proper. His father rolled down the window of his Fiesta and inserted a key into a bronze box and the gate swung open. Then, after they'd parked the cars, walked with Danny's bags across the parking lot, nodded to the doorman—a thin, uniformed black man his father called Jimmy who had skin so dark it shone and a mouth spilling with corn-coloured teeth—they faced a combination in the lobby that could be opened only by pressing a sequence of numbered buttons, like a push-button phone. When all the buttons were pressed, a pair of glass doors, three-quarters of an inch thick, swung open to let them into the bowels of the concrete building. The third lock was on the door of the apartment itself, second floor at the back looking out over the Atlantic.

"You're very secure here," said Boris.

Danny was almost a head taller than his father, he realized as he followed him into the deep pile expanse of his living-room. His father hopped ahead like a bony little bird.

"Well, boys, sit down. Would you like some cola?" He went to the refrigerator in the small galley that ran off the living-room.

It had been more than a year since Danny and his father had seen one another and Danny was aware of needing to go through a ritual that would ease them into one another's territory. Boris' being there made him feel like a third party, but for the time being he didn't mind. He walked over to the window, a large floor-to-ceiling window that occupied almost the entire wall, and looked out past the mangroves and the few palms and the crusty, shell-covered beach at the distance of the pale green sea.

Boris followed his father right into his kitchen and then followed him back out as he brought a tray loaded with glasses and drinks. They took seats at various places around the large living-room and the talk for a few minutes rambled over nothing in particular. Finally, Boris said, "You know, I'm intrigued by this part of the world and I'd like to know more about it. You must have some perspectives on it."

"Indeed I do," said Danny's father. "I've been paying attention to things while I'm down here. I've been learning as much as I can about this little neighbourhood of mine."

Early the next morning, fortified by bacon and pancakes engineered by his father, and overly strong coffee put in a thermos by Boris, they roared off in Albert Hinkle's Ford Fiesta, out of the condominium compound toward the highway. His father was up and rattling around the kitchen before Danny and Boris were even awake. Boris made the coffee, eager to be helpful but careless in his measuring.

"Maybe we should take a day off," said Danny. "We've been driving around this state for the last three days now."

"Nonsense," said his father, holding firm to the wheel and keeping the little Ford tight to the road. "You'll enjoy this trip. It's a spectacular drive between here and Key West." Boris sat in the front seat, his head almost knocking the roof, his knees accordioned in front of him. Danny was in the back seat like a little kid, leaning forward to see between the two heads in front of him.

"The Florida Keys," announced Albert Hinkle, turning west onto the highway, "are a chain of a thousand islands, 62 of them populated, that run for 200 miles from the Florida mainland in an arc curving to the south and to the west, almost to the tip of Cuba. The largest and last of the populated islands is the island of Key West, in Spanish, Cayo Hueso or Bone Island.

"Key West, at 24 degrees latitude, just above the Tropic of Cancer, is the most southerly point in the continental United States of America." Albert Hinkle knit his brow while he delivered the geography lesson. Boris sat forward, listening intently.

"It is on a latitude parallel to East Pakistan, the Spanish Sahara, Riyadh, Saudi Arabia and Canton, China. From the dock on Mallory Street, which is effectively the end of the Florida Keys, it is 90 miles to Havana, Cuba. But psychologically, it is much closer.

"In Key West the resident population supported the South in the American Civil War but the naval station was garrisoned with Union troops, a great number of whom, from places like New York and Massachusetts, perished in a plague of yellow fever in 1862. In 1912 the Florida East Coast Railway, built with the expenditure of $50 million and 700 lives by Henry M. Flagler, a partner and crony of John D. Rockefeller's, made its last island hop along the Keys to Key West.

"Ernest Hemingway lived there, arriving in 1929 with his

second wife, Pauline. I'll show you his house. It's the biggest one in town. American writers seem to like to live there. Playwright Tennessee Williams kept a house there although he had a rough time. I read in an article that local thugs at one point gathered in front of his fence screaming at the closed door for the 'faggot to come out.' He was a homosexual, you know, Tennessee Williams." Boris nodded that he knew.

Danny watched the scenery go by. The warm, salty gulf air blasted his face through the open car windows. They passed through a fishing town named Marathon and soon were climbing the spans of a slender construction which a large sign told them was The Seven Mile Bridge. For long minutes their little car seemed suspended on the long concrete arc while far below them shimmered the bright blue-green of the sea. Then, as suddenly as they had left, they were down again on the hard dust of the highway. The silver knobs of house trailers in seemingly endless patches of trailer courts once again zoomed past, interspersed with the blocks of cement condominiums that seemed to rise like calluses out of the mangrove swamp.

The bridge just passed, his father explained, had in 1970 completed the road link between Key West and the lower Keys and the rest of the continental United States. U.S. Interstate #1 was yet another version of the omnipotent arteries of 20th-century connection. Follow it for 3000 kilometres in the other direction and it would take you to Maine and New Brunswick.

"The coming of automobile traffic to the Keys meant what it meant to any other location on the continent," said Albert Hinkle. Bam! He lifted his hands from the steering wheel and smashed them together. "In Key West you'll see that the old, white clapboard town has been surrounded, buttressed, by a melee of endless sprawling Howard Johnsons and Holiday Inns, jet-ski ports, Winn Dixie and Searstown shopping plazas, radiator repair shops and Chicken Unlimited outlets. Where once it was silent as summer, now it's all automobile mayhem. Once, the wind blowing in one direction brought the smells of the fishing wharves and in the other, the scent of hibiscus. Now it's all the stench of exhaust fumes. You'll see what I mean.

"And tourists," he went on. "The world, boys, it seems, is full of tourists. You're tourists and so am I. Come to think of it, it always was so and I'm sorry I never used that as the theme for a sermon. But that's another story."

They arrived at the town of Key West and drove in past the muffler shops, the shopping plazas, the marinas and the dog-race track. When they got to the old town they looked for a place to park. Albert Hinkle never stopped talking.

"At that beach," he said, pointing to a luxury hotel beyond the pier, "I'm told the tourist women even take their bathing suit tops off and sit there naked as jay birds. The tourists are half-naked even on days when the weather is cold and the local people, who refer to themselves as 'Conches,' walk around with their shirts buttoned to the neck, trying to mind to their business and trying to keep their little community liveable. And they try. Oh they try. They rant away. On the street when I was down here last I saw a Chevy with a bumper sticker that said, 'Inflation hasn't touched the wages of sin. It's still death'." He paused for a brief laugh.

They walked out past the crowded streets of tourists, past the naval station and the cigar factory to a jut of land that pointed toward Cuba. Danny's father, who had been intense and animated all morning, became calm. "Such is life," he said, "on what is at the most a precarious environment. For the Keys are no more than a little finger, a spine of coral and limestone that extends from the swamp of southern Florida out into the sea. A bony little finger. The balance between dry land and water is so tenuous that a good rain storm can diminish the land area excessively. For four miles out into the Gulf at some points the water never gets more than three or five feet deep. On most of the islands, by the same token, the highest point of dry land is perhaps seven or ten feet above sea level and the mangroves that cover the rock have their tentacle roots steeped in salt water. The limestone and the coral are the petrified and fused remains of trillions and quadrillions of tiny marine molluscs cemented together in one huge embrace ten million years ago.

"Can you imagine?" he cried in seeming conclusion, his arms flailing. "Crawling up on top of one another every year over hundreds, thousands, tens of thousands of years and dying?"

They stood in the wind at the very end of the United States. Danny was aware of nothing so much as the rumble of the ocean. His father, exhausted by his speech-making, stood panting. No one spoke.

Then Boris, almost inaudibly, whispered, "Amazing. Amazing," he exclaimed again. He smiled and jumped over beside Danny's father. "I'd like you to write your thoughts down and send them to me," he said. "I like your view of the world." He put his arm around Albert Hinkle's bony shoulder. "Danny," said Boris, "before I leave tomorrow I want you to take our picture, your dad and me." Danny's father grinned, weary but pleased. They turned back toward the car.

"Dan, you'll have to drive going back," said Albert Hinkle. "I'm afraid I'm exhausted.'

16

Danny had visited his father perhaps three dozen times since he left home and they stopped living together. When he was 20 and his father stopped giving him money (and he stopped asking for it), any practical nature or dependence that their relationship had had, ended. From that time on they were independent human beings—tied by their memories and their history and by sentiment—but free to meet one another as men. Yet for ten years they never had.

Danny thought that he and his father had never really known each other. By that, he meant they'd never appreciated the person the other thought himself to be. That might be, he realized, the only true way of knowing someone—giving credit for the other person's image of himself. It made him feel sad. His mind flooded with memories and speculations about how it might have been. Resentments still sat there like undigested seeds in a grape. He hadn't been the best father, he thought, there were things he could have done. No, could he say that? Yes, that's what he meant. For instance, his father was never out playing baseball; he was in his study. He wasn't telling Danny the facts of life; he was busy going to meetings. He didn't know about Susan Benton in grade ten and the way Danny longed for her, and he didn't know how he wished Stephen Copas would break his arm so he could move up from second-string quarterback to full time on the high school football team. His father would surely have reproached him for such thoughts. Even though it was he who gave Danny his first camera, he never knew how much Danny dreaded telling him when he quit university to study photography at the polytechnical institute. Or how he feared, believed, that his father would condemn him for having settled for second best.

But then Danny hadn't done everything, either. There were things he could, should, have done. They stayed only tentatively in touch. For a while, with the zest of a child delivering handicrafts from school, Danny clipped and mailed pictures he had taken which had been printed in newspapers and magazines. Even, he remembered, his first newspaper news-spot photo, a broken, gushing fire hydrant that had been run over by a car. And ads he had photographed—snow tires for a local distributor. Did his father ever know what to say to these offerings? Did he save them? Put them in a scrapbook? Stuff them in a drawer? Or did they get misplaced or thrown away?

Danny would get letters, sometimes, with tiny references: "It looks like you're busy, Dan. Keep at it." But who knows what that meant? Yet what did he want from his father? What would he have welcomed? Copies of his sermons every week?

Danny cringed with pangs of guilt when he realized what

his father had become for him. He was young and healthy
with his life happening all around him; his father was an old
man with his life in boxes and photo albums and diaries. He
sent his letters, his tracts, which Danny greeted first with
perplexity and confusion, then consternation. And then he
joked about them in letters and phone calls to Leslie. With
the arrogance that infects the young like acne he now
presumed to come to see his father loaded with the tired yoke
of obligation, with some affection, as one might go to see an
old pet dog to scratch him one more time behind the ears.

When they were having breakfast Danny looked across the
counter at this man who had difficulty now, with the
Parkinson's, even buttering a piece of toast. The knife shook
in one hand and the piece of toast rattled in the other until
he placed it down, flat on the plate, and applied the butter to
it in uncertain waves. Because of his failing eyesight, he had
to sit back an extra couple of inches from the table. He tilted
his head back slightly and then, his lips pursed intently, went
to work on toast and marmalade. The difference in his pos-
turing was only a matter of a couple of inches, but it and the
intensity with which he applied himself to this most mundane
and ordinary of tasks became a huge exaggeration that both
astonished Danny and overwhelmed him with pity.

His father saw it and tried to make a joke. "You think some
day I'll be sick," he said, "and you'll be stuck changing the bed.
Leslie already has me reduced to the status of patient. But I
guess," he continued wryly, "that would be normal for the
professional medico in the family." He looked up. "Samantha,"
he said, "is the only one who treats me like a man. I guess it's
because we're still quarrelling."

He was always, in Danny's memory, a formidable man. Not
a big man. But so capable and so in control that no thought
of fallibility ever occurred to his children. Even after their
mother died, there was no apparent crack in the composure
and certitude with which he dealt with the world. No matter
what his grief and no matter what blow the world might have

dealt him, it was all part, he seemed certain, of a cosmic plan
in which his place was well-ordained. Every adversity was a
test, he proclaimed both in his teaching and in his life, sent
to enhance you, through which you grew and out of which you
emerged stronger and more serene than ever. To his children
he was basically kind and fair, loving but aloof. As a child,
Danny would have to be preoccupied indeed to burst into his
father's study without announcing or knocking. The spon-
taneity of approaches to their father was qualified indeed.

His discipline had the strength and the tension of
tempered steel. Danny remembered one time when he was 13
years old, sitting in church where he always sat during his
father's services, with a row of his friends in a pew near the
front. The lot of them were high-spirited—full of energy and
an adolescent need to tease one another. And they were bored
to tears by having to sit in church. On this particular morning their energy and zip got the better of them and they commenced giggling and poking, unaware of the commotion they
were beginning to cause. Jackie Pryor started it. He always
had an infallible eye for the amusing or the absurd, and
pointed out that from their vantage point down low in the
pews they could have a good gander right up the skirt of Mrs.
Deacon where she sat in the front row of the choir.

Elvira Deacon was one of those small-town pillars, a great
lump of a woman given to high-pitched chatter and ceaseless
frenzied activity around church bazaars, choirs, home-and-
school associations. She was not one who would ever have
raised with any of them the slightest twinge of sexual interest or curiosity. Yet on this morning, it was she, sitting in the
front row of the choir with her knees splayed wide apart like
a drawbridge, who set Jackie Pryor and then the rest of them
off, just like a row of dominoes. It wasn't even that they could
see much; but they did notice that her stockings stopped just
above her knees, pulled up just above her knees and then
rolled there, big fat rolls of dark stocking and then, spilling
out above that, billowing white tumbles of flesh.

There was nothing lascivious about it in the least, just the ridiculous image of a chubby pillar of churchwomanhood caught unaware with her legs splayed so that a row of adolescent boys could see the roll of the tops of her stockings. They were heaving with the giggles.

Danny's father was reading aloud from Deuteronomy when he stopped in mid-verse. Without missing a beat in the rhythm, he looked over the top of his glasses at the row of them and said, "Boys."

Like a platoon on cue, they turned red and sucked in and bit the insides of their cheeks. But they were on a course that knew no turning back. The fact that his father's warning had put them on probation only made it worse.

The Rev. Albert Hinkle returned to Deuteronomy. Danny grabbed a hymn-book and thumbed through to distract himself. Beside him, his pal Stewart Foley had hunkered over with his forehead resting on his knees, his hands clasped firmly over his ears, the back of his neck red and his body racked with the convulsions of suppressed laughter. Up in the choir Mrs. Deacon closed her legs, crossed them, then absently reached down a hand to scratch her left buttock. Then her chubby thigh slipped off her knee again and her legs swung back to their former position.

Jackie Pryor let out a loud snicker. Danny's father stopped his peroration right in its tracks. He had no idea what it was they were finding so funny, but he knew he'd have to put a stop to it.

"Boys," he said, this time with explicit firmness. "I've had to stop once already. Now I'm not going to go on." There was a death-like pause in the church and something told Danny, as his ears burned red, that a terrible event was about to happen. "Daniel," his father looked straight at him. "I want you to leave the sanctuary."

His mouth dropped open half a space. He couldn't believe it. Me? he wanted to say, pointing at himself on the chest.

"Please leave, I won't continue until you do," he said in the

most quietly dignified, gentle, firm voice Danny had ever in
his life heard.

With a realization that clattered like a load of falling
bricks, Danny understood that he meant it. There would be
no trial, he could not protest his innocence nor the fact that
he was but a second-rate supporting actor. The price had fallen to him. He alone was being sentenced to the exile, the
humiliation. Disbelief flooded over him.

He got up and bumped past the knees of his friends until
he reached the aisle. He set his sights firmly on the exit door
which seemed at that moment to be half a mile of red carpet
away. And he started walking. On legs whose strength came
from he knew not where, he marched one of the longest
journeys of his life.

He didn't know where to go. On any other sunny Sunday
he would have had an enormous list of places he'd rather have
been than church. Now, with his options open for almost the
first time, none of them occurred to him. He didn't go to the
ballpark; he didn't go home; he didn't even go for a walk on
the streets. He went down the stairs to the basement of the
church, circled back to a corner and found the door to the big,
dark, dusty furnace room. Slipping in quietly and pulling the
door shut behind him, he groped around until he found a
wooden orange crate, turned it on end and sat down, alone,
in the black dark.

He sat there for a long time in a silence both so oppressive
and so soothing that at times he felt it made him larger than
the world. He sat there in the cool black of the room, the faint-
ly slick smell of heating oil easing into him. And after a while
he started to hear things. Sounds. Singing from the far-off
distant sanctuary of the church high above him. The sound
was coming down through the heating ducts. Within moments his ears tuned and he could hear everything: the
choruses ". . . Saviour, Saviour hear my humble cry. While on
others Thou art waiting, do not pass me by."

He could hear the shuffle, the rumble as the congregation

stood or sat down, the shuffle of 800 feet on the floorboards, the settling of 400 rear-ends on the oak pews. Finally, he could hear the voice of his father as he intoned the benediction that would send them all on their way. Out into the world.

"And now may the grace of our Lord Jesus Christ, the fellowship of the Holy Spirit, the love of God the Father almighty rest and abide with you from this time forth ... amen," he said. His father giving blessing. At that moment how he hated him.

This was the same man he now accompanied into the U Tote M store on Plantation Key so that they could spend some of his pension money on taco chips, fresh fruit and shrimps, canned soup and a couple of large, lean steaks to replenish the larder.

His father wore his squeaky white shoes and his light blue pants held up by the wide white belt. The rosy crest of his head flaked as wafers of burned dead skin shrivelled and popped loose. The same was happening on the bridge of his nose. The colour the sun had given him, however, made him seem happily healthy despite the frailty of his body.

At the check-out, a smooth yacht of a woman with primped silver curls and a flowing tent of a dress covered with flowers busily sorted through a hand of discount coupons, reading them through the lenses of shell-framed glasses. When Danny and his father approached, she dropped the glasses, which swayed for a moment from a pearl-studded chain until they settled on her heavy bosom. Her face burst into a summer smile. "Why Rev-er-end Hinkle! I do declare. Doin' your shopping?" Her voice rang like door chimes.

Danny's father giggled and stammered. His colour deepened. "Why, yes. Yes. Just picking up a few things."

The lady moored a dainty forefinger in the crease of a fleshy cheek. There was some serious flirting going on here, Danny could tell. He was a little embarrassed. He looked to see if there was a magazine rack nearby so he could leaf through something.

"This is Mrs. . . . ," his father wrestled him back into it. But he appeared to have mislaid the lady's name.

"Garvey," the woman said with the same doorbell chime, only louder. "From Rhode Island."

"My son, Dan," said Albert Hinkle.

They escaped the store with Mrs. Garvey fluttering after and about them. Grinning madly, backing out the door, hugging their groceries, they left her. She waved her coupons after them, tinkling in her high voice. On the parking pad in front of the store, Danny's father practically crumpled. "Widows," he said. "They're everywhere down here."

They walked in silence the rest of the way to the car. But Danny watched his father like a hawk, all his senses tuned. He was immensely curious. His father started the car and said not a word.

For the next couple of days Danny paid close attention. They didn't talk much, just the pleasantries. But he watched.

He wondered at first whether his father was lonely. But after a day he wasn't sure about that. He seemed content, in fact, in his solitude; so much so that Danny thought perhaps his visit was an intrusion. Although his father didn't say anything to that end; he remained busy and cheerful. But Danny noticed that his father was thinking in ways that were new.

"I think, sometimes, that I made a mistake coming here," he offered at one point.

"What do you mean?" Danny asked.

"I hate to fish," he said.

But here he was on this arch of rock and coral surrounded by the sea, where almost every activity had to do with fishing; whether it was salesmen from Chicago grabbing a week and going out to chase marlin in the Atlantic, or the tanned, black-eyed little Cubans who lived in the tin shanties on the other side of the marina, hauling in grouper and yellowtails to sell to the restaurants. Or the big shrimp boats with names like the *Mary Sue* or the *Betty Jane* registered in North Carolina but docked down the Keys at Marathon or Key West, waltzing in from the horizon in the first light of early morning, their big boom arms stretched out like the wings of prehistoric pterodactyls. If you didn't love or understand the sea, there wasn't much reason to be here.

From the standpoint of his father the theologian, Danny might say it was an appropriate place to be. He might say that there was something mythologically perfect for this man to be here. He had spent half his active life attempting to understand and interpret the cosmos, grappling with a set of doctrines that had appeared to lay it all out with some order and purpose. In the other half he had provided succour and comfort to fellow travellers aggrieved and confused by its natural unfoldings. For him to come at the closing of his life to 'land's end,' surrounded by the sea and burned by the sun, to make his home on the backs of a billion years' accumulation of dead and petrified crustaceans, might be totally appropriate.

It was nothing he could have expected his father himself to realize or acknowledge—the governing myths of his father's career, his theology, his ministry, were agricultural ones. He lived in the small towns of Ontario, the midwest of the continent; came from people and lived among people who husbanded the land, cleared land, laid out fields, planted them, killed weeds, domesticated and tamed their animals, feared the wild and kept the wolves at distances ever further from their doors. It was a world populated by humans, overrun by humans, a world in which Old-Testament decrees to Adam's children to procreate and inhabit the earth, to have dominion over and take stewardship of the earth, held sway.

The sea was a more pre-ordinate world, a less orderly, less controlled world; a world whose life pre-dated that of the life rooted in deep loam soils by billions of years. But as Danny watched, he came to believe that it was having an effect on his father. He was being drawn to it in some magnetic, although undefined, way. At some deep level of his consciousness it was bothering him; it would not let him rest; it threatened to somersault all his thinking into arcs and curves that at another time he would never have allowed or deemed possible.

It started with a drawer full of clippings that Danny saw him with on his third day. His father, always a voracious reader of newspapers, magazines and periodicals as well as serious texts and literature, walked to the U Tote M store every morning to pick up copies of the *Miami Herald* and the *News*. Sometimes he bought *USA Today* or even a copy of the *National Enquirer*. Then he clipped until he had accumulated a table-top full of pages and half-pages, columns and long thin strips of newsprint that chronicled the most audacious, the most bizarre, the most lamentable, the most hilarious, the most terrifying, the most pitiable and the saddest events, occasions and actions of humanity on the planet.

Danny surprised him one morning seated cross-legged on the middle of his bed with the current day's offerings spread out in disarray about him, a long pair of clipping scissors still in his right hand. His father wasn't unsettled at being discovered; Danny was, rather, the unsettled one. These clippings, he realized with a shock, were what had been sent on to him, almost at random.

His father did not shy from showing his work, as if sitting on the bed making a scrap-book of reports (some verifiable, some less so) of the world's calamities should be the most natural vocation for a 68-year-old man with a Masters of Theology from the University of Toronto (1938) and (almost) a Doctorate of Divinity from Union Theological Seminary (stopped short due to events of the war in 1941). A man who had been a middle power in the offices of his country's largest Protestant denomination for 30 years; a man who stood by example of word and thought and deed unassailable in rectitude for nearly a lifetime at the very centre of his industrious, careful, orderly community.

"I am compiling a history of our present world, Danny, human and cosmic," he said excitedly from the middle of his bed. "And I find that that world is going to smithereens."

Danny scanned a stack of fresh clippings. In a suburb of Atlanta, Georgia, an ordinance had been passed requiring all residents to own hand-guns for their personal protection. In Battle Creek, Michigan, 17 relatives of a dead man had been awarded $60,000 in a court judgement because the man's coffin fell apart as he was being carried to his grave, dropping the body rudely onto the ground. The coffin lining, relatives discovered, was stuffed with pantyhose and old newspapers. In Arizona, a Pentacostal preacher was electrocuted when the hand-held microphone he carried shorted out as he stood waist-deep in a pool conducting a baptism.

A story datelined Washington, D.C. declared that 200 million tons of toxic waste, almost 2000 pounds for every man, woman and child, are pumped every year into the air, land and water of the United States. If the high-level radioactive wastes from the continent's nuclear power plants continued to accumulate at present rates, another story reported, by the end of the 20th century it would take all the fresh water of the world, two times over, to dilute them. And even then the water would not be drinkable for about 24,000 years.

A story clipped from the *Washington Post* said that of perhaps some five million species of plants and animals inhabiting the world, about 17,000 are killed off each year due to destruction of the tropical rain forests. Seventeen thousand entire species; little-known varieties of trees, plants, animals, fish in Amazon basin rivers or in Peruvian valleys or on Borneo plains.

The next morning Danny went swimming in the Atlantic Ocean.

At breakfast his father had looked peaked; a pallor from some deep-seated fatigue pressed through even the colour of his suntan. His hands shook as he poured cream over his Special K. His mouth looked pinched and white. But his eyes shone bright like emeralds, as though the energy that lit them had nothing to do with the weariness of the rest of his body. At three a.m. Danny had wakened to see a light still burning in the corner of the living-room where his reading chair sat.

"I had trouble sleeping last night," his father said.

"I noticed you were still up," Danny said.

"I read." He paused for a bite of his breakfast. "You know, I read Ecclesiastes. Just started reading it and went on and on. It's been translated, I don't know how many times," he continued. "But it retains such beauty. All those precepts put so succinctly, with such clarity. It is wonderful." His eyes misted over and he looked toward the window. His white lips had converted into a sad, wistful smile.

"Then I started to read Revelations," he said. "I wanted to go with John to see the City of God where the streets are of pure gold, like translucent glass. I wanted to see the great scarlet beast with seven heads and ten horns, the foul spirits coming from the mouth of the dragon, the sea of glass shot with fire, and I started to read it. But I fell asleep, right there on the chair. Didn't even go to bed." He looked at Danny.

When Danny stepped into the water his father was sitting on the beach. He wore his swimming trunks but he sat in a folding chair with a large beach towel over his knees. He never went in the water.

Danny swam out over the coral where the water was only three or four feet deep until he reached a spot where the reef dropped off and the water turned blue and got very deep. The sky before him looked bright as crystal and went on forever. He felt exhilarated with the strength of all the world.

On the horizon at a great distance, a slate-coloured tanker seemed moored in time, although he knew from the smoke wisping from its stack that it must be moving. The swells of the sea rose like breathing and carried him in great rushes on their up-side and then down. Danny was not a great swimmer but he felt as if he could go on forever.

When he turned, finally, his father was a speck on the beach. Danny paused for breath and treaded water, rocked in the swells like a baby in the great liquid arms of its mother. Above him, a covey of seagulls dived and screeched and twirled, white in the sunlight, and were gone again. The steamer had moved 20 degrees on the horizon; he started to swim back.

It was a long way back. He had come much further than he had intended. But he started to swim. The return to shore was markedly different from the swim out, when he had no destination, just the exhilaration of the bright morning and the seemingly limitless stamina and strength of his body. The horizon was forever away, yet it seemed to him that he could reach it. Now the shore and the little dot of his father and the dusty bank of the mangrove swamp seemed as far away as another city, and he could feel the weariness creeping up through his arms and shoulders.

The swells carried him high, then dropped him into their troughs, then caught him again. One caught him badly in mid-breath, and his mouth filled with salt water. He kicked madly but his feet moved nothing but air. A pellet of panic rose in his sternum. He paused, swallowed it, found himself in the water, and took a moment to calm himself. He knew suddenly how people could drown in three feet of water. The feeling of primordial terror is so opposite to conscious, planned, controlled life that it is like being filled with a block of ice that obliterates all memory. He had trouble under-standing how a drowning person could see all the memory of his life move in a flash before his eyes. He couldn't fathom the calm, as water filled the lungs, that would provide the mo-ment for that visionary experience. He took all his strength into his arms and he continued to swim.

In a kick, at last, his toe stubbed against a sharp, hard edge of coral and entangled in a mass of seaweed and sub-merged, rotting lily stems. He swam a couple more strokes and settled to his feet. Finally, standing up, staggering and heaving, he took slow steps toward shore, groping for footing. His lungs ached and he could not inhale the air fast enough.

The water ran off his hair and down his chest, and his arms hung limp and tired as rubber. The breeze blowing offshore was warm and humid.

He reached the shore 20 yards down the beach from where his father sat, wrapped in his towel. Danny sat on a rock of broken coral for a long time, catching his breath and his life. Then he walked slowly, like a racehorse cooling, in a circle a couple of times before heading over toward the little figure on the folding chair. Above him seagulls swirled again, engaged in another episode of their never-ending quarrel.

He approached his father, expecting to sit down on the towel beside his chair and lie back for 20 minutes and enjoy a silence that finally they discovered they could welcome in one another. Although they had not expressed it in words, the urgency their times together had always had for as long as Danny could remember, the edge of tension that made them work hard, that exhausted them in being together, had disappeared. Danny had always been ready to defend himself to his father, but he didn't have to this time; his father had asked him no questions.

Most remarkable of all, he thought, was the freedom with which they could sit in one another's presence in silence, thinking their own thoughts. And once in a while this man, this old man who had guided him through the years of his early life with the rigidity of a captain holding the wheel in a gale, this theologian who guarded the portals of faith and conduct tenaciously, this man who now, almost as far away from his roots as he could take himself, clipped items from the *National Enquirer* even as he read Ecclesiastes all night and fended off, abashed and embarrassed, the advances of the widows who surrounded him, this man who was his father would throw out the most remarkable revelations, the most unexpected, unlinear pieces of information with no warning at all. Little curve-ball secrets from the corners of his life. That he shared such things left Danny speechless with amazement but almost ready to weep with tenderness.

"One time," he had said as they sat in the big chairs of his living-room, interrupting Danny as he paged through an old issue of the *New Yorker*, "one time, before I had even met your mother, I was at a social event. And a girl with flaming red hair and wearing a loose white dress . . . it was summer and a hot, humid evening . . . flirted with me in the most transparent way. I knew her only slightly, but I knew that evening that, should I want to, I could do anything I wished with her. I didn't, of course. But, you know," he said wistfully, not even to Danny, "I've always regrétted my hesitation."

Danny approached his father still breathing heavily. The sour sting of swallowed salt clouded up the back of his throat and trachea. The old man appeared to be asleep, although there was something not right about his being asleep in the mid-day sun, asleep with his body tilted at an awkward angle, his head lolled like a doll's. The towel had half slipped from his lap, and his hand clutched like a claw at the front of his shirt.

Suddenly Danny felt vacant, like a desert or a huge empty ballroom. His father's sunburn had disappeared and he was as pale as the coral. The hand that clawed at the front of his shirt was rigid as wood. His mouth was half open and a trickle of foamy spittle dried on his lip. Danny bent down, afraid to touch him, but his eyes moved and his head lifted weakly. Danny reached to hold his shoulders almost more in awe than in fear of whatever it was that was happening or had happened. Between them the wind continued to blow. His father was either in great pain or he was very weak. He raised his head slightly to fix Danny with water-filled eyes as faded now as limestone. A great panic filled the son and his mind rushed to think what to do, what to say.

His father smiled a little, recognizing the terror. "I'll be all right," he whispered. "I get these now and then." He stopped to rest, to muster strength. He smiled. "Take me home now."

17

When Boris Podolski arrived back at his apartment, the letter box was so jammed with mail that half of it fell to the floor when he opened the little door. He stooped, picked up what had fallen and rifled through it quickly, dropping the bulk, freebies and flyers, into the large black metal basket in the lobby. The rest he held, adding to the accumulation of paraphernalia he was holding already—his suitcase, his brief-case, his light-weight, all-weather trench coat. He pressed the button and waited for the elevator. He did not look like a happy man.

He was a man somewhere in the middle between panic and despair. He had had time to get used to the feeling on the long flight home from Tampa aboard the 737. A doctor from Rio de

Janiero regaled him non-stop in his left ear about how impossible inflation had made things in Brazil. Boris had taken it for a while. Then, "Can you please shut up," he had said. "Can't you see that I'm thinking?"

He had been thinking a great deal. His skin was grey from thinking. And worrying. And not sleeping. The hot sun that should have turned him a healthy tan gave him only a quick burn. And then his problems set in. After leaving Danny Hinkle and his father, he had spent days racing back and forth along the west Florida coast between Tampa and Fort Myers in his rented Oldsmobile. Twice he had flown up to Tallahassee, and once, feeling panicked and in a hurry, he chartered a small plane when no other flight was available. It had come to nothing. He looked for lawyers; he looked to find a crooked legislator. No one could help him.

More times than he could count he had stood in the long grass and ankle-deep mollusc shells of the shore while the brackish water filled his Gucci shoes, and he had stared out into the mangrove swamp of Pine Island Sound, trying to discern in the tangle of roots and pelican droppings and salty, silty, briny water the boundaries of the subdivision he'd optioned with $400,000 (American) of Sidney Blumthorp's money.

Every time he entered the musty, echoing halls of the Lee County land office a clerk gave him roughly the same response. "I'm sorry, there's no mistake. How many of those lots did you say you bought?" Then the look crept over their faces. The look he hated. One chubby, pallid little functionary in a checkered sportshirt had actually put words to it. "Mebbe you can sell 'em lots to gators, ha ha ha ha ha ha ha."

And when he sought, both in Fort Myers and in the state capital, the permit number of the agent who, four weeks previous in a hotel in Chicago, had sold him the options, he got the same answer: "I'm sorry, no such name exists on our files. We've never heard of the man."

The one thing he hadn't done was phone Sidney

Blumthorp. He would have to do that now. He thought of his white Cadillac parked in the basement garage, two weeks of dust settled on it. He thought of Sidney Blumthorp's redheaded secretary. He felt ill from the top of his head to the very pit of his stomach. Boris did not look like a healthy man.

He had to perk himself up. He had a reception to attend in three hours. The annual meeting of Peter Alverstone's constituency association; seventh-floor ballroom of the Hotel Fort Garry. A reception and drinks at seven, then a speech by the Minister of External Affairs. Then the meeting itself. Four spots on the constituency executive to be filled. Five candidates.

He dropped his heavy bag inside the door of the huge, empty living-room of his apartment and hung his raincoat on the room's only chair. He laid his briefcase down flat on the floor beside his red push-button phone. He pulled down the knot on his tie and undid the top two buttons of his shirt. He walked to the bathroom and turned on both faucets full blast to fill the tub, then threw his jacket on the floor on the way to the kitchen. In the kitchen he drew a full glass of water and swallowed two Tylenol capsules.

He had his ticket to the meeting, an embossed card with the Party's insignia in the upper left-hand corner, a picture of Peter Alverstone in the upper right, tacked on the bulletin board beside his phone. He didn't need the card to remind him of the meeting. It had been on his mind for weeks. For the four openings on the executive he, Boris Podolski, lawyer, agent, media consultant, promotions manager, entrepreneur, was candidate number five.

He had worked like blazes to get into the position where he could get the nomination. Kissed ass like crazy. They didn't like him, those people. They resented him—too new, too brash. Stern the senator, it was, who finally got him in. The old lawyer, still a senior partner in his firm although he no longer did any work. Spent all his time now in Ottawa or Israel. He must have felt sorry for him. Or maybe he saw something the rest of them didn't see. Or didn't want to see.

Stern had scrambled up the hard way too, but now he could tell them to go fuck themselves. Once, Stern had pulled him aside after a frustrating committee meeting. "This is the party that has room for everyone but where everyone has his place." The hand on his arm, the wry grin. Boris could have wept. "Well, I'll screw them too," he thought.

He should get his phone messages. He was so depressed about the Florida business he didn't want to get his phone messages. There'd be calls he couldn't answer right away. Sidney for sure. Sidney. He took off his trousers and his shirt and his socks and eased himself into the tub.

Although he had got the nomination, he hadn't campaigned. He was off in Chicago; he was off in Florida. He hadn't been around to grease the wheels, oil the palms, put balm on the waters. That bothered him, although he wasn't sure what he would have done as a campaign, whom he would have seen and how he would have moved them. Maybe it was just as well. They were either going to vote for him or they weren't. He'd give a speech. Stern and his friends were irritated enough with the ruling clique to vote for him just for spite. He smiled at the thought. Alverstone and his people— he didn't know how they would go. Things with them were more complicated. More variables at play. They were happy enough when he got them billboards and talk-show invitations during the campaign but he couldn't tell how that would translate tonight. Sometimes he got the feeling Alverstone the MP didn't really want to be seen with him. One lousy invitation to Ottawa. Ah, screw 'em. He sunk deeper into the steamy water of the tub.

With a big green towel wrapped around him and his hair still wet and plastered to his head, Boris sat cross-legged on the floor and played back the tape on his answering machine. His wife in Toronto wondering if he was still coming for a weekend. Sylvia, the little receptionist in the mayor's office he'd been seeing sporadically. He smiled. Sidney. Sidney once,

Sidney twice, Sidney three times. Sidney's secretary. Burrows. An ad writer who needed work. Marc Lachance, Alverstone's right-hand guy. Stern. "I need to talk to you before the meeting. Get in touch with me any way you can. It's critical."

Bzzzz. Nothing more on the tape.

What could Stern want? He looked at his watch.

For an hour before the reception he tried to reach Stern. No answer. The Florida business bothered him immensely. It was a dead bird hanging around his neck. He had gone there on his own, a hunch. Blumthorp's expense account, of course, but he had gone without clearing it with them, without discussing it with Edward Burrows or with Blumthorp.

He was pleased with his and Danny's photo expedition. Something would come of that, for sure. They would be pleased. But the land business was terrible. What had gone wrong? Had he done something wrong? Had he missed something that should have been obvious? He went back in his mind over the events.

Something about his exchange with Thomas in Chicago had bothered him; something about the papers, something about the maps. He couldn't quite put his finger on it because on the surface things looked in order: three packages, all worth virtually the same money, all looking good on paper. He had looked at them this way, that way. Thomas claimed never to have seen the properties either but what the heck, he had said, "we're just rolling over, aren't we?"

Boris had selected one and paid the money. Then the unease had set in. Had he picked the right one? Had he checked enough? Had he asked the right questions? He himself would never consider buying land without looking at it. Perhaps this was the instinct that kept him a small-timer; people bought stocks, after all, without touring the factories. So he tried to dismiss the feeling, shrug it off. But he couldn't. He lay awake for a night. Then he decided to go have a look on his own. To satisfy himself. So he went to Florida.

And, holy smokes! The land was a swamp. A mangrove swamp. He couldn't tell for certain where it began and where it ended. It might be out under the ocean. The lands and the deeds and the surveys existed all right, they were authoritative. But the land was worth maybe a tenth of what he had paid for it. Or it was worth nothing at all. Nothing could be done on it. Panic like a green sickness filled him up. What would he say to Blumthorp, to Burrows? Oh my, oh my, he thought.

He shaved. He tried again to reach Stern on the telephone. No answer. He got dressed and tried again. No answer. He had a drink. He thought of climbing in the Cadillac and zipping out to Stern's house in River Heights, but that would probably be pointless since there was no one answering the phone anyway. He called again. A woman answered; one of Stern's daughters.

"He's already left," she said. "Can I give him a message?"

"No," said Boris. He went blank for a moment, staring at the far wall of the apartment and through the big window at the forest of trees that obscured the tops of all the houses of the city. "I guess I'll catch him there."

The reception was already in full swing when Boris hurried into the seventh-floor ballroom of the Hotel Fort Garry. He had ruffled his hair with the blow-drier but it was still damp and wet curls clung to the back of his neck. He had panicked for a minute, thinking he had no clean shirts. Then he found one and put on his dark blue suit, the one that made him look bigger at the shoulders than he really was.

A Party wife at a table just inside the door pinned a name tag to him and tried to sell him a roll of drink tickets.

"Not just now," he said.

He scanned the room, anxious to find Stern, to find Alverstone, to get in and get going. He would have to forget about Florida for the next four hours; this meeting was his priority now. He felt drugged. The whisky at home on top of the Tylenol. The anxiety, the lack of sleep; he felt airy, light in the head, as if his fingers and toes weren't part of the same body. It made him want to jump around.

He spied Stern's white head in the crowd at the same moment Stern saw him. Stern's chubby hand went up with a beckoning motion and he elbowed his way through the crowd toward Boris.

Boris started moving toward Stern. Stern looked pissed off, his mouth set in a sort of twisted scowl, his thick eyebrows lowered. From the corner of his eye Boris could see Marc Lachance, Alverstone's assistant, tall, skinny, brilliant Lachance, the manoeuvrer, striding from the other side of the room like a big gangly stork. His suit hung on him like laundry.

Stern got to him first. "Excuse us a minute, Marc," he said, brushing Lachance aside. The aide looked surprised.

Boris gave him an apologetic shrug. "In a minute?" he asked.

"Sure," said Lachance. He stood with his mouth moving but no sound coming out.

The senator steered Boris off toward the cloakroom. As soon as they got into the relative darkness of the hallway, he exhaled a long breath and his face relaxed. He dropped his grip on Boris' arm.

"You sonofabitch," he said.

Boris' mouth dropped open, astonished. He stood a full head taller than Senator Stern and had to crouch with his head jerked forward to look him in the eyes. Besides, it was so dark in the hallway behind the cloakroom he could barely see him; they were not much more than shadows to one another.

"What?" said Boris.

Behind them the noise from the ballroom increased as more Party people crowded into the room. Perhaps the Minister of External Affairs had arrived.

"You have to drop out," said Stern.

"What do you mean?" Boris' throat went dry. He was confused. He didn't think he'd heard correctly.

"Have you been doing business in the States?" Stern nailed him with his pale blue eyes.

"What? Yeah. . . . Well, I just got back from Florida." Panic rose inside Boris' chest.

"And out west?"

Boris swayed. The Tylenol had made him dizzy. He needed to eat something; he hadn't had anything since breakfast.

"Not for myself. Well, not exactly. Some land. I bought an option. For another party."

Stern's mouth set. He took his hand off Boris' arm. He moved back half a step.

"My boy," he said, "you are screwed." He said it the way a teacher tells a student he's failed an exam. Boris looked at him in disbelief.

Stern looked at him long and hard and then his eyes softened. "You're not kidding me, are you?" He moved back another half step and he and Boris had one another fully in frame.

"What do you mean?" Boris asked. His mouth felt like chalk.

"You were in the States buying land," Stern continued. His hand touched Boris' arm again.

Boris nodded.

"Some of it was Indian land. . . ."

Oh no, Boris panicked. Was that illegal? Was there a diplomatic problem? Had that one screwed up too?

Stern moved closer so that his breath was stale against Boris' face. He looked him right in the eye. "Boris, you didn't buy any land at all, did you?"

Boris' mouth dropped open again.

Stern continued quietly. "I mean, you bought land, but you didn't buy land. Nothing that's worth anything near what you paid for it. Am I right?"

Boris was stunned. He felt pale. "How did you know?"

Stern was quiet for a moment. He looked bereaved. He glanced to the end of the hall where Marc Lachance was still waiting and waved his hand in some anger, motioning him away. Then he returned to Boris. He spoke slowly, measuredly.

"Boris," he said, "because of my position I'm privy to some information. There's an investigation going on and there may be some charges laid, if they get enough information to make them stick. Two men at least. Do the names Burrows and Blumthorp mean anything to you?"

Boris felt himself blanch beneath his sunburn.

Stern smiled. He continued. "Some cocaine, a considerable amount, seems to be arriving here secreted in the hulls of sailboats destined for the boat show. The boats—and the Guatamalan drugs—come from Florida. There haven't been charges laid yet but I know the investigation is working toward it." He stopped and then started again. "The police have been waiting a long time for these guys."

Boris needed to sit down. He reached for the top of a cigarette machine and leaned on it. "I had no idea, believe me," he whispered. Stern, he thought, looked compassionate. Or was it disgusted?

He shrugged. "Maybe not," he said. "You can put two and two together, though, can't you? When you were buying bogus land what you were really doing was paying the freight."

"A courier," Boris said. "Laundering."

Stern nodded.

The top of the cigarette machine felt unstable, as though his hand would disappear into its plastic. The world felt surreal for a long moment. Who knows? he wanted to ask but couldn't get the words out.

"You may not believe it," Stern continued, "but I'm doing you a favour. When I learned that the cops had your name I persuaded them to let me check it out; reach you first, you might say. I suspected you might be an unwitting dupe."

"Alverstone?" Boris asked. "Do they know?" His mouth was dry as sandpaper.

Stern smiled. "Lachance wants to talk to you but all he knows is that you bought water rights to some Indian land in Idaho and they got calls about that. They frown on it, they think it'll embarrass them down the pike and probably figure they can't afford you because of it. The Idaho senator called State Department, State Department called External, External has you listed with Alverstone. They want to talk to you about it. They have no idea about the other." He gave a wry smile, the only one of the two of them still able to muster it.

Stern had taken hold of a button on the front of Boris' suit and drew him forward like a pull-toy. Then he let go, let him roll back.

Boris stepped back. He needed air. He needed something to lean on. He turned his head and saw Marc Lachance come into the narrow hallway and stride toward them. Stern moved from his side and held up his hand, palm flat, toward Alverstone's man.

"It's okay," he said. "It's solved." He gave Boris a pat on the arm, then took Lachance and they both walked out to the meeting.

Boris was left, still needing air, leaning on the cloakroom wall.

18

The political meeting was on Tuesday night. The next
morning Boris didn't know what to do. Finally, he walked
to a phone booth down the street from his apartment building and dialled Burrows and Blumthorp's office. He put his
hand over his mouth to disguise his voice. Lydia, the redheaded secretary, answered and said no one was there; Mr.
Blumthorp was not expected in that day. Later that morning
Blumthorp and Burrows were arrested. It made the third
page of the afternoon papers.

At three in the afternoon Boris' phone rang. After a brief
hesitation he answered it. It was Lydia.

"Mr. Podolski, you called for Mr. Burrows this morning. . . ."

Boris panicked. "Don't call me," he shouted. "I don't want to hear from you."

"Calm down, I'm not calling from the office."

This put Boris marginally at ease but still he looked over his shoulder as if to make sure no one was standing in his kitchen watching him. "All right," he said. "I've seen the papers. What's going on?"

"Bail is being arranged. Mr. Burrows and Mr. Blumthorp have a hearing in the morning. I think they should be back at the office tomorrow. I am to tell you . . .," she paused, "that Mr. Burrows believes it is imperative that you talk to no one and he urged me to convey that message to you. The present matter, he asked me to reassure you, has nothing to do with you."

"Like hell it has nothing to do with me," Boris blurted.

"Please, Mr. Podolski, remain calm." Her voice was smooth. She was a very steady lady. "Mr. Burrows will get in touch with you."

"No," said Boris.

"Yes," said Lydia. And Boris hung up the phone.

For the rest of the day nothing happened. The next morning Boris had a phone call from Edward Burrows. He sounded cheerful, his old self. Boris was petrified. "I should see you," Burrows said. Boris tried to figure out if the cheerfulness was forced. "Let's have a steam, or lunch."

"I'm not sure I should see you," said Boris.

"Relax," said Burrows.

"How can I relax?" said Boris. "I saw the papers. I know what I was doing in Chicago."

Burrows' pleasant voice turned hard. "Relax," he ordered. Then, softly, "Let's have a steam. You know where. Same time as last time. It's better to talk in person." He hung up.

At noon, before he had a chance to go out, Boris' door buzzer rang. Two mounties from the special investigation squad. They wore suits and were as big as football players. When they came into his living-room Boris' legs started to jump and he feared he might burst into tears.

The mounties asked him questions and Boris, sweat running like cold coffee down his neck and into his armpits, answered as best he could. The mounties had nice neat moustaches and flat eyes. They both took notes. Boris stood during their entire conversation as did both of the mounties. It didn't even occur to him to invite them to sit down. He offered rote answers to all their questions. He felt no desire to hide anything but he had an overwhelming feeling that he didn't know anything. Boris felt his whole life was rolling up, snap, snap, snap, like a badly creased map. The mounties acted as if they were doing nothing less routine than a check into an overdue parking ticket.

They didn't charge Boris with anything, although they alluded to the possibility. They also alluded to the possibility of a deal: become a crown witness in exchange for no charges. Boris knew all about it, he was a lawyer. He needed a lawyer.

When the mounties left it was two o'clock. He would be late to meet Burrows at the steam room. He shouldn't meet Burrows, he knew. He didn't know what to do. He pulled his blinds, unplugged his phone, went to bed and pulled the blankets up black over his head.

The next day he felt more normal. He went out to a restaurant for breakfast and read the paper. It reported that a couple of men who were believed to be the biggest dope smugglers the city had known in years were out on bail.

When he got back to his apartment the phone rang. It was Lydia. "Boris," she called him. It was the first time she had ever called him Boris. "Don't worry, I'm not calling from the office. But if you're worried about your phone, you can call me back." She gave him a number.

He walked to the phone booth at the corner and dialled the number.

"I'm frightened at what might happen," she said.

Boris felt suddenly concerned, protective. "Are they after you?"

"No. But it's awful in the office, the tension is terrible." She paused. "And I'm worried about you."

Boris was touched.

"You're all right, aren't you?"

"Yes," said Boris.

"Edward is concerned about you. He said you were supposed to meet him but didn't come. He was worried that something had happened to you."

Boris told her about the mounties.

She sounded distressed. "Oh Boris, be careful," she said. "Mr. Burrows seems convinced that none of this can touch you, that you are in no difficulty. There's no need for you to do anything rash . . .," her voice trailed off, giving Boris a moment to think about what she had said. Then she continued. "Even Mr. Blumthorp is concerned about you," she said. "Stay in touch with us," she pleaded. "Stay in touch with me."

She hung up the phone.

19

By afternoon Danny's father seemed better. "We've got to see a doctor," Danny told him.

"No, I'm all right," he said. "It was just a little spell."

Danny was afraid. He didn't know what he should do. "I can't leave you down here," he said. "In two days my ticket takes me home."

His father paused as if sensing a need to mollify him, to put him at ease. "All right," he said. He agreed to make arrangements to fly back to Canada instead of driving up alone in his car. And that as soon as he got back he would check in with Leslie.

Two days later Danny was back in Winnipeg.

Rita met him at the airport.

When he came down the escalator from the arrivals gate he saw her standing there and he could feel a warm rush inside him, a nice little tingle. He wanted to smile and wave, embrace her and lift her off her feet. But when he got close to her he could tell something wasn't right. "Hi," she said but she wasn't quite there. They both felt awkward while they waited for his bags. "How was your trip?" she asked.

Bellows had been calling from Toronto, asking when he would be back. Boris had been calling at all hours of the day and night.

"What does he want?" Danny asked.

"I don't know," said Rita. "He never says. He just asks if you're back and then he hangs up when I tell him no. He doesn't leave a number, either. He just calls; at all hours, sometimes in the early morning or in the middle of the night. It's making me uneasy. I hope you'll do something about it."

Something in the air between Danny and Rita bothered him. He watched her as she drove her Toyota through the afternoon traffic. She seemed tense, sitting straight as a soldier. Her knuckles were almost white from grasping the steering wheel so hard. It's funny, Danny thought, being apart for a long stretch, you feel awkward, you have to re-establish yourselves.

"How's it going?" he asked.

"What?" It was as if he had jolted her out of a reverie.

"How's it going? How are you?"

"Fine."

"How's everything?"

"What?"

"Everything. Work. How's work?"

"Fine."

"Your committees. How are the plans for the demonstration coming along?"

"You don't have to be so critical," she flashed.

"Critical? I'm not critical. I just. . . ."

"You called it a demonstration," she interrupted. "It's not a demonstration. It's a rally." The little car was moving along quickly, rounding corners into downtown streets. Rita looked straight ahead out the windshield. "And the plans are going just fine."

"Rita . . .," he said, an appeal.

She looked over at him. Her eyes were bright and her mouth quivered. She looked pale, but then everybody Danny had become used to seeing over the last couple of weeks had been brown. The car hurried through a street corner and a giant puddle of water, splashing a cascading shower over a middle-aged man in a light coat waiting on the sidewalk for the light to change. He jumped back but got it anyway. Danny half-turned and over his shoulder could see him shaking his fist, yelling at them, livid.

"I'm sorry," said Rita. Danny hoped she was speaking to him but maybe she meant it for the man on the street.

"Well, I wasn't criticizing," he said. "Why would I be criticizing? I've never criticized you. I admire you; I admire what you do."

"I don't know, Danny," she said, her tone resigned. "Do you?"

"What do you mean?" He was astonished. "Of course I do. Listen," he said, "I just got back from a trip. We should be happy to see each other. What's going on?"

"Let's not talk about it," she said.

Danny looked at her. What the hell was going on?

Rita dropped him at his place but waited only long enough to see him and his bags in. She couldn't stay.

"Later?" he asked.

"Not tonight," she said. She was already going down the stairs.

"Okay," he said.

She stopped at the bottom, before the door. "I'll call you tomorrow and maybe we'll have lunch," she said.

"Okay," he said.

For a long time he sat at home, his bags still packed, trying to figure it out. He had to call Bellows, he had to get in touch with Boris; but he sat thinking about Rita. Didn't they have good things going with each other? Were there tensions around her work? Around her work on all her committees? Was there something he was missing, that he had failed to think about?

Later, when she saw him, it all seemed to burst forth.

"Maybe if you would get involved in something yourself you wouldn't resent me so much," she said.

"I don't resent you."

"Yes you do, I can see it in the way you act."

"How do I act?"

She was on her way to another meeting. Her eyes flashed with anger, her jaw was set, the muscles in her neck throbbed. "Sarcastic, cynical. . . ."

Danny protested, indignant, "I am not!" This was manifestly unfair, he thought.

"Yes, you are, Danny. There may be things to criticize in what I do, in what Robert does. But at least we're doing something. We're trying," much emphasis on this word *trying*, "to do something. You're a watcher."

"A watcher?"

She threw up her hands, arched her eyebrows. "A watcher. You watch. You take pictures."

This made him angry. "Of course I take pictures. That's my job!"

"But that's all you do. You do nothing else. Nothing. . . ." She was so intense by this point that he could see the white all around the green iris of her eyes. "With you nothing can be done in this world; the world unfolds as it does, controlled God knows where, somewhere off in space or not controlled at all and the best you can do or believe anybody can do is watch it go down. Taking pictures of it. Do you remember the thing in the news when the man who was unemployed called the TV station and told them he was going to set himself on fire? They sent a cameraman."

"Hold it, Rita." She had gone too far and Danny figured she realized it. She softened quickly and looked contrite.

"I'm sorry," she said.

He thought about it. It wasn't that he didn't want the world to be saved. In his heart of hearts he was terrified of the impending doom. Terrified and furious. When he read in the newspapers or in *Time* magazine the statistics about the build-ups of the arsenals and the spreading 'nuclear capability,' he wanted to weep with helplessness. A few times he wakened in the middle of the night at the sound of a plane rumbling low overhead and, filled with terror, thought, this is it. The thought of some wacko in Moscow or Washington or wherever sitting down and at some moment, for God knows whatever reason—fear or cracked ideology or wounded pride—pressing the button, sent him regularly into inarticulate rage. It was like knowing that his landlord was toying with the idea of burning his apartment down to collect on the insurance.

He knew about the environment. He read the papers every day. Invariably on page two there was news of a new study itemizing the devastation of acid rain. It was killing the maple trees now, for God's sake. Then, just as sure, on page four, almost a parallel article quoting some cigar-puffing congressman from a coal-producing state about how they couldn't possibly do anything without more study. And then, a few pages later, the fat business section of the paper with talk only of new jobs and new profits from one monumental environmental rape after another. He could see the inconsistencies, for Christ's sake. He could get angry too.

But he also feared he had less heart than Rita. Or he saw

things less in black and white. His feeling was one of paralysed helplessness. He couldn't feel optimistic, as Rita seemed to, that they could get out of it, that it could be turned around. He thought of his father's clippings. He thought of the teenagers whom he saw every day, their loyalties latched onto their respective rock groups, serious in their belief that they had maybe a year left. No wonder they could be so cynical, the kids who didn't shave yet, who were just having their first periods. Walking around with those blank, awful, empty looks on their pimply faces.

Rita cited all the hopeful people. "Man made this; man can unmake this," she would say. Danny wanted to think she was right, but to him there was also a sort of cosmic destiny involved, everyone riding the little globe and hurtling toward the end-game. Telling jokes and firing the empties overboard along the way. The magnitude of the stupidities already involved, already set in place, seemed too great. He knew the South American rain forests were going down and with them, supposedly, the world's right to oxygen. But he also knew that half the population in those countries was below the age of 15 and living in searing poverty. Was Rita going to tell them, all those millions of big-eyed teenagers, that she wasn't going to allow them their Big Macs, their pollution-belting Chevys and the nuclear-powered microwave ovens we'd all enjoyed for so long because such things weren't in the end good for them?

But he went along with Rita, sometimes, to her world-saving meetings. A gesture toward her, or a gesture toward his own guilt and the deeply ingrained need, despite himself, to be responsible.

It was, in part, curiosity; he wanted to find out, if they were going to save the world, how they were actually going to do it. How would these good people who lived so responsibly—taking their old newspapers to the recycling boxes, always reading the labels on the things they bought so they could at least be aware of the poisons and the synthetics therein, never buying grapes from Chile or wine from South Africa—how would they pull off the great turn-around when to him the momentum, the great snowball of history, was rolling with such force in the other direction?

At the end of March Danny went with Rita to a lecture, part of a series of seminars leading up to the great environmental and anti-nuclear rally scheduled to be staged in front of the legislative building in the spring. If it was successful there, it was to be repeated in Ottawa and in Washington.

The seminar was held in a room in the back of an old downtown church. They drove in Rita's Toyota and parked in a lot behind Eaton's. Robert would lead the seminar. Robert, the professor of religion at the university; Robert, whom Rita had come to hold in the highest regard over the time she had been able to observe him and learn to know him. Robert, who had turned his whole life over to 'causes' and who, Rita told Danny every chance she got, was "the most committed man I've ever met," this said with her eyes glazing over just slightly.

Danny felt a pang of jealousy. No, it wasn't jealousy; it was the kind of confusion he always felt in situations like this. An internal contradiction, part awe and part envy of Robert, the most committed man Rita had ever met, when a corner of himself wished that people could say that of him, Danny Hinkle. And part scorn, a well-developed skepticism and anticipation that Robert wouldn't come off at all as heroic, that he would just seem naive. That, he felt, would almost be worse.

As they walked toward the church on the chilly winter's evening, Rita had no idea of the contradictions that boiled inside him. She just thought, he suspected, that he was basically a good fellow who was too blasé to get involved.

The meeting was small, maybe 35 people milling around, drinking coffee out of styrofoam cups. Many of the people knew Rita and they greeted one another with the informal familiarity of colleagues. A number of people had been able to distill their biases into single catchy phrases which they wore on buttons attached to their clothes. Others used buttons bearing slogans to advertise both the alliances to which they belonged and their opinions or positions. "Feminists Against Imperialist Domination," read the button on one young woman's chest. "Students Opposed to the Seal Hunt," said another on the lapel of a smooth-faced young man's tweed jacket. Somebody's button declared "Self-Determination for Poland," and Danny was caught for a moment trying to fit that sentiment into the general bent of the meeting.

At the front of the room, surrounded by a cluster of intent followers, looking strangely fragile, gentle, almost cervidian, was the man Danny remembered from Sarajevo Restaurant. A pale face framed by wispy grey hair, watery blue eyes behind thick, plastic-rimmed glasses, a small-framed body clothed in a sport coat and open-necked shirt, delicate hands turning his coffee cup. The professor of religion, the guru of at least one little group of people who would turn the world around. The man of causes, the most committed man Rita had ever met. He watched him for a long moment. The people pressed in on him like groupies. Reflected glory or a way to establish connection, identification or support. And then they faded back and he was left with a circle of space around him, placidly turning his coffee cup in his delicate white hand.

Rita came up beside Danny. "Alverstone is here," she whispered excitedly into his ear.

"Why would he be here?" He turned to her quizzically.

She shrugged. "Don't know," she said. "Martin says he thinks it might mean the government is coming around on the nuclear issue even before the rallies. Though I doubt it." Rita was getting good at sounding like a back-room strategist; tough and not to be fooled, accounting for all possibilities. "On the other hand, he could be here for purely personal reasons. I mean, he doesn't live far from here. Or he might be trying to make a showing simultaneously on every side of the

question. He's such a fucking liberal," she added in disgust.
"Is he going to speak?" Danny asked her, starting to get
caught up in the drama. He always liked a bit of a show and
if Peter Alverstone was going to speak, this would be a show.
"Don't know," she shrugged. "Martin doesn't know either."
A couple of Marxist-Leninists squeezed past them, burly
but at the same time badly nourished young men with dark
circles under their eyes and very white skin. They carried a
red cloth banner which Danny suspected they would try to
unfurl at the back of the room. He had seen them do it at other
meetings. Sometimes the meetings tolerated them, other
times they were asked to put their banners away. Those in-
terchanges could also make for interesting little side-shows.
"Who are those guys?" he asked Rita, pointing to two dour
men in dark suits sitting at the back of the room by the door.
"Where?"
"Over there. Those two with the thin ties."
Rita squinted. "Fascists," she said.
"Mounties?" he asked. Perhaps all of them, including the
Hon. Peter Alverstone, would have their names and descrip-
tions entered into black notebooks.
"No, nothing like that. Right-wingers. Some Balkan
nationalist organization that loves Ronald Reagan and thinks
we ought to be actually declaring war on the Soviet Union."
Rita's friend Martin called the meeting to order. Robert
walked to the front of the room, shuffling his notes medi-
tatively. The Marxist-Leninists stood quietly at the back of
the room, their red banner still rolled up. The Balkan
nationalists looked severe, eyeing with suspicion the Marxist-
Leninists and Robert in turn. Peter Alverstone looked well,
the healthy tan on his chubby face (he had been in Brazil, the
newspapers said, checking into working conditions for a
United Nations committee) set off marvellously by his pale
blue shirt and grey suit.
The meeting started smoothly; there were no surprises.
Robert, the theologian, was against nuclear war and had done

his homework. Methodically he rhymed off his most up-to-date estimates of over-kill capacity. They were numbers everyone had heard before; the problem was, as always, their abstractness. Trying to imagine the globe being burned to a crisp 17 times over is even more difficult than trying to imagine infinite time and space. It always left Danny reeling, his mind couldn't stretch that far. His house, maybe, or his street. But everything? Even the Great Lakes? It was like being able to imagine himself dead but not everybody. The whole world all at once. All the people in Newfoundland and all the people in Hollywood. All his neighbours, the people in the Armenian bakery, Prissy. . . .

Robert had taken on the mission of making the abstract seem more real. So he read for a while from eye-witness accounts of the first days after Hiroshima and Nagasaki. Chilling and agonizing vignettes of horror and wretchedness; steaming rubble, burned flesh, green pools of radioactive water, wailing motherless babies, and the stench of dead bodies starting to decay.

That was another problem—nobody wants to imagine such horrors. The realities of such things are kept at arm's length, in the abstract, for very good reason; if they weren't, the nightmares would drive the population to suicide. The aura of fatality and futility is so great that everyone, even the best, is truly paralysed. What can we do to turn the scenario around? Danny wondered. Is there any basis under the sun for hope?

Robert appeared to believe you must be strong and not give up hope. But it seemed to Danny that to presume hope brands you immediately as a naive, childlike Pollyanna. When he watched Robert standing in the front of the vestry room—his pale hands shaking and his glasses beginning to fog as he pleaded for the West to unilaterally disarm and for the Canadian government to withdraw its support from the United States and from NATO on the matters of nuclear armaments, and for the Canadian people to insist the government do these things—all the articles he'd read in *Time* and the *U.S. News & World Report*, all the discussions he'd seen William F. Buckley chair on "Firing Line" on television, flooded in to scream at him about what a silly, naive, unrealistic, unpragmatic man this Robert was. He could tell with a quick glance that the two members of the Balkan nationalist organization felt the same.

Someone called, suddenly, on Peter Alverstone. "Maybe the minister will tell us," queried a thin grey-haired man who sat on the aisle near the front, "how the government will interpret a great pouring out of public sentiment through the vehicle of the forthcoming rallies." He spoke precisely in a clipped, almost English, accent, his eyes fixed on the tanned face of the cabinet minister. "And will he tell us for now," he continued, "the rationale for the warm hospitality our government seems to be showing toward the American plans to test their bomb-carrying missiles right here in our country, in Alberta?" He sat down and puckered his lips like a prosecuting attorney who had just posed the case-sealing question.

Peter Alverstone, of course, was not flustered. These were his sort of people. He had grown up with people like this and in their company he had formed his ideas and his views of the world. Peter Alverstone had come into politics not via the corporate boardroom or the big law office, but through academia where he had taught political science and urban planning, and through social planning councils, church groups and organizations predicated on social good and selfless public welfare. Peter Alverstone was only 38 and in some ways still the darling boy of some of this set. Peter Alverstone would very much have liked to give more money to the handicapped, and many of the ladies who first heard him give public speeches when he was in grade ten still wanted him to be Prime Minister.

Peter Alverstone rose and, as he talked, edged his way toward the front of the room. He possessed a very good sense of how not to just answer a question, but how to take over a meeting. "Of course the government will notice your rallies," he said reassuringly, "we're pretty tuned to public sentiment in this country." Someone in the corner guffawed. Alverstone pretended not to hear and continued, not missing a beat. "But it would be presumptuous for you to think and for me to say that government policy on this enormously detailed and complicated issue could turn around," he drew a circular gesture in the air with his right hand, "on the basis of some public demonstrations. There are some in cabinet," he went on (it was becoming a lecture now), "who on the basis of the very detailed and complex information available to them believe that our present defence stature is the correct and necessary one. There is a core of what you might call 'hard-liners' within the cabinet who believe, sincerely, that our position is, in fact, very weak and that our support for the United States ought to be much more extensive. And there are our NATO commitments—which exist, which are on paper—we have obligations there that we can't possibly try to get out of . . . nor should we."

"And where, in the cabinet, do you stand?" asked a woman from the other side of the room.

"I'm a pragmatist," Peter Alverstone answered with the faintest hint of a shrug.

"What we need, perhaps," interrupted the man with the English accent, "are not pragmatists but leaders." His voice rose like a diving board, sprung on the word *leaders*.

Peter Alverstone puckered his lips and looked perturbed.

Robert seemed to see the moment opening for him and promptly jumped in. "What I want to make you understand, Peter," he pleaded, calling the cabinet minister, an old university colleague, by his first name, "and what I think we need to make the government understand is the sheer lunacy of the present situation. The lunacy of the original assumptions from which the so-called pragmatic decisions are taken. You can be as pragmatic as you like, but if you are working from original assumptions that are absurd, then of what worth is your pragmatism? We want our country," he was becoming emotional, this was not an academic discussion for him, "to take the leadership in telling the rest of the world, the United States first, that the assumptions of the nuclear-arms race are insane ones, that life itself on this planet is what is at stake, and that our pragmatism and nice Canadian sense of rationality and cooperation will do us no good when we are all dead."

There was applause from a few people. The Marxist-Leninists at the back of the room stamped the butts of their sign-posts on the floor. Briefly, then stopped. The room became silent. Robert was almost in tears. Peter Alverstone looked peeved. He clearly felt that he was not, after all, where he would like to have been. Danny could tell he would rather be on television playing the humanist gadfly to generals and conservative defence theoreticians from the Brookings Institute. He would like to be the hero rather than the apologist. Being the idealist had always sat well with him; happier in opposition than in government. Here he felt manipulated into a position he would rather not have to defend.

But here he was, in government, the apologist—having to play the general while others got the roles he would like. He became petulant. For a moment his cool slipped. "What would you have us do?" He addressed Robert more than the crowd, in the manner of a football coach with carping reporters when the team is down in the fourth quarter and the star quarterback has just suffered a shoulder separation.

"Lead," said Robert, undaunted. "This is the time to have courage, to take courage." He was becoming passionate again and was hitting Alverstone, whose campaign posters (ordered by Boris) promised Courageous, Innovative Leadership for Our Time, where it hurt. "This is the time to look at this world of ours in new ways. This is not the time," he turned to the audience, "to be frozen into traditional ways of thinking and dealing. The future of our planet, of our children, of everything we cherish is at stake." Rita gave Danny a nudge; she was smiling beautifully.

Alverstone looked distressed. He pursed his lips. He interrupted when it seemed that Robert might go on. "That is a fine speech, Robert," he said. "I laud the sentiment." He was more impatient, Danny sensed, than sarcastic. "But if you only knew," he flashed, "how complex the world is; if you could only appreciate what a luxury you have to sit there and make your idealistic pronouncements uncomplicated by commitments to allies, compromises in cabinet, responsibilities to constituents. If you only knew what a free ride that is." He was angry now and speaking quickly. Robert had taken one step back and looked surprised. Even a little hurt. "In the end I need to be pragmatic. Balance is my business." And almost as an afterthought, "I would rather be pragmatic than foolish. I'm very happy being pragmatic." He sat down. He looked very unhappy.

20

Danny would have liked to have gone straight home after the meeting but Rita would have none of it. She was wired, full of adrenaline. "Come on," she said. The hard core of the committee was going to Martin's apartment, a short couple of blocks away over downtown streets. When she backed the Toyota out of the tiny parking lot, she was still glowing. Her eyes shone, her hands on the steering wheel trembled with suppressed excitement. Danny felt depressed.

"What did you think of it?" she asked.

"It was fine."

She looked surprised. "You didn't like it?"

Danny looked ahead at the dashboard and avoided her eyes. "It's not a matter of liking it."

"Right," she said. "It's pretty awesome." Then she brightened. "They really stuck it to Alverstone. Wasn't that incredible?"

Danny winced.

Rita continued. "I've never seen Robert so articulate as he was in that exchange with Peter Alverstone. The points about leadership were right on. It was marvellous."

Danny paused a moment. Then he said, "But I think he was right."

"Of course he was right."

"No, Alverstone."

The car lurched as Rita almost drove up on the curb. "What do you mean, Alverstone?"

Danny looked at her, gathering courage. "Alverstone was right. I mean he was right to say it's a complicated matter and he hasn't the same luxury that some of the rest of us have to be so definite in our positions. I have some sympathy for his point of view."

Rita looked incredulous. "Sympathy! Danny, he's a fucking politician!"

"Of course he's a politician. That's what I mean, he's in a tough spot."

She pulled the car into a parking spot on the street and looked over at him. "I can't believe," she said, "that you're so, so naive! No, that's not the right word. . . ."

"Damn right that's not the right word."

"But our point," she interrupted, "is that we have to see things clearly; we have to see things in new ways. It's not the same world. If we keep thinking in old ways, we're doomed." Her voice trailed off and she started the car again, silent.

Martin's apartment was on the third floor of an elderly building that was waiting to be demolished. On three sides it was surrounded by glass office towers and bordered at its entranceway by weeds and broken bottles. A window on the second level of the stairwell was smashed, allowing a steady, chilly breeze to push into the hallways.

When Danny and Rita arrived, about 20 people from the meeting were already crowded into the tiny abode, some holding bottles of beer, a few with glasses of wine. Martin, a burly, hairy, happy man with a bushy black beard, greeted Rita with an embrace that lifted her right off the floor. He met Danny with one of those soul-brother handshakes (grasping his thumb and his arm simultaneously) invented in the 1960s. "Glad you came," he said. "Come on, I'm making a big pot of tea too."

They elbowed their way deeper into the apartment.

Danny could tell from the general hubbub that everybody in Martin's cramped apartment felt pretty good about how the evening's meeting had gone. None of them seemed to share either his distress or his sympathy for Mr. Alverstone, with his government jet and his nice grey suit. The mood of the place was like a victory party. "Here, have a beer," said Martin, shoving a warm bottle into Danny's hand.

The replays were being rehashed, mostly in the kitchen. Robert, of course, like an exhausted, conquering prize-fighter, was the centre of attention. He slumped uncomfortably on a kitchen counter, his head ducked sideways to avoid bumping the shelves. His hands caressed a warm mug of Martin's tea.

Rita headed straight for the kitchen and Danny manoeuvred his way into another room, a room filled with books and walls covered with posters. At the far end he found an upturned Coca Cola crate and sat down on it. He nursed his beer. It was warm in the room and a ribbon of perspiration dampened his hair along his forehead and against his ears. Behind him was a fake fireplace, one of those whose heating coils glow against a metal reflector. Seated on the floor beside him was a slender young woman with long, straight, auburn hair. She held a match and was trying to light a stick of incense that she had placed in a jar. After she succeeded, she looked up with a half-sleepy gaze. "So you're Rita's old man," she said.

After 40 minutes his beer was gone. He could have used

another cold one. Or he could quite happily have gone home. The crowding in the room had not let up; the heat had forced him to pull off his sweater.

The woman beside him had disappeared into some sort of trance. Her head was bent forward and her eyes were closed, her hair fell limply in front of her shoulders. Beside her, on the floor, the incense wisped, the stick half-burned. Danny felt as though he was back in university, almost a generation ago.

He got up and headed for the kitchen. There was still lively talk in the living-room but action-centre, in the kitchen, seemed to have slowed down. A couple of voices were laughing and somebody, he was astonished to hear, mentioned a basketball score. But the reassessment of the evening's action seemed to have ended. He turned a corner and saw that only five people were left in there: Martin and two fellows near the door who were speculating on the basketball game, and, in the background, Robert, now no longer sitting on the counter but straddling a chair turned backwards so that his arms leaned, folded, on the chair back. His chin rested on his arms and his eyes were closed. Standing behind him, her eyes closed too, her fingers massaging the muscles of his neck and shoulders, pulling hard at all the tiredness, weariness, tension, was Rita.

21

At 8:30 the next morning Danny was propped up in bed
looking out the window at the grey sky. He didn't have
anywhere to go, but Rita had already gone to the CBC to
produce her interview program. He had had no idea how it
would end the night before, but eventually the two of them
had arrived back at his place. And she stayed over. Now he
sat alone in the chilly, white morning.

The women's movement had been working through two
decades, the 1960s and the 1970s, preparing the ground so
that a new generation, of whom Rita was almost a classic
type, could emerge in the 1980s. In 1960 Rita was two years
old. Now she had a career, her own apartment, a larger and
more stable income than either Danny or many of his friends,

a fistful of credit cards, a string of past 'relationships' more
or less similar to the one they now had (although she would
say each one in turn lasted longer than the one before) and a
vocabulary of negotiating phrases which she could haul out
regularly to keep a guy like Danny on his toes.

And he, Danny, had a profession that sometimes seemed
to him more like a hobby; sometimes paid the rent and sometimes didn't. No credit cards; a little string of past relationships, none of them as good, whatever the shortcomings, as
what he had now, and the awful feeling that somehow he must
have been out of the classroom when they were studying
negotiating phrases.

Nobody has to reiterate, he thought, that these are
strange, marvellous and convulsive times on the man/woman
front. In his short lifetime the whole world of human and social relationships had gone kerflooey. He hardly knew anyone
younger than his parents who was married, or still married,
or at least married to the same person they started out with.
His pal Boris wouldn't spend more than one night consecu-
tively with any woman who lived closer than 1500 miles.
Roger, on the other hand, was so confused his complicated
romantic liaisons would require an investigator to sort them
out. Most of the people Danny knew were perpetually on their
way either into or out of relationships. It was like a carnival
where the ferris wheel kept stopping to let people on or off. It
was hard to keep track of who was where, so nobody even
tried very hard.

Rita wanted to be independent and involved at the same
time. She adamantly maintained her own apartment although she 'visited' Danny two or three nights a week. She
maintained her own circle of friends and would balk at
describing herself and Danny as a 'couple.' Yet from time to
time she could become obsessively preoccupied with their
'relationship' and every two or three weeks dragged it out like
an old quilt for a good airing. Danny dreaded those moments
like the plague. He'd rather be down for the weekend with

influenza, he thought. It was like a dissection in zoology class—everything laid out and examined, turned over two or three times, raked around, poked, prodded, given a little kick.

The first few times he didn't know what was happening, why she was upset. He thought he'd done something wrong and tried madly to figure out what it was. Eventually, he found out that, yes, he had done something wrong; for a day and a half he'd taken 'their relationship' for granted.

"You haven't been very affectionate to me," she said.

"I'm reading a book."

"You've been reading for two hours."

He looked up. Warning lights were on but he was slow to recognize them or heed them. "I'm a slow reader." An attempt at a joke.

Silence for a long moment.

"What do you mean, I'm not affectionate to you? You know I'm affectionate to you. Have I ever been unaffectionate to you?"

"Yesterday."

"What?"

"I'm going for a walk." And she headed for the doorway.

"Wait a minute. What do you mean, yesterday? What did I do yesterday?"

She turned in the doorway, pushing a strand of hair away from her face. "Do you remember when we were walking from the library and a girl, some young student girl, passed in front of us, do you remember what you did?"

He didn't remember.

"You leered. You leered at her and you said, to me, 'What a marvellous ass.' "

Silence again. Did I say that? he thought. I might have.

"I was joking."

"It was disgusting." She made a face as if she was going to bring up her dinner. "I was disgusted, Danny. I was appalled."

"Rita." He got up from his chair, putting the book down. "I was joking. Or if I wasn't joking, it was just a passing comment, an aesthetic observation. It doesn't mean anything beyond that."

"It may not to you," she said. "And perhaps that's the problem. . . ."

And on it would go, one thing leading to another and it could last all night.

Another time: "Where do you think our relationship is going?" This, totally out of the blue.

"What?"

"Our relationship. You and me. Where are we going?"

"Would you like to go to bed?"

"Danny, I'm serious."

"Okay, I'm sorry." Pause. "I don't know where it's going. Why is it so important to know where it's going? Can't we just enjoy it as it is?"

"I can't just enjoy it as it is. I have to know that it is going somewhere, that a commitment is building."

"Do you want to live together?"

She looked perturbed. "I don't mean that. It's not that easy. That wouldn't resolve the question. I'd still have to ask the question; we'd still have to have this conversation."

"Oh. Then you tell me, where is it going?"

"Sometimes I don't think it's going anywhere."

"Rita, come on. What do you mean it's not going anywhere? How can you say that? We're here, we see each other, we enjoy each other, we trust each other. . . ."

They got through these orgies of self-examination, flagellation, negotiation. But for Danny, each one was like a new skirmish in the Middle East. It was the price they had to pay, he decided, for the late 20th-century mode of coupling. For women, in the absence of the marriage contract or the longevity social expectations put on liaisons in former and not so distant times, it was their struggle for security, mostly, and meaning and depth. For most men he knew, it was an exercise in negotiation that they would sooner not have to go through. With an articulate woman—and Rita was an articulate woman—a guy would sooner go into a room to face the head of the United Steelworkers Union.

He knew that somewhere out there must still be a batch of those tidy little units—mom, dad, two and a half kids and Rover. Maybe in a museum. But he himself didn't know many of them. He hardly knew any of them. The people he would best peg as having a stable, happy, till-death-do-us-part marriage were his kid sister Leslie and her husband John, who lived in Kingston. But the last time he'd seen them Leslie announced, almost triumphantly, that they'd decided they were never going to have children. Just as matter of factly as that. That was one of their 'options,' just as buying a Volvo was, and they'd decided to go with it. On the other hand the only person he knew really well who had a child was his other sister Samantha, who lived alone and had for four years.

What a world, he thought. And where was he in it? No more sure of anything than was anybody else. Floating along like a little rubber duck.

Something about it depressed him; filled him with unnameable anxiety. He didn't know what he wanted to do about it; he didn't know if anything could be better. But he felt himself groping with a desire to change something. He'd like to try the roller coaster for a while but he couldn't get off the ferris wheel.

He'd never known what he wanted. He felt certain that he would not want the wife who doted on him, who waited with the seven children and the dog for him to come home after a hard day and pick up the pipe, paper and slippers. "What would you like for dinner, dear?" "Are you comfortable?" He couldn't imagine that anyone would ever ask him those questions. And he would not want to be Hugh Hefner with a different bunny every night. If he made it big, the rich and famous world-class photo-journalist invited everywhere, he didn't know if he would have the stamina to cavort around the world, intriguing one smart and dazzling woman after another. He didn't know that he would even like it.

He didn't know what in the world he wanted. He knew, though, that never, in any fantasy he had ever had of his life, did he imagine that he would be sitting alone in bed in the middle of the morning at the age of 29 not knowing what he wanted.

He looked at the clock; Rita would just be at work. He reached for the phone.

It took a couple of minutes for the call to trace its way through the labyrinth, the switchboard, the extensions; for them to locate Rita.

"Hello?" her small voice said finally at the other end of the line.

"Let's get married," Danny blurted.

"What?"

"It's me, Danny. Let's get married. I want to get married to you."

She laughed. "I know it's you. But I'm at work; you've got to stop kidding around."

"I'm not kidding," he said. He felt, suddenly, hurt. "I'm calling you and telling you this because I want to wake up with you every morning for the rest of my life. Just like this morning. I want to sit in bed with the *Globe & Mail* and watch you get dressed."

"Danny!" Her voice took on an edge of nervousness as if she had started to realize that perhaps this wasn't a joke or a prank.

"I want to have children with you. I want to grow old with you. I want to meet your parents. I want to save our money in a joint account and buy a summer cottage and go on trips."

"Danny, I'm working. Can we talk about this later?" By now, he knew, there might be a whole crew gathered around the phones in the CBC studio, eavesdropping over her shoulder. He didn't care. His rashness was growing, not diminishing.

"No," he said. "What's there to discuss? You know me, I know you. Two hours ago we were asleep together, I was curled against your back with your wonderful bum snuggled in my lap. . . ."

"Danny," she interrupted, "I can't. I have to work."

"Just say yes or no!"

"No."

"What?"

"No. Not now. I mean, maybe sometime. But there's so many things right now. Danny, I like you, I love you. But . . . I don't know. I've got to go back to work. Bye."

The phone clicked before he could say anything else. He sat still for a long time; he felt strangely buoyant, strangely immune. Strong. No matter what transpired now, he had said something, rash as it may be. And it was all out there now. His gesture was out there floating around the cosmos along with all the other gestures anyone had ever made. She could respond however she liked but he'd done his bit.

He got out of bed and walked around the room. It must have surprised her. It must have been the last thing, he thought, that she would expect to come from him. The shoe had been dropped. In one fell swoop he had changed it all; he'd thrown in the new dimension, he'd changed the rules of their game. Rita must be reeling. He was starting to reel. Good God, what have I done? he thought. He could feel a cold sweat breaking. A wide tube of panic expanded his insides.

He walked out to the kitchen where the big glass jug of orange juice still sat on the counter next to the sink. And she forgot to turn the coffee off. In the bathroom her towel was draped over the vanity instead of being hung up on the rail where it was supposed to be. No, it wasn't her towel; it was his towel. She used his towel! He folded it over his arm and hung it up. He went back to the kitchen and put the orange juice away. He emptied her ashtrays. Danny couldn't do anything until the place was neat as a pin; Rita could be happy if the walls were falling down around her.

He thought about other things. When they went somewhere she was always late. Never more than a few minutes, but it always irked him. He'd be ready to leave and she'd be starting to get dressed. And when they would be out at a party he'd be tired or bored and ready to go home, and she'd just be getting started. She would have found someone to talk to about changes in the civil service or travelling in the Yucatan, or she'd be ready to get up dancing. Maybe he was a lot happier going to things by himself. He had done so in the past. Lots of times. The thought unsettled him.

Later in the day he walked across the bridge over the river and turned up the street to Boris' tall high-rise apartment. He rang the buzzer in the lobby and after a moment a nervous voice over the intercom asked who it was. When he told him, the door opened and he went up in the elevator and walked down the hall to Boris' apartment.

Boris was sitting on the floor in the middle of the room. He looked terrible. His hair was dishevelled, his skin was grey from lack of sleep or from worry, he hadn't shaved. Two suitcases lay open in the middle of the floor and clothes and papers were all over the place: some of them stuffed in the suitcases, others lying crumpled in heaps on the floor. Boris sat in the midst of this, cross-legged, crumpled. He looked as though he'd been crying.

"What are you doing?" Danny asked.

Boris looked up. He looked so weary Danny thought for a second that Boris didn't recognize him.

"Packing," he said.

"Where are you going?"

"I don't know."

"Boris, what the hell's going on?"

"Come on," he said, pushing himself to his feet. He found a woollen sweater in the pile of clothes and pulled it on over his head. Then he slipped his bare feet into his Gucci loafers and started toward the door. Danny followed.

They travelled back down in the elevator all the way to the

basement and walked through a couple of short, empty, jail-like halls. Boris pushed open a heavy steel door and they were in the parking garage.

"Come here," he said. He padded like a sleep-walker through the maze of parked cars and empty stalls in the cold, echoing garage. They toured through what seemed to Danny like the entire basement. Then, at the far end near the door, he could see it, parked all by itself. The Cadillac. He could hardly believe his eyes.

It looked as though it had been in a demolition derby. It looked as though somebody had taken a hammer to it. There was not a spot, not a square foot on the hard, smooth, sleek, white body that had not been hammered. It had dents and blisters all over it; it looked like a huge, cracked egg. It looked like Old Testament Job with boils.

"Holy smokes," he said.

When they got closer Boris stopped and just stood there with his hands on his hips. Danny touched the car gingerly, running his fingers over the pocks on the hood, the fenders, the door. Nothing else; the glass was okay, the windows, the headlights. The grill, the cloth of the roof. But the metal of the body, in its entirety, had been banged to smithereens.

"Who did this?" he asked.

Boris walked around the car, opened the door on the driver's side and bent to look inside. The yellow of the interior light illuminated his haggard face. Tears glistened on his cheeks. He backed out, slamming the door. It closed with a quiet, firm thud. Boris leaned on the hood.

"Sidney's guys," he said.

"What?" Danny said.

Boris turned. "I don't know how it could all have turned out so bad." He put his hand to his forehead. "I couldn't have planned everything to come off this bad."

Danny stayed silent.

Boris looked up at him. "You really want to hear it all?"

Danny nodded. He wasn't at all sure, but he nodded. Yes.

"I made an agreement," he said. "I got scared, I didn't know what to do. I should have known they'd do this; I don't know what they'll do next.

"Sidney," he continued, "was into many things. But among the things he was into was dope. You may know," he said sadly, "if you've been reading the papers."

"Jesus," Danny said. His memory snapped. He'd seen something in the newspaper but had failed to connect the names. "The guy whose office you took me to."

"I didn't know, Danny," said Boris. "Unbelievable as that may sound." He spread out his hands on the car hood. "I had no idea. I thought I was a messenger putting together land deals. Using my savvy," he said bitterly.

"Are you in trouble?" Danny asked, then realized how naive the question sounded as soon as it was out.

"Of course I'm in trouble. What do you think this is?" Boris pointed to the car.

He went on. "I'm not charged. But the reason I'm not charged is because when the mounties came and the prosecutor came I said yes I'll talk, yes I'll get up in court. I called Weinman the lawyer; he says, 'It's your only alternative, you have no other choice.' So I said okay." He lifted a finger. "Don't think for a minute that I like it. It's a terrible thing to do, a terrible position to be in."

"And Sidney," Danny said, putting it together, "is trying to persuade you otherwise."

Boris nodded. "The cops say don't tell Sidney anything, act natural for a while. Go to see him if you have business to finish. Like fuck, I say. Sidney'll find out, Sidney'll kill me. No, they say, we'll protect you.

"So I go up to the office once to see Edward Burrows. First I get mad. I say how could you involve me in this, unwittingly. I thought I was buying land for you. How could you send me out with no notion of what was going on, with no chance to say no, no chance to protect myself. He just shrugged. I'm sorry, he says. That's all he says. I'm sorry. Fine. He's all out of steam, I guess; he's looking at time. He doesn't say much. Finally he says, they'll be after you to talk, Boris. If they haven't already. I know they will.

"Then I went out. I was mad. I was confused. I was scared. On the way out the woman at the desk, Lydia, gives me a little smile. I can tell she's scared too.

"A couple of days later she calls me. She's sympathetic. I think maybe she's in the same spot I'm in, no idea and then, pow. She'd been on the phone to me already a few times like she had no one else to turn to. This time she says, meet me at such and such a restaurant and we'll have dinner. I say yes, I'm so grateful to her just for calling me; the stress is getting terrible, I have no one to comfort me. So I meet her at the restaurant and we have a drink. She's real nice, it seems she feels sorry for me. This is a terrible position for you, she says. I know how this must upset you. I'm so grateful for the kind words I could almost cry. They're after me to talk, she says. The prosecutor. I don't know what to do. What should I do? I look at her and shake my head. You may have to, Lydia, I tell her. They're after me too. We have no choice.

"We sit there for a few minutes. But before we can order dinner she says she's not hungry. Let's go back to my place, she says. If you're hungry I can fix you something. So I drive her to her place, an apartment building in the north end, almost out of the city. Park here, she says, showing me to an alley behind her building.

"So I leave the car and we go upstairs. In the elevator going up to the apartment she puts her hand on my neck. She has these deep brown eyes and that rich head of red hair."

Danny nodded; he remembered.

"When we get into the apartment she makes me lie down on the bed. It's one of those women's apartments, you know, chintz this, chintz that, fluffy little pillows and a pink bathroom. The bed had ruffles all around it. But booze; expensive booze all over the place, lots of it.

"Before I knew it she had my clothes off. Then she had hers

off and was on top of me. She was having her period but she wanted to fuck anyway. She was all over me, I was going crazy, all this anxiety inside of me needing to get out. We went at it for a long time.

"When we were done she said, all sudden-like, 'You should go now.' 'What?' I said. 'Can't I stay?' I said. 'No, you should go,' she said, 'I'm expecting somebody.'

"I was kind of numb and I couldn't understand what was going on. She hurried me to get dressed. She didn't even give me time to go to the bathroom; she just hustled me to get out of there.

"When I was going down the hall I turned a corner and there was this black guy, a boxer, a kid I'd seen one time with Burrows at the gym. I thought it was kind of funny to see him there in Lydia's building but I didn't stop. I went down the elevator and walked out of the building and went around to the alleyway. And there was my car."

Boris stood up and stepped back from it.

"Holy smokes," Danny said.

"I couldn't believe it. I looked at it, I walked around it. I got terrified. I headed back to the building. Then I realized, holy shit, she's in on this. I was crying, I was laughing, I was running around. I could still smell her on me. I didn't know what to do. I looked everywhere; there was no one around. Then I looked in the car; there was this note on the seat."

Boris reached into his pocket and handed Danny a small, typewritten note: "For you to talk," it read, "would be a very bad idea."

"Holy shit," Danny said. He looked at Boris.

"So I drove it back here. What could I do?"

"Now what?" Danny asked. He was appalled, he was sickened. The whole thing was too bizarre. The whole thing was like a bad movie.

Boris handed him a set of keys. "I want you to take the car," he said. "I want you to hide it. I can't leave it here, I can't get it fixed. Take it to the country or something, I don't care. Just put it away somewhere until I can figure out what to do. Will you? Danny, you gotta help me."

"Sure," Danny said. He didn't know what he would do with it, and he didn't know if he was doing the right thing, but he didn't know what else to say. "But what about you?"

"I'm leaving. I'm going to Toronto," Boris said. "But don't tell a soul."

22

Over the next few weeks things happened in rapid-fire succession. Unlike some years when it lingered on and on, winter disappeared almost overnight. And spring came in like a bomb.

Rita's rally was a huge success; 20,000 marchers. The day after, the papers showed pictures of the crowds on the front page. On page three there was a heroic photograph of Robert, his hair blown askew in the wind, exhorting the throng from the steps of the legislative building. They would be off to Ottawa, he was quoted as saying, "like a mighty tide that could know no containment." Even the premier of the province had stood with them on the podium.

Danny got busy with lots of little bits of work. From time

to time Boris would call, not leaving any forwarding numbers, just hurried, whispered, urgent calls. Usually to ask if his car was all right. Danny would reassure him and return to work. He thought sometimes about calling Bellows to see what was up with their northern Indian project, but decided to wait.

After the success of the rally, Rita was slated to go to Ottawa to help some of the others arrange things for the rally on Parliament Hill. In the week before her departure she bustled around, excited as a kid going to camp. Four days before she left she started to talk to Danny about joining her there, going along on the trip. She brought it up wistfully at first, in the sort of 'wouldn't it be nice if' vein. Then she became more definite. By the end she was saying "please come along, we could have a wonderful time." Danny agreed; they had begun to grow warmly affectionate again.

A day before she, they, were to depart, Bellows called.

"We're on," he announced. "I have things all set. Can you get your cameras packed, and your gear? I'm sorry for the short notice. . . ."

Danny's mind flipped through its catalogue of pages. "I don't know, I'm supposed to be leaving for Ottawa," he said; he didn't tell Bellows it was a holiday trip with his girlfriend. "When do we have to go?"

"I'm coming Monday. We can head north on Tuesday morning. This is the best possible time for me; you know how difficult it's been for me to get away, how busy I've been."

"Yeah," Danny said. Why now, with Bellows? He'd have to talk to Rita. He resented Bellows, he resented his cameras, he resented the Indians. "All right, you come out. I'll change my plans; I'll be ready for you."

He let out a long sigh when the phone was hung up. He looked around his room. He'd have to take all the Ottawa stuff out of his bags and put all the northern stuff in; heavy sweaters, mitts. Rita'd probably be upset, he hated the thought of having to face her. But maybe it was best. He had his work too, after all.

An hour later he walked over to Rita's. He went up to her apartment, the three-storey walk-up in the picturesque old building. He surprised her with her suitcase on the floor and her things scattered. She was packing.

"This is going to be wonderful, Danny." She got up and came across the room to kiss him on the cheek. "I can hardly wait." Then she looked at him. "What's wrong?" she said.

"I can't go."

"What do you mean?" She looked stunned.

"Bellows called." He shrugged his shoulders and let out a deep breath.

"And. . . ."

"And we're going up north. Finally. Tuesday."

Rita looked at the floor.

"I'm sorry." Danny went over to her; she started putting things into her suitcase.

"I'm really sorry," he said. "But I have to do this. Maybe we can go another time."

"It's all right," she said, too forcefully. She looked at him, her eyes were glistening.

He reached to touch her but she pulled back. "Rita."

"It's okay, I said," she said. But she didn't let him get close.

Rita was gone a day and Danny thought he was going crazy. In his studio the pile of paraphernalia for the northern trip seemed to grow on the table in front of him: film, batteries, lights, filters, outdoor gear. The day was warm and the heat of the sun, streaming through the windows, filled the front room of the studio. Heat from the bakery downstairs pushed up like a cloud through the floor. He took his shirt off. He couldn't keep his mind on the preparations.

In the afternoon he left and dropped by to see Samantha. She was cleaning her refrigerator. She wore an old grey sweatsuit and had jars of salad dressing, cartons of yogurt, heads of lettuce strewn the length of her kitchen counter. Danny noticed how tired she was starting to look, and old. He should give her $40 to go to the hairdresser. She'd look better if she'd exercise and take off some weight. She should get some new clothes. She should stop smoking.

Since his return from Florida they had only talked briefly. He wanted to tell her about their father. Not just the standard stuff about his health, about his spell on the beach, about his flying home to Canada for the summer; he wanted to find some way to tell her about the man he had found there, the man he barely recognized but in some way liked better than the man he might have expected to find. But he didn't know if he could say it in any way that would make sense; he didn't have it sorted out enough yet in his own mind. He wished there was some way she could just see him. Then she'd understand. Then, he felt sure, they'd be able to make some kind of contact with each other.

Something was going on with Samantha. Despite her dumpy appearance, there was, still, more life in her eyes. As if she had been thinking about things, or doing things. He couldn't quite put his finger on it. She seemed more gentle.

"Maybe I should have tried to go," Samantha said, wringing out the dishcloth with which she had been wiping the insides of the crisper drawers of her refrigerator. This made him listen. "God knows I'd love to pull Prissy out of kindergarten for a few weeks and go get some sun." She smiled. "But I don't know how I'd arrange it." Then, in a slow, given-up voice, "Somehow it'd be . . . you know. It wouldn't work. Dad and me. I mean, I don't think we're ever going to be able to say more than 'hi' to each other."

"No, Sam," Danny said quickly. "I think you're wrong."

She looked up at him, startled. But not with her usual, weary, half-accusing 'here it comes again' look.

"No," Danny blurted. "It's not what you think. I just think. . . . Something's happened . . . I don't know quite how to explain it, but he seems like a different person."

She gave him the chance to go on.

"Maybe it's the heat, maybe it's getting old. I don't know."

He was going to continue, but he didn't. He looked at Samantha to see if she looked encouraging, as though she wanted to get into it. But she had backed off, the curtain had gone up across her eyes again.

Danny became hesitant. Every time he thought about what she had said at their last meeting, the one before he went to Florida, the night Rita was there, he felt badly. He should apologize, perhaps, but he didn't quite want to. It would be, he thought, like apologizing for the whole of their lives. But at the same time he wanted to do something, make a gesture.

Samantha didn't offer the chance; she changed the subject. "I've got to get this done," she said, looking at her half-cleaned refrigerator. "Then I've got to get at the books. I'm a couple of days behind. And tomorrow Prissy wants me to take her to the Shrine Circus Parade."

Danny saw this as his chance. "I'll take her," he said.

Samantha looked startled.

"Please," he said. "Let me."

She looked blank, then a bit brighter.

"What time?" he said.

"Morning," she said. "It starts, I don't know, around nine or ten. Are you sure you want to?"

"I'll be here at nine," Danny said.

That night he tried to reach Rita. He had no idea where she was staying. He called several people from the committee. Finally he reached one who thought she knew the name of the hotel in Ottawa where all of them—Rita, Martin, Robert—were staying. She gave Danny a name.

He called. Yes, she was there, but she was out. He left a message.

Half an hour later the phone rang. He grabbed it. It was Roger. He was stammering with excitement. "They took it, Danny."

"Took what?"

"My book. They're going to print it."

"Hey, that's wonderful, Rog." He summoned a facsimile of excitement that wasn't really to be had, although he owed it to Roger. Roger was so excited himself that he didn't notice.

"December," he said. "Christmas."

Danny battled to keep down a pang of jealousy. It embarrassed him. "Great, Rog. Let's get together."

"Shit. Yeah."

He poked around his apartment, trying to stifle a well of despair that kept pushing up inside him. He didn't know what to do. He didn't want to stay in; he didn't want to go out. He walked in circles in the room that was too small. He should have been more generous and enthusiastic in talking to Roger. He was happy for Roger, but now he had a book. Even though Danny had his own possibility for a book with Bellows finally coming to town, he couldn't keep his mind on it. He wanted to talk to Rita.

A little after midnight the phone rang. It was her.

"I've changed my mind," he said. "I want to come and see you."

At the other end she hesitated.

"Can I come and see you? I'm going to call Bellows and tell him to stuff it; put it off. Tell him I can't do it, or I can only do it if he'll wait."

"Danny, are you sure? When did you decide this?"

"Just now. Yes, I'm sure. I miss you."

"Why don't you wait and come to Montreal?" she said.

Danny was stopped short. Didn't she want to see him?

She jumped in quickly. "I'm going to go down there for a little holiday after we're finished in Ottawa. You and I can have more time. The others won't be there, I won't have to be working. God, it's been busy here, there are a million things to do. In Montreal we can just be together."

"Okay," he said. "I'll be there in a week."

Rita gave him an address, and suddenly there didn't seem to be anything more to say. They hung up.

Danny sat in the chair in front of his phone for a long time. He'd acted so impulsively he wasn't sure what he had done. There was something inside that still made him feel desperate and he couldn't seem to keep it down. He felt enormous confusion and loneliness. He stared at the wall as if he were watching all his energy running out the bottom of an hourglass.

Eight hours later he felt completely different. The morning was clear and bright and he felt buoyed by a mood as fresh and uncluttered as a new-mown lawn. He drove over to pick up Prissy. It was parade day; the circus had come to town.

"I could have got her there somehow myself," said Samantha when he stepped into her apartment. "Maybe we could have gone with Cathy and her girls."

"Take the morning off," Danny interrupted her, a self-confident firmness in his voice. He winked conspiratorially at his six-year-old niece. She gave a big smile back. She had lost her first tooth, one at the bottom, and when she grinned open-mouthed, it gave her face an oddly checkered look like a Raggedy Ann doll.

"Okay," said Samantha.

They went out and got into Danny's car.

Danny thought he knew the best place for them to watch the parade. It was still early enough that they could go to an A&W restaurant on Portage Avenue, put the car in the parking lot, go in, get a hot dog for Prissy and a coffee for him, and still get a good spot on the boulevard.

Danny looked over at Prissy, who seemed half a mile away, tiny, down at the other end of the long bench front seat of the Pontiac. She was babbling away like a chipmunk.

"The only thing I don't want," she was saying in that instructive way of six-year-olds, "is for the clowns to come in that car that makes the noise."

Danny thought for a minute, then remembered that when

she was four they went to the circus, and the clowns came into the ring in a multi-coloured Volkswagen that miraculously held 11 of them. And while they were piling out, stumbling and falling over one another, it bounced and jolted around in a big circle, letting off periodic and unexpected backfires, huge noises with a burst of flame and a puff of smoke reminiscent of artillery fire. The noise had terrified Prissy; she had covered her ears, clung to him and howled with fear. She still remembered.

"Don't worry, honey," he said. "I expect today the clowns will be walking."

"What I want to see most are tigers," she said emphatically. "There'll be tigers, won't there?"

"There'll be lots of things," Danny said. He looked over at her—her earnest, excited little face, her hands folded in her lap, her bony knees, her running shoes with one of the laces already undone.

His mind shifted to his own parade, the parade of his wishes. If Samantha would only go to see their father, by herself, before it was too late, before he died; if Bellows could somehow adapt to his need to change their plans, briefly, and if they could still do the book and see it through to publication, to honour and glory. If Roger's book actually got published this time. And if he could maintain his cool long enough to let them do it, without panicking and yanking it back, becoming stubborn and stupid and hoarding it away, becoming a recluse again. If Boris could iron out his difficulties and move back to the big, empty, grey-carpeted apartment where he used to live in this city, where Danny used to be able to drop in on him, or Boris on Danny, with his big booming halloo and a slap on the back and something surprising and wacky up his sleeve. If the telephone would ring again and it would be Rita. . . .

They got a good place on the boulevard, Prissy and he. The sun would be hot later, already the day was becoming warm. Prissy pulled off her jacket and gave it to him to hold. People were lining up along the boulevard on both sides of the street. Collecting like crows in a cornfield; fathers and mothers and little children and teenagers working at being indifferent. They drew in like flies to syrup from all over the city until they massed in lines, five deep, jostling for position; until the whole crowd was a sea of rolling bodies all up and down both sides of the broad street as far in either direction as one could see.

Danny edged over until they reached a newspaper coin box, then lifted Prissy up so she could stand on top of it. "How's that?" he asked.

"Great," she said.

Policemen arrived in front of them and stationed themselves out at 20-yard intervals with their arms spread, white-gloved hands pushing back to hold the crowd in place. In the distance, toward downtown, Danny could see the on-and-off red flash of a fire-truck's roof beacon.

"Lookit, they're coming," said Prissy.

Within minutes the parade started to roll by. Shriners in funny hats, Shriners on horseback, Shriners in convertibles, Shriners on motorcycles, Shriners dressed up like the Keystone cops, Shriners on roller skates. Top-down, gleaming Cadillacs rolled by with lettered signs on the doors: Grand Lumpen Potentate This or That, Enigmatic Omnipotent Governor Which or Whatever. Chubby, rosy-faced men waved from within. A squadron of drum majorettes imported from Aberdeen, South Dakota, strutted by, jerking chubby, tanned thighs high like trained horses. Then, a Scottish pipe band, oddly out of place in the middle of the prairies, although there must be dozens of them, all in tartan, blaring "The Campbells Are Coming Yo Ho, Yo Ho."

"This is great!" shouted Prissy.

The woman who did the weather at 6:00 p.m. on CTV rolled by, waving from the back seat of a green Buick. A group of boys, navy cadets with wooden rifles painted white, marched by, a third of them out of step. Then came a band of middle-aged men all in maroon blazers and straw boater hats, playing "New York, New York" on kazoos.

At a similar parade Danny once saw two paunchy, red-faced Shriners, shining scimitars clasped to their waists with silk sashes, crimson vests glittering with decals and buttons and jewel-bestudded medals, earnestly attempting to explain to three bewildered Egyptian or Syrian or Libyan-looking students the significance of the Shrine's Arab motif. They went on and on, these big, blubbery, grand masons. The tassels swayed from their purple fez hats while the young Egyptians, dressed conservatively in pressed slacks and sweater vests, shiny black-framed spectacles, listened intently, looking from one to the other in the most awesome effort to fathom what this was all about. Behind them the parade rolled by.

And in front of Danny and Prissy the parade rolled by. Big guys in orange silk jackets drove miniature cars the size of lawn mowers, each run by a black 12-volt battery strapped to its chassis, in figure-eights up and down and all over the street. A clown tossed candy kisses into the crowd, much to the delight of Prissy, who missed all that flew her way, her hands and arms all over the place like a windmill, trying to catch them until she nearly fell off her perch on the newspaper dispenser. Danny trapped two in the grass before the other children could usurp them and he gave them to her.

"Can I eat them now?" she asked.

"Sure," he said.

"Here, you have one too," she said.

A band went by; more Shriners in white jackets and red, puffed pantaloon-style trousers, all blowing on trombones. Then a flatbed truck; a huge Kenworth, gleaming white, pulling a trailer upon which sat a gilded cage guarded by four, smiling, painted-up circus ladies in glittering costumes. And in the cage, yawning either with boredom or satisfaction, the largest tiger beast he had ever seen.

23

Danny felt lucky. He said to Rita, "We might not be rich, we might have no money and no security, but the world is more available to you and me than to almost anybody who has ever lived. And perhaps anybody who lives now."

He was so exuberant he caught himself going on about it a bit too much, but he couldn't stop. He stood on the narrow balcony of Marielle's apartment. Marielle was a friend of Rita's and that's where they were staying in Montreal. Marielle had left town to teach rich kids at a camp in the Laurentians so they had her place for the few days they were going to be there. Down below was Rue St. Urbain, the street Mordecai Richler made famous in his novels, but which was now no longer Jewish but everything: Italian, Vietnamese.

Up and down the street the cars whizzed like space toys through the golden sunlight of late afternoon. In Marielle's bedroom their bags lay open and their wrinkled clothes spilled out onto the glossy varnished hardwood floors. Danny had stashed cameras beneath a table; he'd dragged them all this distance just in case. It was hot, one of those hot, early spring days; Rita had taken off her clothes to accommodate the heat and stretched out her long brown limbs on Marielle's sofa beneath a print of something by Raoul Dufy, a crowd of people in boater hats and blue blazers pushing up to the edge of a pier to get a good look at the river below. The hundred leaves of a big potted umbrella plant, bursting with health, dappled dark shadows up her legs. She stretched luxuriously, arching her hips and causing her pleasant white breasts to rise.

He tried to identify the music that charged through their open window from an apartment across the alley. Z Z Top. The apartments in this neighbourhood around Mount Royal were small, old, three-storey buildings with steep metal staircases, some of them painted gun-metal or bright green, or turquoise, purple and orange. The apartments crowded up against each other like barnacles on a ship's hull. They were tight together and hot days made them seem even more so.

Danny leaned out on the balcony, the palms of his hands flat against the moulded wood of the rail, his heels squared against the door jamb. The balcony was tiny, just big enough to turn around on. Yet up and down the street whole families were sitting out on similar ones, escaping the air from their stuffy cooking and laundry-filled apartments.

Across the street, a large man who looked as if he lifted weights for a living and threw longshoremen around for a hobby sat on a small chair, his huge bare gut spilling out over checkered shorts. Below him the concierge of Marielle's building sat on the concrete front step, puffing, airing her toes. Her shapeless grey tent of a dress was pulled up to her fat knees and her yappy black poodle, tied by a chain to the handle of the propped-open door, ran in circles. The day before, Italy had won an important World Cup preliminary soccer game. The neighbourhood had celebrated wildly. Cars still whizzed by with the tri-colour red, green and white flags flapping from their radio aerials; young black-haired men sticking their heads out the windows grinned madly.

Just a short way down the street, three children squatted low on their haunches like Zulu chieftains in a circle around a crater in the sidewalk that they had filled with water. They poked the water solemnly with short sticks as if goading the cavern's monster back into his cage. Across the street from them an old man dragging a garbage bag shuffled along, talking to himself. Periodically he broke into a brief, quick-stepped jig. And once he did an entire pirouette. Then, the spurt of joy dissipated, he continued to shuffle.

So many people. Danny felt as if he was at the movies. What adventures had they had? He felt that Rita and he should go on forever like this. On their first day they were all lovey-dovey. A long walk in the streets, love-making on the floor in Marielle's living-room. Dinner out in the twinkling city. The second day was not so good. Old patterns emerged. Rita accused him of being self-absorbed. She had wanted Danny to spend the afternoon at a lecture at the Musée des Beaux Arts. He thought it was too nice to spend the afternoon sitting in a big room; he wanted to walk instead, and maybe find some shady table under an umbrella where he could sit and have a cool Perrier, watch the world go by. He didn't mind going off by himself; in fact, he preferred it. Maybe that's what upset Rita. "Can't you be interested in something I'm interested in?" she said. "Don't you want to learn something?" One thing led to another in the way that arguments always unfold until she, in a burst of her own exasperation, turned on him, called him self-obsessed and accused him of being a cynic.

But he was not a cynic.

And he wasn't self-obsessed in his walks. He was world-obsessed. He was watching and listening like crazy, every pore, every nerve-end wide open. He wanted to be everywhere, go everywhere, be everyone. In his imagination he was hopping around like a jack-rabbit. He wanted to slip his hand around the smooth waist of the cool young woman at the next table and feel the bone of her hip shift under his fingers as they set off down the bricked street toward lord knows what adventures. He wanted to turn the key and shuffle into the close little room and sit on the sagging bed with the old folks, open up the treasures wrapped in newspaper that they kept in the satchel at the back of the closet and weep softly along with them for all the children who never came to visit.

He wanted to ride with those cocksure young Italians, beating his chest and whooping away, waving the flag because his country, 3000 miles away, had come up with a big football match when nobody expected it. He wanted to be the young women, their dark hair cut nicely in front and all piled up in back and perfumed, tottering on high heels past the boulangeries of St. Laurent Street, knowing that the young guys were watching. He wanted to be the construction worker trudging home, dangling his big lunch-bucket carelessly from the last joint of his finger, his shirt with the tear in the shoulder filled with cement dust, his face streaked like a drought landscape where rivers of sweat traced their way through the cake of dirt, his feet so weary, his body so tired at the end of a shift it slung along like ropes with a momentum beyond consciousness.

He wanted to be that hot and that thirsty for the big brown litre bottle of Molsons stashed in the door of the whirring refrigerator. He wanted to be them all. He wasn't obsessed with his own life like some lost explorer who could never find his way out of his own jungle no matter how energetically he hacked away; if anything, his life wasn't big enough. He wanted more; he wanted to see it all. Why couldn't Rita understand this? Why couldn't she see this in him?

Danny was already home when Rita got back a second time from the Musée des Beaux Arts. She marched straight through the apartment and started gathering her things, throwing them into a pile on the bed.

"Are you still upset?" he asked, standing in the doorway.

She turned to face him and pushed the damp hair back from her forehead. Her face looked stern, severe. "That's not the right word," she said. "I'm not upset."

"What are you doing?" he asked.

"I'm going," she said. "I have to go. And I don't want you to come with me." This, after a brief pause. He was stunned.

For a minute they stood like two fencers, poised and alert, rigid. Then she sat on the edge of the bed, her hands clasped in her lap, her shoulders sagged. She looked so small, she looked so helpless, he wanted to go to her and put his arms around her. Everything, he wanted to say, will be all right. I'll do whatever you want me to do; you want me to do something, I'll do it.

"It's not going to work, Danny," she said. "I can't do this anymore." She looked up. Tears welled along the bottom of her eyes. "I don't love you," she said.

Danny felt that time had stopped. He felt that he'd been clubbed on the back of the head but his eyes were still open. On Marielle's bedroom wall a line ran from ceiling to floor where it had been repainted, but the new paint job didn't quite match the colour of the old paint right beside it.

"Oh, this is so hard to say." Rita wrung her hands. She stood up. "I like you. It wouldn't be hard if I didn't like you. But I like you. . . . You're sweet."

Danny could feel anger building inside him like a furnace.

"You're gentle." She came toward him. He stepped back. "Maybe I even love you, but it's not right," she blurted finally.

"What's not right?" he said. Not gently.

"Us."

"Oh."

"There are so many things in this world I just ache," she said quickly, "and I can't talk to you about them. It's like we don't have quite the same language."

Danny thought quickly about Robert. That goddamn puny little theologian with his simplistic crusades.

"It has nothing to do with Robert," Rita said as if she had anticipated his thoughts. He looked up. "Not really, anyway. It has to do with you and me. Us." Rita looked pale but strong. Danny suspected she was stronger than he, and that irked him. He wondered what he looked like at that moment.

"Oh," he said.

She exhaled and reached for his arm. He pulled it back.

"You're right," she continued, returning to sit on the edge of the bed. "There is something naive, innocent about Robert and about what we are doing, are trying to do. But there is also something incredibly wise and deep to it, to him. You never appreciate that. Don't you see how it hurts me, frustrates me that you don't appreciate that? Robert is an incredible man and it would be so easy for me. All I would have to do is let myself go. God knows," she looked away at the corner of the floor near to where his cameras were, "it would be easy enough should I want to." Then she looked back at him, bravery filling her face, setting her jaw. "But I didn't do anything."

"Why not?" Danny said. Accusing. God, she couldn't be saying this.

She had an answer ready. "It would be too easy."

He looked at her. His mind was a whirlwind. He knew from all the experiences of his life that it would be impossible for him to muster thoughts, feelings, into anything remotely articulate. Rita had said what she wanted to say, lips pursed, sitting there. Danny resented suddenly the ease with which she could get things out. "And it was too easy with me too?" he asked.

She looked as if she was about to agree.

"Or is it," he continued, "at last too much of our old quarrel;

you the doer, me the watcher and that never being quite good enough."

She opened her mouth to speak.

"Not enough passion for you," he said, angry. "The dilettante; the voyeur."

"Some of that, yes," she said. He could see that he had surprised her. She was actually fearful. He was encouraged, emboldened.

"Rita," he said, "you're really starting to piss me off."

She looked stunned. He stepped past her.

"What are you doing?"

He got down on his hands and knees and rummaged through his things crowded under the bedside table until his fingers touched the firm, smooth, cool body of his Minolta. He reached into his bag for a lens and pulled back, attaching it to the camera body. He checked the indicator, lots of film left. He looked at the room for light.

Rita sat on the edge of the bed, bewildered. Now it was she who couldn't figure out what was happening. He smiled at her brightly.

"What are you doing?"

"I'm going to take your picture."

Her mouth dropped open. Then she jumped up, eyes flashing. "You son of a bitch!" she said.

"No, no," he said. He raised the camera. Click.

She grabbed some clothing off the bed and flung it at him. He ducked. Click. Click.

"You bastard," she yelled and lunged at him. Click. She hit him with her fists on the chest and shoulders. He raised his left arm to protect himself but kept the camera aimed with his other hand. Click. Click.

He fell on the floor, the camera cradled like a touchdown pass close to his face. Rita fell right on top of him. She was laughing, crying. "You bastard," she panted, pounding him, bruising him, he was sure of it. He pushed the camera aside and took hold of her arms. She was strong and continued to flail at him, but finally he had a hold on her. They wrestled until they were both exhausted. They exhausted themselves, but it did no good. As making love would have done no good. Their physical exhaustion left the shell into which could fit their terrible, if yet not fully realized, loneliness. They rolled off one another and lay separately for a time longer. It was not, in the end, enough.

Danny got up and walked to the window. The front of his shirt was ripped. Sweat from the exertion and from the heat of the apartment bathed his chest. He looked back and Rita was crying softly, huddled next to the bed, her arms wrapped around herself. "Go then," he said gently. He wanted to make it easy. "I understand," he said. "Maybe it wasn't the right time." Rita wiped her nose with a Kleenex. "It's okay," he said, "I understand." He didn't understand at all.

He watched Rita carry her bags to the taxi. Come back, he wanted to say, let's try one more time. Let's hurt each other one more time. Let's misunderstand one more time. He didn't say it. He stood on the sidewalk and watched the driver put her bags in the trunk and watched her slide into the back seat. And he watched the taxi move away down the street. For a long time it rose and dropped out of sight and then reappeared over the hills of St. Urbain Street until, in the shimmering light of late afternoon, it was swallowed by the traffic and the distance. It was like the end of a movie and he waited for the credits to roll by.

At first he didn't feel anything. Not sad, not stricken, not empty. He didn't feel desperate, he didn't feel happy, he didn't feel relieved. A little fearful, perhaps. Maybe, deep down inside, he was as happy she was gone as he was sad. Maybe that was what made him fearful. And he had some retrospective anger. The thought that he might not see Rita again, ever, didn't even occur to him. He wasn't sure what to do. In the absence of anything else, he started to walk. And it wasn't until he started to walk that a terrible hurt and loneliness came like a waterfall and held him in its surge, keeping him so that he could barely get his air.

He walked up the street past Marielle's apartment building and rounded a corner that went up another two short streets and ended at the big sprawling park that flanked the side of the mountain. He wanted to get going and then keep going forever. The trees shadowed the street beside the park like a broad canopy. People were jammed into the little yards that fronted the heavy stone apartment buildings. Children dodged the cars that whirred by. Tanned young people played tennis on the dozen park courts in the heat of the late afternoon sun and 20 individual soccer games covered the broad field, each of them with groups of adolescent boys crowded around a white and black ball. He passed a slender young woman pushing a baby in a pram and he kept on walking, all the way down to the end of the street, across a broad field and up a hill, the side of a ravine.

He scampered down a concrete abutment and waited at the side of the highway for the busyness of the traffic, evening rush hour, to ease before sprinting across. He walked down narrow streets built on hillsides and sneaked in around the periphery of McGill University. He walked until his feet were sore and he wanted to take his shoes off. He walked until the warmth of the city made his clothes sticky and seasoned with a thin powder of grime. He walked until his body felt wrung out, empty, cleansed; until his head felt clear; until he was hungry, thirsty, tired, weary with the fatigue of having worked in serious physical ways. He walked until darkness came, suddenly, and the city lit up like a midway. On St. Catherine Street, he ordered a cup of coffee just so he could have an excuse to get three tall glasses of cold water which he chugged back as if he were watering the lawn. When he went to pay for the coffee he discovered he had no money in his pocket; it was all back at the apartment. He sat down again. A little panic. Then he waited until no one was looking, and raced out the door and down the street until he was quickly lost in the throng of shoving bodies that moved along the night street like a sea.

He walked on. He walked with the hookers, the street guys, the musicians. He stuck his head into bistros and got caught for a minute in the embrace of three drunken sailors from Norway, all in white naval suits and little pancake hats, singing their hearts out in foreign chorus. One of them took an icy, sweating bottle of beer off the counter and thrust it into his hand. He took a long, grateful swallow. He found a urinal at the back of the bar and stood in the poisoned stink, feeling a most blessed calm drain down through his body. Then he was back out on the street.

He walked north. He walked all night and when the sky was beginning to lighten, when the air that breezed up from the river had a damp, fresh smell that covered the stale stench of the city like the thinnest of cotton sheets, when the birds were chirping furiously, he rounded the corner to Marielle's apartment. He lifted the phone just inside her door and dialled the railway station.

"Je voudrais un billet à Toronto à six heures si c'est possible," he struggled. "Merci."

In an hour he was settled on the train, fitfully asleep.

24

Two days later Danny sat on the edge of the bed in a nondescript motel room in rural Ontario, an hour or so north of Toronto. The colour and pattern of the wallpaper in the spacious room was the same as that of the drapes and the bedspread. The bed covers were still neat, barely rumpled. He had slept quietly. On the table by the bed lay a brown Gideon's Bible and a thin rural Ontario phone book with a picture of an old-fashioned grist mill on its cover. Through the window he could see black and white cows on the other side of a fence that ran along the motel. They grazed at the short green grass, periodically lifting large bovine heads for a slow look around, this way and that way, jaws methodically chewing from side to side. He wondered what it would take to complicate the life of a cow, what it would take to make them emotionally overwrought. Half a mile up the road, his father was in the St. Joseph's Care Home, probably at this hour being fed his breakfast. He'd gone to visit him the night before.

Twenty-four hours earlier Danny had been in Toronto, looking for a phone booth.

He thought that if he looked in the phone book perhaps he could find the number for Boris' gap-toothed, Lauren Hutton look-alike wife. The train trip while he slept made the transport between two worlds seem too easy. Five hours of fitful lost images of Rita and suddenly he was in another city; disoriented, weary, baffled, fatigued, but in Toronto.

He was seeking comfort and lost ends. But very specific ones. He had passed through Kingston on the train and it did not even cross his mind to get off and call his sister Leslie. But when he arrived in Toronto, he knew he must go out of the city to see his father and he must find out about Boris. Was he all right? Was he still here? Had he gone back to turn himself in, to the mounties, to the prosecutor, to the machinery that would grind out a disposition of Blumthorp and Burrows and an industry built on midnight drug runs? Was he hiding out? Did he have plans? Danny felt an overwhelming need to contact a world that was familiar, even if troubled.

In the phone book he found one, two names actually, that were possible. When he dialled the first one a man answered the phone. He recognized Boris' voice immediately.

"Hey, hey," he said. He sounded like the same old Boris; no hint of the terrified, cornered man Danny had seen in the grey bottom of the parking garage in Winnipeg a mere month ago. Boris sounded as though he had done what he always did: taken the world by its tail and turned it around. Danny felt oddly disappointed.

"I'm in Toronto, Boris," he told him.

"Great," he said. "I'll meet you in an hour."

What Danny really wanted was to ask if he could come to

his place, his wife's place, and have a sleep. But Boris snow-balled him.

"I'll meet you at the Eaton Centre," he said. "We can take it from there. Gee, it's good to hear from you."

After Montreal it was strange to be in Toronto. Montreal had made him exuberant and careless; Toronto made him nervous and hyperactive. His skin tingled; he was so tuned up he was almost in a panic. On the way out of Montreal the old buildings of St. Henri lay heaped and stacked like a chaotic woodpile, held up only by the washlines strung between them; big round domes and spires of churches stuck up between the neighbourhoods. "It looks," said the young Lebanese student in the seat opposite him, his face pressed to the train window, "like Rome."

But Toronto, when they rolled into its eastern limits, looked all business—neat and orderly. Even the inevitable drab of industry seemed, somehow, more tidy. The buildings were all square; the churches looked like high schools. Everybody was off and running with the glint of business in their eyes; things to be done, products to be moved, money to be made.

When he pulled himself out on Yonge Street, it was worse. King Street was a mass of people, uniformed in three-piece suits, running in every direction, brief-cases wielded like weapons, clearing the way.

"So how are ya doing?"

He looked the same old Boris, standing in the Eaton Centre with the buttons of his jacket undone. He had brought an umbrella along with him.

"I'm not so good," Danny said. He told Boris about Rita.

Boris shrugged. "So what did you expect?" he said.

Danny looked at him.

"C'mon," said Boris. "We're going up the street."

"What?" Danny said.

"I'll fix you up. We'll go watch some ladies taking their clothes off; that'll take your mind off your girlfriend."

This caught Danny off guard. That wasn't what he wanted to do. It was the early part of the afternoon.

"C'mon," Boris insisted. He was hopping around like a jack-in-the-box.

They threaded their way shoving and weaving through all the afternoon shoppers in the huge, vaulted, glassed-in concourse and made it to the street. The afternoon was hot and muggy. Danny was still tired. He tried to keep up to Boris, who was moving in a light jog ahead of him. They dodged past a newspaper seller and an unshaven beggar with no legs rocking back and forth on a skateboard. Boris stopped short. "Give me a dollar," he ordered. Startled, Danny found one and handed it to him. He gave it to the beggar.

They passed a couple of girls selling necklaces from a board propped up on two chairs. They jogged past movie houses, burger broilers and dirty magazine stores, Boris tireless in the lead.

"Why are we doing this?" Danny asked when he caught up, puffing.

"Because it will do you good," he said. "This will put it all into perspective. And besides, I'm horny."

"Jeez," Danny said, "you're always horny."

"I am," he said. "I'm like a fire-truck."

"And I don't think it will do me any good." Danny felt glum but lacked the energy to dissuade him. Maybe Boris was right.

They reached a building with a bank of flashing lights. Upstairs, music blared from behind a black door. They went in, groping in their pockets for five dollars for the guy at the counter.

It was the same place Danny used to go when he was a student. The same smoke-filled, red velvet curtains hung over the stage; the same four rows of theatre seats, more deeply sagged now from a decade of use, lined up so that your eyes were right at stage floor level. The same scratchy top-forties records—Sinatra, Elvis, Stevie Wonder. The memory was palpable; a catch in his breath, a wave of longing in his groin, a tickle of excitement in his throat. The same rows of glistening bald heads and furtive students, once his eyes adjusted to the low light. Only the girls were younger. He looked over at Boris. "Great, eh?" said Boris, his enthusiasm in marked contrast to the lethargy, almost somnolence, of most of the clientele. In a chair in the back row one man was sound asleep with his head thrown back and his mouth wide open, snoring softly.

Danny and Boris stood with a half-dozen other patrons against the wall facing centre-stage, the four rows of theatre seats in front of them. Danny knew right away it was all a mistake; he didn't want to be there. It wouldn't do him any good; it wouldn't dismiss Rita from his mind. He needed to get Boris out of there.

The women paraded up and down the narrow stage under blinking coloured lights, disposing of their clothes as they went, 15 minutes per act. Some danced rather well, others badly, to the canned music. In the last song or two of the act most spread a furry rug on the little abutment of the stage and rolled around on it. At this point the bald-headed guys lined up to sneak dollar bills into the elastics at the tops of stockings.

Most of the girls were plain—they looked like waitresses from east-end restaurants who chewed gum, had bad teeth and stringy hair, and seemed to share a sad, plaintive view of the world. Occasionally, a woman was exceptional—of stunning good looks or exceptional talent. Or, at least, she showed some lusty enjoyment of her profession. One of those usually woke up the crowd. Boris was beside himself when a Germanic-looking girl named Lana panted on her furry rug and crossed and uncrossed her long slim legs. "Holy Moly," breathed Boris when she winked at him.

In a front-row seat was an old man with an enormous gut. There was something wrong with him, a thyroid problem or something. His arms, face, neck were of slender proportion but his girth was huge. When he stood, it looked as if the upper part of his body had been drained into a gigantic barrel, as if he was wearing the barrel although what he wore was simply a pair of XXXL trousers held up by suspenders. He was a regular; he knew all the girls and had a couple of dollars ready for each as they completed their acts. At the same point in each performance the girl would come forward on the stage and kneel down, putting one pretty leg out so the old guy could lean ahead and nip a dollar bill in the stocking top or inside the band of the frilly garter. When he got up to go to the bathroom, nobody took his seat.

Everybody in the burlesque house was deliberately, painstakingly polite. No catcalls. The customers were docile in their plush theatre chairs or along the back wall. They stepped back to make room when a girl, dressed in jeans, sweater and jacket, emerged from the dressing-room at the end of her show to go outside to buy, perhaps, some cigarettes. It was as if they were in awe of them.

"Hi, howya doin'?" Boris said to a tall black woman who not seven minutes before was panting, sweating, flopping around on a little red bathroom rug under the hot, bright lights, her legs splayed wide.

"Fine," she said as she trekked past.

The old man with the overgrown belly waddled back from the washroom toward his seat. "Wait till you see who's up next," he stopped to tell them. "My girlfriend Carol." He went to sit down.

"Isn't this wonderful?" said Boris. He was laughing like a kid in anticipation of Christmas.

It was easy to see how Boris could like this. The burlesque put the whole womanizing side of his life into fast action. One naked lady after another parading past with only a howdy do; rich possibilities for fantasy and only the most minimal engagement.

But Danny couldn't take it any longer. He took Boris by the arm. "We gotta get out of here." Boris looked at him. "This isn't any good for me, I really want to get out of here."

Boris looked disappointed, as if he had failed his friend. "Okay," he said.

On the way out Danny looked back at the fat man, moored in his seat. He was arched forward and his hands trembled on the arms of the chair. His face flashed the changing orange, green and purple of the stage lights, and his eyes glistened as the dancer he had been waiting for folded and unfolded herself in front of him.

She tossed a gauzy scarf which caught on his head and fell down over his ears on both sides like a babushka. He looked startled. Then pleased. Everybody in the place laughed. He laughed. Then he took the scarf off his head, folded it up and clutched it to his breast. The show went on.

Outside it had started to rain. Black clouds boomed in overhead and large drops of rain splashed on the hot sidewalk. Boris opened his umbrella. They dashed back down to the Eaton Centre.

"We gotta meet Lucy," declared Boris, looking at his watch. "C'mon, we're late." He pushed his way through shoppers and browsers. Again, Danny jogged to keep up.

They turned into a small, dimly lit cocktail lounge just off the promenade of shoppers. When Boris stopped abruptly in the middle of the room to look around, Danny bumped into his back. Then Boris spotted a woman sitting alone and bee-lined for a table along the wall, beside a window that looked out onto an old brick church surrounded by the chrome and glass of the shopping centre. "Darling," he said, kissing her on the forehead, then straightened up, beaming.

She was truly lovely, Danny thought. Lucy smiled a warm, gap-toothed smile and lifted her left hand to her chin, like a model raising her face for a more direct profile. Her eyes were blue as the sky and her hair a tawny golden bundle of curls. "So what have you two been doing to make yourselves late?" she asked. Quite pleasant, indulgent, the smile still warmly in place.

"I've been showing Danny around," said Boris. "The tower, the new stuff they're doing on the waterfront. He's never been inside Roy Thompson Hall, he's never seen the stadium."

Lucy smiled and looked at Danny. Danny couldn't believe his ears.

Boris ordered some drinks and they settled into meaningless chatter. Lucy remained ravishing; Danny could understand her hold on Boris. When she excused herself to go to the powder-room, Boris sat back, still beaming.

"Why did you do that?" Danny demanded.

He looked perplexed. "Do what?"

"Tell her you showed me Roy Thompson Hall, the waterfront, or whatever the hell it was."

Boris looked for a moment as if he had forgotten his wallet. "Did I say that?" he said.

Boris wanted Danny to stay for a while; a few days, a week. When Danny told him he had to go, he crumpled. "Stay," he pleaded. His face looked as if it would dissolve; his hands started to tremble.

"I can't," Danny said. "I have to see my father."

"But you could wait a day," he protested.

"No, I have to see him tonight."

"I'll drive you," said Boris. "Lucy has a car."

Before long they were heading out of the city, battling the evening rush-hour traffic on a freeway 20 lanes wide, directing themselves toward the vague smoky blue of the hills to the north.

Boris had his foot to the floor of Lucy's grey Audi but they drove in a kind of pleasant, pensive silence. Danny looked over. In profile, Boris seemed sad, almost wistful. The scenery flickered past and Danny thought of his father.

The spell his father had had on the beach in Florida set off a series of traumatic, mysterious seizures. He had a second spell a couple of weeks after Danny departed and it left him unconscious for a few minutes on the floor of the laundry room in his condominium before someone came along and called a doctor. A week later he was flown home to Canada.

"They're not sure what they are," Leslie explained over the phone. "They're like strokes but the doctor says they're just blackouts, though I said if they're not strokes, what causes them, and he said he didn't know. We wanted him to come here and stay in the University Hospital, but after a couple of days they said that if he would be happier closer to home he might as well go. As long as he would be someplace where they could keep an eye on him. John and I don't know what to make of it. I think he's getting weaker, thinner. I know it's not just my imagination. . . ." She paused for a moment to catch her long-distance breath. "I wish he was closer so we could drop in on him but he insisted on going back there. You know how he is. We try to get up every second weekend or so but we're busy too. Maybe in the summer."

His father sent Danny a letter to tell him he had returned to Treeton and had taken a unit, as they called them, a tiny bachelor apartment in a sprawling one-storey building expressly for senior citizens and invalids. It was so he could be close to the doctor and the hospital where he was to go five times a week for treatments and observation.

"It's not such a bad place," he wrote in his letter. "I get a comfortable though narrow bed and the window in my room looks out over a sort of playing field for one of the schools; a field that runs all the way down to the river. I can also see the A&P store and, if I crane my neck, part of the post office. For my meals I walk down to the end of a long hallway to a rather cheery dining-room where we are seated four to a table. On days when I'm feeling particularly chipper I can walk to the hospital. Other times I have to take a taxi, or get one of the men to drive me."

He knew his father was not well. There might not be other visits, more times to see him. But as they drove along in Lucy's Audi, speeding now past fields and hardwood forests, past neat farms and villages, he felt as calm as he could ever remember being. Tenderness choked him, much like he could feel Christmas Eve, hearing the voices of a choir go high in the descant in the third verse of "Hark the Herald Angels Sing." He wanted to talk to Samantha. He felt that if he could see her, then magically to his lips would come the one exact right sentence to make sense of it all: all their history, all their past, all their present, all their future.

He wanted to be forgiven. He wanted to say he was sorry for everything he had done or not done, intentionally or by accident, with will or without. And he wanted to say that they, everybody, must continue to try to start again, fresh, a clean slate. But also he wanted to give a cheer for the world as it was; the imperfect world of his father's sermons and even of his crazy clippings, Boris' chaotic world, the world of Samantha's struggles, the flawed world Rita wanted to right, the world that would never be put right, yet was always right. It would go on; accept that and then go on too. That there seemed so little time was no illusion; it was one of the only reliable truths.

Then, suddenly, Boris spoke in the gloom across the front seat of the car. "She's a wonderful woman," he said out of the blue, meaning, Danny realized, Lucy. "We've been getting along famously. I can hardly believe it." Danny remained silent, which Boris took for agreement and continued.

"If it weren't for her," he said, "I wouldn't be here." Danny looked at him. "I'd be," he waved a hand, "in Brazil or Mozambique or some place like that. I'd have run even further. That's how much this has affected me."

"Are you going to come back?" Danny asked.

Boris looked almost despondent.

Danny felt a sudden inspired resolve. He didn't know where it came from, but suddenly he saw Boris' future, if not his own. For a brief moment Boris' whimpering disgusted him. He fixed Boris in his gaze, waited a moment. "If you don't come back," he said, "I'm going to the lawyers myself and tell them where they can find you."

Boris looked over at him; there were tears coursing down the side of his cheek. Danny felt surprised, pleased with himself, important.

"Did you notice what this is?" his father asked when Danny arrived at his room.

"What do you mean?" Danny said. "An intermediate care home?" That's what the sign had said, just under the crest for the province of Ontario.

"That too," he said. "But Catholic. St. Joseph's Care Home." He chuckled feebly but with irony, and sat down on the one chair in the room. Then he got up. "Here, you take the chair, you're the guest. I'll take the bed."

"Maybe there's a lounge we could go to," Danny said.

"Naw, it's always full, busy. I'd rather stay here. I'd go for a walk but I feel weak today. In the knees. Breath, too; not much breath." He pointed to a space of green wall above the door where a tiny crucifix hung. "There were always Catholics here," he said, "even years ago. But in the last ten years, my oh my. When they built the potato-chip factory the Italians moved in and now the town's three-quarters Catholic. Now isn't this something?" He looked up at Danny. "An old Methodist preacher like me ending his days in a Catholic home for invalids and old folks." He laughed.

"You're not ending your days, Dad," Danny said.

"I don't mind," his father added quickly. "I think it's kind of funny, actually. The second day I was here a nun came to see me, a sister. Chaplain here, she says. We had quite a good chat." He drew in his papery-thin cheeks, pursed his purple lips. Then smiled. A sparkle was still there in his eyes.

Danny looked around the room. The walls were light green like in a hospital. There was a bed covered with a patchwork quilt, a table, the easy chair, a small shelf for books and a sink. Two doors led into a bathroom and a closet. There was a small, intricately woven scatter rug on the shiny tile floor. His father followed his eye to the floor.

"They don't have carpets in the rooms because too many people make messes, mess themselves, and it's easier to clean up the tiles."

Danny looked back at him; he didn't know what to say. He searched the room again for things that belonged to his father. There weren't many: a few books, a picture that used to be in his study in the manse—a print in a dark frame of Millet's *Angelus*, people praying in a potato field.

It was getting late. "Can we have some supper?" he asked. "I mean, can we go out? I'd like to take you out."

"Of course we can go out," his father said. "I'm not an inmate. We'll have to tell them, that's all. I'd like to go out, but I don't feel like walking too much."

"We'll take a taxi," said Danny.

They went out. His father was right, the town had grown and changed. He barely recognized it. Ten years ago it had been a safe, stolid WASPy Protestant town with red brick houses and sturdy beech and maple trees lining its streets. The taxi, driven by a middle-aged man in a turban, took them to the broad, two-acre parking lot of a shopping mall so new the red earth pushed back for the development still lay in huge raw piles not yet grown over. They entered a rose-coloured restaurant that advertised pizzas and veal. "I'd like an omelette," his father said, "but I guess you can't get one here."

Minestrone soup, he settled on, and a small green salad. Then, at the same moment, they both set their hands, palms down, on the thick weave of the red tablecloth, a gesture, in unison, spontaneous, of tentative resignation. His father didn't miss it. Quickly he pulled his hand back and turned toward the waitress, a big, dark, high-school girl who was taking orders at the next table.

"Miss," he said. She turned. "I think we'll have a couple of glasses of wine here as well."

For a long minute they sat across the table from one another, Danny and his father. Above them on pedestals stood a row of half-clad, alabaster, phoney Roman statues. Venus de Milo, David, even a bust of someone supposed to be Leonardo. Leslie was right, their father was thinner, he had lost weight even since Florida. The collar of his shirt hung loosely around his bony, corded neck. Scrawny was the word that flashed through Danny's mind before he dismissed it quickly, with some guilt. Brown liver spots blotched the backs of his father's hands; his hair, what was left of it, was dry and wispy. He saw Danny studying him and smiled.

"Heart," he said.

"What?"

"It's my heart." He took a drink from his glass of water. "They say they don't know what's wrong with me; I go in every day and they give me tests and take samples and put me on machines. Give me this pill, that pill. They say they don't know what it is, all those doctors in their long white coats hurrying around trying to seem cheerful and serious at the same time. But I know what it is. Heart." He touched himself on the chest with his second finger. "It hasn't been working right and it's not going to work much longer."

Danny felt a shiver of fear tremble up inside him. He wanted to tell him he was wrong. He wanted to say "Come on, Dad, you've got 20 more years. A couple of weeks here and they'll pin-point something, maybe put you on medication. You'll be back in your own house good as new. Gosh, I'll even come to see you again next winter in Florida. . . ." But he didn't say anything. Something in his father's eyes stopped him; in the steady way they held him there, the dignity, lack of fear, matter of factness of his own observation. Danny didn't say anything.

The high-school waitress set their glasses of wine before them. His father reached with his thin, papery hand. "Let's have a little taste of this," he said.

In the motel room Danny sat silent on the bed. A tap in the bathroom dripped; the air conditioner let off a vague hum. When he and his father had parted at the entrance to the St.

Joseph Care Home he had suddenly leaned over and brushed
the dry skin of the elderly man's cheek with a kiss. Then he
had stood for a long time in the parking lot, looking back at
the building until the window in what he was sure was his
father's room had gone from light to dark.

He looked at the beige telephone on the desk beside the
bed. Long distance, dial 8. Rita would be at work now. He
smiled to himself as he imagined her picking up the phone
and hearing his voice. He thought of Bellows. He should buy
an additional lens, a medium-range lens, if they were going
to do that job right. He would pick one up in Toronto. He
touched the warm plastic of the phone. He looked up and out
through the window. The pasture and the grazing black and
white cows were framed perfectly. F 11, 125th of a second, he
thought automatically. "Click," he said under his breath.
Around him all the world was as still as could be.